THE CROSS I BEAR

JOSEF KRISTJANSON

Table of Contents

Chapter 1

Her bedroom was never that bright in the morning — *never*. After all, her window faced north, not east. Not only did the unusual brightness force Viktoria out of her much coveted Saturday morning deep sleep, but it also made her eyes ache just to open them.

"What the—" she moaned as she turned in bed. The blinds were still open.

"You have got to be kidding me," she muttered as she rubbed her eyes. "Could the sun be any brighter?"

Her hands collapsing on her stomach, the magazine she'd been reading the night before was still there. She could only imagine how mortifying it would have been had her mom walked in and seen what she was reading.

Note to self: Remember to close the blinds before curling up in bed late at night to read. Oh, and read something else just in case you fall asleep.

She looked at the cover of the magazine. It was four months old; the May 1986 issue. She had already read it a million times. Still, she couldn't get enough of it. It was her favorite issue, and *Pro Wrestling Illustrated* was definitely her favorite magazine, though she would never admit it to her mom, dad, or Teri. Only Dylan knew.

The two men on the cover were shocking. Three — yes, three — mohawks: One man had one mohawk and the other man had two. Both donned studded, spiked, black leather hand wraps and dog collars. They had to have been around

275 pounds each, but no, it wasn't fat. They were obviously putting in their work at the gym.

Anyone could look at what they wore and see why a girl like Viktoria would be attracted to their style. It went well beyond the studs, spikes, black leather, and attire, though. Thanks to Dylan, she had seen them on TV countless times. It was who they were and what they did that breathed new life into her just over four months ago on June 1, 1986.

Just like on the magazine cover, their faces were painted like savage, post-apocalyptic warriors during every TV appearance. With brute force, fearlessness, and stone cold focus, they commandeered their battleground and dominated their enemies with no mercy.

To many individuals, especially children and those seeing them for the first time, they appeared frightening and monstrous. Viktoria could relate to that. She and Teri often had a similar effect on the same demographic.

She could also relate to the frightened ones, though. There were monsters she feared.

Her monsters, though? There were no leather and spikes for them. They were the 1986 suburban Phoenix, Arizona normal: athletic, charismatic, wealthy, and beautiful.

These monsters hid in plain sight, in all ages and cliques. They disguised themselves in the latest fashions, letterman jackets, cheerleading outfits, business suits, and stunning hairstyles. They lurked in the subdivisions, joining together in their matching clans, going out in search of their prey, which was anyone who did not fit in with them. For years, Viktoria, Teri, and Dylan knew that all too well.

The irony of her favorite magazine issue being May 1986 was not lost on her. That was also the month she realized just how powerful those suburban monsters could be. The damage they were able to create could be irreparable, devastating, and life-altering.

Reality hit that month, and it hit hard. Until then, it was just schoolyard kid stuff. Viktoria knew and accepted it. She, Teri, and Dylan were the outcasts, and the monsters were the bullies. It was a cat-and-mouse game played by children all across America that would somehow vanish when they reached adulthood.

Tragically, in May 1986, a fatal line was crossed, and the game prematurely ended. The thing is, only Viktoria and Dylan knew it was over. To Teri and the monsters, the game was still on. The roles remained the same. With the stakes even higher, the adults joined in. Well, either they joined in, or the game never ended with adulthood after all; they just played at a higher level.

Regardless, to Viktoria, the game was over. As of June 1, 1986, it was war.

The monsters were no longer mere bullies, they were the enemy. Life was no longer a disheartening daily grind with distant better times only to be hoped for — life was the battleground.

Above all, fear was no longer her protection. It was her greatest enemy. The most powerful weapon for all other enemies to use against her.

She didn't know how she was going to win the war. She only knew she had to. Not only for herself, but for Dylan — it was her promise to him. After all that had happened, she was going to see to it that her little brother had what he so rightfully deserved.

Resting the magazine on her stomach, she turned to her radio alarm clock. She couldn't believe the illuminated red numbers. It was only twenty minutes past seven. Way, way too early for a sixteen-year-old on a Saturday morning.

After tossing and turning for another thirty minutes, she realized with irritation that she was awake for the day. Sitting up in bed, her eyes returned to the magazine cover. The 550-plus pound, two-headed, three-mohawked wrecking machine took her right back to a half-hour before, and so many other times since June 1.

It was another day to go to war; to soldier on. With her grandmother's cross above her heart and Dylan by her side, she knew she could turn everything around. She could win the war.

A lifelong plague of fear and self-doubt was a hard nemesis to defeat. Four months had already taught her that it wasn't going to happen overnight. Still, though, failure was not an option.

She knew one role would never change: hers. She would always be an outcast, strange and different. Then again, many of the true greats in humanity were viewed in that light. That's how the two beasts on the magazine cover were viewed. Yet it was obvious Animal and Hawk, The Road Warriors, were going to be among the true greats. What was there to not embrace?

Outcast. Freak. Vampira. Call her what they will, she knew her role. Her titles would surely remain, but she was going to flip the script.

The gaze of Animal and Hawk pierced her from the magazine cover, challenging her to become one of them. To put on her warpaint, her black, silver, and gold attire, and march to the battleground with laser focus and fearlessness.

Joining Animal and Hawk, becoming a Road Warrior — an adventurous life of fearlessness and triumph — was what Dylan wanted more than anything. Through Viktoria, it was still possible. That reality was just on the other side of victory.

Still, each day must begin one step at a time. It was early Saturday morning. With a couple forceful blinks and a headshake, Viktoria finally pulled herself from her bed. She stumbled down the hall, making her way to the kitchen.

She froze at the shifting sound of newspaper pages turning at the kitchen table. With her stomach suddenly in knots, she closed her eyes and groaned.

Ugh, I promised Teri. How am I going to do this?

She was famished and groggy, so breakfast and coffee had to come first. After that, she would face what she thought would be the biggest challenge of her day and get it over with. Still, it was a most formidable challenge: dealing with her mom.

Chapter 2

Her mother, Olivia, was at the table, reading the newspaper and nursing her coffee as she did most Saturday mornings. Whether it was the dreaded conversation looming ahead or just typical teenage sulkiness, Viktoria was not in the mood for her mom's superhuman morning cheeriness.

Olivia worked as a closing cashier at a grocery store on Friday nights and had a midday shift on Saturdays. Still, though, she was always up before sunrise. That particular Saturday, she actually had a day off, and she was still up that early. *On her day off!*

"Viktoria!" Olivia turned from her newspaper and beamed. "I can't believe you're already up. Before eight o'clock? On a Saturday? I usually don't see you until 9:30, if I'm lucky. What's going on with you?"

"Yeah, yeah, I get it," Viktoria mumbled, rubbing her eyes again. "It's just too bright in my room so I couldn't get back to sleep. I accidently left my blinds open."

"Well, perhaps you should leave your blinds open on school nights as well. The sun is obviously much more effective than your alarm clock. That'd save me from having to drag you out of bed so you can get to school on time."

Olivia was right, but that didn't make her banter any less annoying. Viktoria wasn't going to let her bask in being completely right.

"Well, I'm also already awake because I'm starving. What's there to eat?"

Snatching the *TV Guide* off the kitchen counter, Viktoria flipped through the pages as she waited for her mom's response. After about a minute of silence, she turned to her.

The newspaper was set aside as Olivia held her coffee mug with both hands close to her chest. With her head tilted, she was in another world as she gazed aimlessly out the window.

"Mom."

With a quick gasp, Olivia turned to Viktoria.

"Mom, you're spacing out. Again, is there anything to eat?"

Looking at her for a few seconds, Olivia shook her head as she grabbed the newspaper, turning to the next page. She mirrored Viktoria's dismissive mood with her response.

"There's some coffee cake I got from the bakery department before I clocked out. It's on the counter. In fact, it's right in front of you. You're welcome."

Viktoria snapped back at her. "Mom, at least give me a chance to thank you. You know I always do."

Setting the newspaper on the table, Olivia repositioned herself, turning her chair in the direction of her daughter. Leaning forward with her arms resting on her folded legs, she let out a heavy sigh.

"You're right, Viktoria. You always do. I didn't give you the chance to say thank you and I should have. I just jumped to the conclusion that you weren't going to because of how flippant you've been toward me so far this morning."

Viktoria sighed. "Mom, I didn't mean—"

Olivia raised her hand. "It's OK. Trust me, I get it. Believe it or not, I have my rough mornings too. I also know that things haven't been easy for you as well lately."

Olivia folded her arms as she looked out the window again. Following a brief moment of silence, her eyes, heavy with exhaustion, turned again to her daughter.

"I'll be honest. Last night's shift was a rough one. I also put in some long hours. I can't tell you how tired and hungry I was when I got home. I remember dragging myself in from the garage, and you were still on the couch, watching TV. I'd be lying if I said it didn't hurt when all you did was mumble a halfhearted '*Hi Mom*' to me and then just shrugged when I asked how your day was. After walking down the hallway to my bedroom, did you see me come back out?"

Avoiding eye contact, Viktoria hung her shaking head. "No."

Olivia placed her hand on the kitchen table where Viktoria was staring, causing her to look up again. Leaning forward more so their eyes could meet, Olivia's voice remained soft, yet strong.

"That's right. You didn't. After my shower, I dropped on my bed and passed out. No going back to the kitchen. Nothing. I can't tell you how tired and hungry I was when I woke up this morning. Still, I have things to do today, so I had to get myself up and get on with the day. Nobody was already up, having breakfast ready for me. I could've been down and wondered why I didn't have that luxury. Instead, I decided to look on the positive side and be grateful for the things that I do have. That's what you need to do, Viktoria. Who knows? Doing so, you just might find out you're a morning person after all."

"Yeah, I don't see that happening," Viktoria said with a sarcastic grin before the instant gleam in Olivia's eyes and her infectious smile caught her off guard.

"What are you talking about? You're definitely a morning person. You just forgot you were. What about all those mornings when your dad and I dragged ourselves into the kitchen to find you already whipping up some big decadent breakfast for us?"

Viktoria continued to avoid eye contact with Olivia, whose voice changed from lively to concerned. "Why don't you do that anymore?"

Knowing where her mom was going, Viktoria continued to look away. "Mom, I just don't want to anymore. It was just a phase, and I outgrew it."

With her eyebrows raised, Olivia sat straight up in her chair, cracking a smile. "A phase you outgrew? Cooking is not a passing phase. Believe me, I'm a mother. Come on, Viktoria. You have a gift. Those breakfasts, dinners, desserts — well, everything you made for us — were unbelievable! Remember how happy you were making those amazing dishes with your grandma? You could have your own TV show. You also blew your dad's coworkers away with what you could whip up in the truck stop's diner. I loved seeing you so happy and carefree while doing something you are so amazing at. I miss that."

Looking out the window, Viktoria shrugged her shoulders. "Yeah, well, I don't. Those days are over."

The silence that followed her words was too thick and heavy to ignore. She turned again to Olivia, whose voice matched the intensity in her eyes. "I don't ever want to hear you say those words again. Understood?"

"What's wrong with that, Mom? I was just saying those days are over. That's it. I like what I'm doing now."

"What's that? The bare minimum at home and school and having a terrible attitude?"

It looked as though Olivia's eyes were on fire. Shocked from the sudden tension between them, Viktoria's eyes grew as wide as saucers.

"Mom, are you serious? Where is this coming from?"

Picking up the newspaper with one hand, Olivia waved her off with the other.

"I'm done, Viktoria. I still can't believe what you said. You need to go back to your room and not come out until you find a better way to start your day."

Viktoria's jaw dropped, and she shook her head in confusion. "Mom, all I was saying was—"

Olivia lifted her hand again. She didn't look away from the newspaper, but her forceful voice was directed at Viktoria. "No. I said go!"

It was rare for Olivia to snap at her, or anybody for that matter. If it ever reached that point, someone had gone way, way too far. Not only that, but it took a lot of buildup and came with plenty of warning. That morning, it was instantaneous. Viktoria had never seen that. Between the kitchen and the hallway, she paused in the living room, trying to make sense of Olivia's sudden flare.

What just happened? Where did that come from? What did I say that was so bad?

Suddenly, it hit her. Her heart sank as her stomach burned. She wished nothing more than to go just a few minutes back in time and not say those terrible words.

Those days are over.

She didn't mean them in that way, but she realized how Olivia had received them. With her head bowed and brow furrowed, Viktoria pinched the bridge of her nose. Too angry to forgive herself, she could only think of what those terrible words meant to Olivia, and then to her.

Those days are over.

Dad.

Grandma.

Dylan.

Oh, Dylan. What was I thinking?

Chapter 3

She was sure over ten minutes had passed, but Viktoria still didn't move a muscle. Even on carpet, she didn't dare take a step. Breathing as lightly as possible, she didn't want Olivia to know she was still in the living room.

When Olivia hurt, Viktoria hurt. It was so much worse, though, when she knew she was the cause of her mom's pain.

Olivia's sniffles at the kitchen table grew unbearable. Quietly wiping tears from her cheeks, Viktoria tiptoed back to her bedroom. Picking up her spiked dog collar from her nightstand, she took hold of the cross hanging from it as she closed her eyes.

I shouldn't have said what I did, Dylan. I didn't mean it that way. You know that, right?

Are you still there? Mom really needs us right now. Please help me help her.

Opening her eyes, she reached behind her neck, lifting her hair to latch the dog collar. She quietly made her way down the hallway toward the silent kitchen.

She paused in the living room and breathed a sigh of relief when she heard the newspaper pages begin to shuffle again. The sound of Olivia taking a sip before setting the coffee mug on the table was even more welcoming. Signs that normalcy was returning. A new beginning for Viktoria and her mom.

OK, Dylan. Let's do this.

Her return to the kitchen was quiet and slow, as was her approach to the table. Viktoria's voice was soft and contrite.

"I can go back to my room if you want, Mom. But, before I do, would you like some Norwegian crepes? I'd love to make some for you."

With forgiving eyes and a wistful smile, Olivia looked up from the newspaper. Her voice was quiet and comforting. "Nah, we have coffee cake. That's enough sugar for me. Maybe some other time."

Viktoria nodded. "OK. I'm getting some milk from the fridge. Would you like a glass?"

Olivia smiled again and winked. "No, thanks. I'll just have my coffee with my coffee cake."

Viktoria raised her eyebrows, snapping her fingers as she pointed at Olivia. "Ooh, nice play on words."

The two of them snickered. As Viktoria turned toward the refrigerator, Olivia set the newspaper down and sighed. "I'm sorry, Viktoria. Last night was a rough one for me. You know — customers. They were driving me up the wall. I even had Mr. Thompson, of course, show up with his usual gripes. He was yelling at me because we don't take competitors' coupons. He was just going off on me, saying for the millionth time that he was never going to shop at Safeway again — I wish! Meanwhile, I had four other customers in my line and, somehow, it was my fault that Lisa decided to go use the restroom for the umpteenth time and leave me with the only open register. Everybody got so mad at me for the long wait, but Mr. Thompson wouldn't let it go. There was nothing I could do. Good heavens! Was there a full moon last night or something?"

Pulling the milk out of the refrigerator, Viktoria rolled her eyes. "What's going on with Mr. Thompson lately? I swear he goes there every night and chooses your line on purpose to make a scene. It's like he has some sort of personal vendetta against you."

"Well, you know as well as I do how that wouldn't be anything new to us these last few months. Things have really changed since May. Everybody has changed. It's not fair, Viktoria. Not for you or me. I wish I knew what to do."

Pouring milk into a glass, Viktoria slightly raised her eyebrows, nodding in agreement. "Yeah, you don't have to tell me."

A couple bites of coffee cake, followed by some milk, brought Viktoria much needed relief. Leaning on the counter, she thumbed through an old cookbook of traditional Norwegian dishes her grandmother had given her the previous Christmas. Realizing it had become unusually quiet, she turned toward the kitchen table.

It suddenly became evident to Viktoria that Olivia had lost even more weight. She was always a slender woman, so she had none to lose in the first place.

With dark circles under her eyes revealing exhaustion, both physically and emotionally, Olivia gazed aimlessly out the window. Reaching up, she wiped a tear from her cheek.

Olivia's hands, cupping her coffee mug, were all that appeared strong — strong from working so hard.

Viktoria's dad's checks provided them with both necessities and comforts, and still, Olivia continued to give her all at the grocery store, despite the heavy toll the previous four months had on her. Why? It was all for her daughter's college education and any other advantage she could provide for her once high school was over. Viktoria knew it was all for her.

Looking down at her feet, shame overtook Viktoria. Beating herself up for being so selfish and crabby toward Olivia that morning, she wished she could take it back, but she couldn't. She could only begin again at that moment.

Looking up as Olivia wiped away another tear, Viktoria bit her lower lip as her heart opened her mind. She knew exactly what to do.

"Who knows, Mom? Maybe Mr. Thompson has a crush on you and he's looking for some way to get your attention. Maybe he's trying to create some sort of, I don't know, sexual tension between you two."

That did it. Viktoria couldn't help but break into laughter at the horrified expression on Olivia's face.

"Oh, Viktoria, that's gross! Ugh, that's disgusting. He's got to be around forty years older than me. Where do you think of this stuff?"

Viktoria, still snickering, did an exaggerated shrug, raising her hands to her sides. "Come on, Mom. He's a widower, retired, and has the nicest house on the street. Accept it — he's your sugar daddy. He's your ticket out of the grocery store."

Olivia could only grimace. "Ugh, stop, Viktoria. Please! I do want to eat, you know."

Viktoria was on a roll. She couldn't stop. "I'm telling you, Mom, I see and hear it all the time. I see how men look at you. Even the guys at school think you're hot."

With her eyes closed and visibly nauseous, Olivia held up her hand as if to tell her daughter to stop while she was ahead.

"Don't even think of going there. I am a happily married woman and still very much in love with your father. Let's leave it at that and change the subject. Now."

The two of them shared awkward grins and laughed. It was the beginning of a lighthearted, enjoyable breakfast together. It was a moment they both desperately needed.

Another battle won, Dylan.

The emotional tension the two of them bore together just a moment before was gone. Olivia's bright green eyes sparkled as she laughed hysterically at her daughter's uncanny ability to imitate some of the more eccentric patrons at the truck stop's diner.

She especially loved Viktoria's imitation of Marla, a woman from Mississippi who had been team driving for the company with her husband for the last ten years. She had the thickest Southern accent, and her chipped front tooth made her whistle every time she pronounced any word with the letter *s*. It made Olivia laugh so hard she had to wipe away tears. For once, they were tears of joy.

It had been months since Olivia was so relaxed and full of laughter. Viktoria knew she was on a roll. If there was ever an opportunity for her, it was then. She had to take it.

The butterflies in Viktoria's stomach overwhelmed her. A bead of sweat rolled down her back. With the jovial mood Olivia was in, how could she say no? With nervous confidence, Viktoria knew the time had come. Teri was counting on her.

Chapter 4

Resting her head against the back of the chair with her eyes closed, the carefree laughter left a beautiful smile on Olivia's face. With the bright sunlight through the kitchen window, she glowed. For the first time in four months, she was completely at ease.

Viktoria took a nervous drink of milk. There was no better moment, yet her lips refused to move. Her teeth clenched in frustration.

Come on, Viktoria. What's wrong with you? Don't fear. Remember June 1? This is your new life — yours and Dylan's.

It's easy. Just open your mouth and ask.

She was half right. She opened her mouth — that was easy. Still, her words refused to escape.

Disheartened, Viktoria sank in her chair. Her stomach churned.

The crushing irony hit hard. A new, adventurous life of fearlessness and conviction had been burning within her for four months. Still, though, she had made no effort to reinvent herself. Not at home. Not over the summer. Not in the first several weeks of her junior year at Peoria High School.

In fact, she had regressed further into her depression, becoming more lethargic and introverted. She was even more accepting of the ridicule she received at school and around town. Again, she touched the cross hanging above her heart.

What's wrong with me, Dylan? We were going to turn it all around starting June 1. What have I done? Nothing! Look at me right now, sitting in front of Mom, too afraid to ask for permission to do what teenagers do all the time.

Olivia looked over at her. Through her smile, she spoke with concern, "Hey, I know that look. What's bothering you?"

Viktoria's lips stiffened as her stomach twisted. Olivia was about to leave for the day to run errands. It was now or never. Taking a slow, deep breath to finally muster the courage, she proceeded to force the words out.

"You know how Teri and I like to watch her brother's band rehearse in their garage, right?"

"Sure," Olivia said. "In fact, Chris played a song for me when I dropped off those basil plants for his mom last week. He's an amazing guitar player. Why?"

Viktoria chewed on the inside of her lower lip before continuing, "Well, they actually have a gig tonight. There's a party at a house on Comet Avenue and they've been asked to play there. It's their first gig and Teri has been begging me to go with her."

Olivia's smile was replaced with one raised eyebrow. "A party? Viktoria, Chris and his band are all college aged. You know better than to think that I would allow you to go to that kind of party."

"No," Viktoria shot back. "It's not like that. It's a birthday party for Collin Larsen. He's in my grade and his friends are all from his church. They call his dad 'Bishop Larsen.' Seriously, they take early morning Bible classes. Trust me, I'd be lucky if I got a Coke to drink at that party. Look, when Collin finally got his parent's permission to have a band at his party, he called up Chris because he's probably the only guy he knows who has a band. They're just excited to play somewhere else besides their garage. Teri seemed even more excited than them. When she told me at school yesterday and pleaded for me to go with her, well, I, you know."

"Pretend I don't," Olivia said with both eyebrows now raised.

Viktoria winced as she shut her eyes. "I sort of promised I'd go with her."

Olivia sighed, running her fingers through her thick, strawberry blond hair, visibly searching for the right words. "What about our plans for tonight?"

"What about tomorrow night?" Viktoria negotiated. "You're off at six, aren't you? Can't we just move our night over one day this week?"

Olivia sighed again. "Oh, Viktoria, it's not about that. Although, I've been looking forward to tonight all week. I know waiting one more night's not going to kill me. It's just, well, it's just the other things."

"Mom, I know where you're going, and it's not fair. You let me go to parties with Teri all the time before May. Since then, you haven't allowed me to go anywhere at night. All I can do is have Teri over. Think of all the times Teri and I went out on the weekends last year and nothing bad ever happened."

Leaning forward, Olivia rested her elbows on the table. "Things are different now."

"But it's still not fair," Viktoria persisted. "Can I tell you what will be different? I'll be at a house with parents, surrounded by church kids. I'll also be with Teri and the band. I wouldn't be in the dark, outside the school's gym, being ganged up on by a bunch of punks because I was alone. What my circumstances will be tonight couldn't be further from the ones Dylan was in."

Afraid she had just gone too far, Viktoria paused to gauge Olivia's reaction. There wasn't one. She just looked down at her hands resting on the table.

Viktoria continued to state her case, "Come on, Mom. You went to parties all the time when you were in high school. That's how you and Dad started to get to know each other outside of school. You've told me that story a million times. Well, I'm that age now. I want to have fun, make memories, and experience life like a teenager should. Just like you did. You can't let what happened to Dylan hold me back from living my life. It wouldn't be right, and you know he wouldn't want it that way. In fact, we both know he would want me to have the fun experiences he can't have now."

Olivia looked up. As her eyes welled up, she turned them toward the window.

"You're right — you should be with people your own age, having fun. It's time," she said softly as she turned to Viktoria. "I guess I'm just not ready yet. But don't worry about me, I'm going to be just fine. Like you said, there's always tomorrow."

The fake smile plastered on Olivia's face betrayed her thoughts, but Viktoria was more relieved she wasn't going to let Teri down. It would have weighed on her, though, if Olivia were left at home that night feeling disappointed and abandoned. Viktoria needed to resolve that concern.

"Mom, I promise, tomorrow I'm all yours. You choose the movie, the food, everything. It'll all be ready as soon as you get home. Look, I know I let you down, and I'm going to more than make up for it. I promise I won't do this to you again."

"Tomorrow for sure? It's a deal," Olivia said with a half-smile. "You know, I do want you to have fun, be free, and enjoy your teenage years, just like I did. Even more. I just wish what happened never happened. I don't want to feel so scared for you, or so alone."

Viktoria took Olivia's hand. "There's no reason to be scared. Like I said, I'll be with Teri, Chris, and the band, surrounded by other good people. Also, you're not alone, Mom. I'm here. You also have Dad."

"Do I?"

Olivia's sudden, sharp response, and her raised voice and piercing stare cut deep into Viktoria's heart. Turning away from her mom, she walked back to her bedroom, slamming the door shut.

Sitting on her bed, Viktoria looked out the window, imagining her dad's tractor trailer pulling up in front of the house. She hadn't seen that since June, and she wiped away tears knowing she wouldn't see it that morning as well. Hugging her pillow against her chest, she rested her face on its edge. It was about five minutes before three gentle taps on her door were followed by the sound of it being cracked open.

"Viktoria? Can we talk?"

When there was no answer, Olivia came in, sitting on the bed next to her. She put her hand on Viktoria's back, gently rubbing it.

"I'm sorry, Viktoria. I shouldn't have said that. Sometimes I get scared, and I say things I don't mean."

When Viktoria didn't respond, Olivia continued, "Just know that your father and I love each other, and we both love you. We're just adjusting to the transition he made at work, and, sometimes, it gets the best of me. You're right, though. You're here and, guess what? We're all going to get through this. He'll be pulling that big truck up to our house before you know it. I promise. Until then, remind me of that whenever I get impatient and say stupid things I don't mean. Can you do that for me?"

Looking up at Olivia with a slight smile, Viktoria nodded. "Yeah."

"OK," Olivia said softly. "Look, I know you were starving this morning. Did that coffee cake and milk do the trick?"

"Honestly? Not completely."

Olivia leaned in closer to her, putting her arm around Viktoria's shoulders. "Well, it's not even eleven yet," she said with a caring smile. "Teri's not expecting you for a few hours. I think we can make a quick run to Kelly's Frozen Yogurt. I can get you back home a little after noon. You can jump out of the car, and I'll go run my errands. You'll still have enough time to dust, vacuum, and then meet up with Teri. Sound like a deal?"

"Absolutely," Viktoria said with a full smile. She looked down as quiet anxiety constricted her stomach before turning again to Olivia.

"I hope it's a good time to go. The football team and cheerleaders are at the school today gearing up for next week's homecoming game. I know it's their tradition to go to Kelly's after every practice and, well, you know how they can be with Teri and me. I'd just prefer to not see them when I don't have to."

"Trust me, you have nothing to worry about," Olivia said, running her fingers through Viktoria's hair. "I was talking with Nancy in the bakery department last night. She said her daughter was complaining about all the preparations she, the other cheerleaders, and the football team are making today for next week's game. They're expected to be at the school until three o'clock or so."

A sigh of relief loosened the knot in Viktoria's stomach. "Oh, well, that's good."

Olivia agreed with a smile. "That's what I think. Kelly's just opened at ten, so we'll beat the lunchtime rush. I bet we'll be the only ones there. We have nothing to worry about."

Chapter 5

No fruit. No nuts. No whipped cream with a cherry on top. Despite having the title of "The Master Chef" at home and the truck stop, Viktoria's personal tastes were quite simple, especially when it came to desserts. She was very content with the cup sitting in front of her — a mix of chocolate and vanilla frozen yogurt, hot fudge, and M&M's. Olivia's cup, on the other hand, looked like a fruit and nut salad.

The two of them hardly said a word as they enjoyed what they jokingly called "breakfast part two." Looking out the window at passing cars and people, Viktoria could only smile to herself, grateful she could be with her mom just a little longer that morning.

Viktoria scraped the bottom of her cup to get the very last bit of yogurt.

"That's the most depressing sound ever," she said, looking up at Olivia. The two of them laughed.

"Yeah, but did it hit the spot for you?"

A satisfied Viktoria grinned. "Oh yeah. That'll carry me until I get something later at Teri's. What's taking you so long? You're only about halfway done."

"Well, look at mine. I got all the good stuff in it. You only got, like, two toppings. I could've saved my money and made that at home for you."

Viktoria rolled her eyes as Olivia smiled and continued, "So, are you and Teri meeting up at the park as usual?"

"I'm actually meeting her at her house," Viktoria said as she looked out the window. "That movie *Over the Edge* is on channel 10 at two o'clock and you know Teri — she'll never miss a chance to see a Matt Dillon flick, especially that one. She loves it when his hair is longer. After that, I'm sure we'll head over to the party. It's a good walk from her house. Hopefully, we'll get there before Chris and the guys get busy setting up their gear, so I can get some one-on-one time with their new lead guitarist." Turning to Olivia with a grin, Viktoria playfully raised her eyebrows. "Teri says he's pretty hot."

Olivia leaned in toward her. Not amused at all, she locked eyes with her. "Viktoria?"

"Mom, I'm kidding. You know that, right?"

"Viktoria." Olivia didn't budge. The intensity in her eyes and voice only increased. "You know the rules. No dating college aged guys while you're in high school."

For a second, Viktoria could only stare at Olivia in disbelief. "Are you serious? Mom, I know the rules. You've rehearsed them with me a million times. Trust me. You have nothing to worry about. I mean, look at me. I couldn't even get a high school guy to go with me to a Sadie Hawkins dance if my life depended on it. I'm a freak."

"Don't say that." With a pained concern in her eyes, Olivia reached over the table, taking her hands. "You know I hate it when you put yourself down like that. I wish you knew how beautiful you are, and I mean both inside *and* out. Look in a mirror right now. Without all that makeup, you are downright stunning."

"Yeah, Mom, I know where you're going with that, but I like my look. It means a whole lot more to me than getting the attention of some high school guy, which I couldn't care less about. They're all immature pricks."

The awkward silence that followed coupled with Olivia's persistent concerned look caused Viktoria to shake her head with a disarming smile.

"Mom, trust me. I'm not just going to up and run off with the band's new guitarist or whatever. Think about it. *Teri's* the one whose saying he's hot. We know her. He's most likely just a greasy, unkempt, Matt Dillon lookalike. Like I said, you have nothing to worry about."

"Uh-huh," Olivia responded with a slight nod, though her eyes expressed the experienced warning that anything could happen.

Wanting the subject off Olivia's radar, Viktoria looked at her watch. "Look, Mom, it's 12:10. We better get going so I can get my chores done and head over to Teri's."

"OK," her mom said as she as she stood up. "I've got a lot to do, so I'll just drop you off in front of the house."

Olivia then looked around the yogurt shop. Nobody else was there except one employee behind the service counter a good distance from them. She leaned closer to Viktoria and said softly, "Remember what I said. You know the rules. Go to the party, watch the band, and have a fun time."

She then leaned in even closer, raising her eyebrows again. Her voice, though it remained quiet, was more strained to get her message across. "With Teri."

"Yeah, Mom, I got it." Viktoria's whisper was forceful to get her frustration across as Olivia grabbed her purse off the table, looking content for clearly making her point.

As Viktoria grabbed her empty cup, it slipped through her fingers and fell to the floor. Reaching down to pick it up, she heard Olivia's purse and keys drop on the table. As she stood back up, Olivia's ice-cold glare pierced past her toward the entrance. A powerful chill rattled Viktoria's spine. Something was wrong.

The bell above the entrance door chimed as it opened. As Viktoria turned around, a boy walked in wearing a Phoenix Suns jersey and a brand new pair of Nike Terminators.

It was Jason Davis, followed by his mom. Always in a dark pantsuit, her high heels and large red bouffant hairstyle made her appear taller than she really was. Even with a nice figure, excessive jewelry, a white Corvette, and a husband who worshipped the ground she walked on, nothing seemed to cure the perpetual resting scowl on her face.

Viktoria's reaction was no different from Olivia's. The mere sight of them sent a jolt of rage through her as well. To her surprise, though, she had the mindset to press down on her anger as her heart raced and her nervous, clammy hands shook.

At first, Jason was looking at his mom. He said something to her, and they both smiled and laughed. Looking around the dining area, the sight of Viktoria and Olivia instantly stopped him in his tracks. His smile faded as he hung his head and stumbled to a front counter stool. Putting his elbows on the counter, he rested his face in his hands, not responding to the employee's greeting.

As Jason sheepishly responded to their presence, the heat of Olivia's stare burned the back of Viktoria's head. The glare toward them from Jason's mom, Linda, held just as much contempt.

After her eyes shifted between the two of them and her son a couple of times, Linda folded her arms. Her eyes pierced just past Viktoria, directly at Olivia. They were ice cold and callous. Her eyebrows pulled down, and her already narrow lips became even thinner.

Click-Click, Click-Click, Click-Click, Click-Click

The sound of Linda's high heels striking the tile floor along with the clanking of her jewelry grew intolerably loud as she approached Viktoria and Olivia.

With her heart pounding and entire frame shaking, Viktoria froze herself in place. She wanted to stand her ground as a defensive shield for her mom from the oncoming threat. After all, that's what Hawk and Animal would do. The enemy was approaching.

From just a few feet away, the overwhelming stench of Linda's perfume, makeup, and hairspray made Viktoria want to vomit. Still, she refused to stand down. From behind, Olivia's hands gripped Viktoria's upper arms, gently moving her to the side.

Chapter 6

With her arms still folded, Linda Davis stood uncomfortably close to Olivia, who didn't budge. Their eyes remained locked on one another. Viktoria couldn't tell whose glare was colder. After only a few seconds of frigid silence, Olivia's eyes shifted back and forth between Linda and Jason.

Linda turned her head to where her son was sitting, and then back to lock eyes with Olivia.

"What the hell is wrong with you, Olivia?" Sounding like she was scolding a child, Linda's sneer toward Olivia could not have been more condescending. "Don't look at my son that way. In fact, don't look at him at all. We were having a perfectly fun Saturday together and now, because of you, he's sitting over there, moping and feeling horrible about something he had absolutely nothing to do with. Nothing at all."

Still resting his face in his hands, Jason's sniffling was constant. Still, though, Viktoria had no compassion for him.

She refocused on the two women as Olivia said, "Something he had nothing to do with?" Olivia's bright green eyes were as wide as saucers. With a bewildered half-smile, her look toward Linda was one of utter disbelief. "You know why your son is sitting over there with his head down. It's because he knows what he and his friends did was beyond horrible, and so is the irreversible loss and grief it caused. He also knows there is absolutely nothing — nothing at all — that his overprotective parents can buy, say, or do to take away that reality."

Linda's flush face tensed with a forced rush of air through her flared nostrils. For once, she was speechless, and her scorching glare did nothing to stop Olivia from continuing, "So, go enjoy the weekend with your son. Heaven knows that because of him and his friends, I won't be able to do the same."

"Olivia!" Linda's eyes narrowed as rigid cords formed in her neck. "Jason and his friends had nothing to do with . . . What happened at the dance was something kids, especially boys, do all the time. It's normal. They outgrow it. And there was no way for them to know what was going to happen afterward. For all any of us know . . . Look, there is no proof the two unfortunate events were related. I'm not trying to trivialize the pain you're going through, Olivia. Really, I'm not. But my son and his friends are good kids. It's not fair that they are punishing themselves for something they, I'll say it again, had nothing to do with."

It seemed to Viktoria that the look Olivia was giving Linda Davis could have struck her dead right there. Still, her voice remained calm, cool, and collected. "'Normal.' 'They outgrow it.' 'There is no proof the two unfortunate events were related.' That's interesting, Linda. Judge Gerald Hall, who, it's no secret, runs in the same social circles as you and your husband, used those same words when he dismissed the charges."

A smug grin formed on Linda's face. "Judge Hall didn't make his decision based on who he socializes with. Which, by the way, is his own right and business. He did so because, well, he was right — bottom line."

It took no time at all for Olivia to counter. "No, Linda, he was half right. Sure, it's normal. Kids torment, fight, and bully one another. Judge Hall was wrong, though, when he said, 'they outgrow it.' No, they don't. *It* only takes a different form when they become adults. Just look at you and the other parents. The case was dropped. You won. Still, you keep coming after us. Just look at yourself right now."

Linda opened her mouth, as if to refute, but remained silent as Olivia lessened the space between them.

"Oh, Linda, and *it*, as adults, can involve even more individuals who can also pass it on to their children. I can honestly say that I didn't know how much influence you and the other parents had until we pressed charges against your son and his friends. I underestimated how much children listen to their parents. But now I know, and so does my daughter."

With her eyebrows pulled even closer together, Linda's lips moved up and down, as though she were trying to put all the words in her head in the right order before she spoke. "How could you—"

Olivia suddenly cut her off. "Raise two wonderful kids? It's easy, Linda. Instead of teaching them to look down on and mistreat others who are different from them, I taught them to look at those differences as opportunities to grow, expand, and make friends who would teach them things they couldn't have learned on their own. I'm sorry Jason and his friends never learned that in their homes. It would have saved them from the horrible burden they will always have to carry. They see beyond their parents' denial. They also know Judge Hall was wrong when he said, 'there is no proof the two unfortunate events were related.'"

"Hey!" Linda snapped. "We are great parents — all of us. And Jason and his friends are sweet, wonderful boys. What happened at the . . . What Dylan chose to do after . . . Look, haven't you put these kids through enough?"

With her eyes still locked on Linda's, Olivia grabbed her purse and keys off the table. Her voice was quiet but remained strong. "You have two children, Linda. A daughter and a son, both the same age as mine. Heaven forbid, but if there comes a time when you would have to bury one of them, that's when you can come to me and tell me when it's enough."

Viktoria didn't look at Linda, Jason, or the server as she followed her mom out of Kelly's Frozen Yogurt. Without saying a word, she got in the car when Olivia reached over and unlocked her door.

On the way home, Viktoria looked out the passenger window in silence as Olivia aggressively shifted gears in their old Datsun 1800. Just a few blocks from the house, she turned to Olivia, who wiped tears from both sides of her face as she kept her eyes on the road. Shaking her head as she gripped the steering wheel, Olivia's voice shook with emotion. "You know, I think about it all the time. If there was just one thing I could go back and change, it would be to not talk Dylan into going to that stupid school dance. He never wanted to do anything social. I thought it'd be good for him. I thought it would, I don't know, help break him out of his shell. I was so wrong, so very wrong. I wish I knew what he was going through."

With the pain in her mom's words, the sorrow in Viktoria's chest threatened to swell beyond its limit. She managed to hold them down, though, so Olivia wouldn't have to be a mom for once. She could finally be with someone who would just listen to her as she grieved, even if it had to be her daughter.

As the car pulled up in front of the house, Viktoria knew what she needed to do. No other option existed anymore. Unbuckling her seat belt, she turned to Olivia.

"Mom, I was just thinking. I see the band play in Teri's garage all the time. I'm not really in the mood to spend my Saturday night watching them play the same songs, just in a different location. I'd rather spend it quietly at home, eating pizza, and watching a movie. Just us two."

Olivia looked at her with a warm smile, and said with a soft, vulnerable voice, "Really? You mean that?"

Viktoria nodded with an assuring smile. "Yeah. Absolutely."

"So, back to Plan A for tonight? Are you sure Teri won't mind?"

"Don't worry about Teri. She'll have fun with or without me. I'll pick up a movie this afternoon and you can stop by Angelo's Pizzeria."

Saying *Angelo's Pizzeria* with an overly exaggerated Italian accent, Viktoria was able to get a genuine smile and snicker out of Olivia. She needed to see that just one more time before they went their separate ways for the day.

"Thank you, Viktoria. Well, you better go get your chores done so you can meet up with Teri."

"You got it. I'll be home around six, OK?"

As Viktoria opened the car door, Olivia reached over and took her hand. "I love you, Viktoria."

She squeezed Olivia's hand, struggling to keep her emotions under the surface. "You know, Mom, if I could take back just one thing as well, it would've been to not give Dylan stupid big sister advice on how to approach his secret crush at that dance. He was too good for Candace anyway. If she turns out to be anything like her older sister, then Dylan is way better off with real angels."

With a sweet smile and a soft, comforting giggle, Olivia squeezed back. "It's going to be OK, Viktoria. I promise."

Viktoria nodded, returning the smile. "I love you too, Mom. I'll see you later, OK?" The thoughtfulness in her voice was mixed with a casual tone as well. It was Viktoria's way of wishing them both, especially her mom, a much better remainder of the day.

As Olivia drove off, the peace that fell over Viktoria told her that she made the right choice. Her mom needed her and, for once, she could be there for her instead of vice versa.

Walking toward the front door, another challenge loomed over her. She now had to break it to Teri that she wasn't going to the party after all.

She told Olivia not to worry about Teri. Viktoria, however, who knew Teri better than anyone, *was* worried.

Chapter 7

With only twenty minutes, it wasn't her most detailed work, not by a long shot. The trip to Kelly's Frozen Yogurt with her mom put her far behind schedule. Viktoria, however, managed to get her chores done just before one o'clock. Right on time.

Whether it was her usual work schedule or running errands, Olivia was always gone by the time Saturday afternoon rolled around. It was Viktoria's alone time — with Dylan.

She wasn't worried about missing the first half or so of *Over the Edge*; Teri would be too fixated on Matt Dillon to notice she wasn't there anyway. Nestled on the couch with a glass of cold water, Viktoria turned the TV on to what no one knew was her favorite show: World Class Championship Wrestling, also known as WCCW.

Airing weekly from the Sportatorium in Dallas, Texas, the show featured a number of the large, gruff, sweaty men she saw and read about in *Pro Wrestling Illustrated* beating the life out of one another in a ring.

No one would ever imagine a girl like Viktoria would even think of, much less love, watching professional wrestling, but there were two reasons why she tuned in with anticipation and watched it every Saturday afternoon: Dylan and Kerry Von Erich.

Nobody was hooked on WCCW like Dylan. Every Saturday, he always made sure he had lunch at one o'clock so he could watch the Texas-based professional wrestling program.

Viktoria couldn't stand it. It would drive her up the wall when she was watching another show and Dylan would come in and commandeer the TV. They argued at first, but Olivia then established that, when WCCW was on, the TV was Dylan's. Without a choice, Viktoria begrudgingly watched it with him.

Sitting on the floor with his legs crossed like a pretzel, Dylan would lean forward with intense interest as he watched WCCW. Looking up from the *TV Guide*, recipe book, or some other magazine she was reading, Viktoria couldn't help but smile with him.

When one of his heroes won, or some great performance was taking place in or around the wrestling ring, it both warmed and pained Viktoria as Dylan turned and looked up at her with excitement. The severe scarring on the right side of his beautiful, contagious smile was both a reminder to cherish each moment together and of the reason he never had a friend to bring to their house.

March 10, 1978, just one week past Dylan's fifth birthday, was a horrible night for Viktoria's family. She could clearly remember how hard her heart pounded in the backseat of that Datsun 1800. With her mom driving and her grandmother in the front seat, the buildings and streetlights were just a blur at the speed they were going.

She also never forgot the tight grip of Olivia's hand as she all but dragged her running into the hospital's emergency room in North Phoenix. For a seven-year-old girl, hearing her tall, superhuman dad wince in terrible pain was alarming.

Rushing to embrace him, they were unaware of his broken ribs. "For stramt. For stramt," he said to Viktoria's grandmother before turning to Olivia, who didn't speak Norwegian. "Too tight. Too tight." Putting her arms around his leg, Viktoria would never forget the comfort of her dad's hand on the back of her head, pressing her against his hip.

"It's a miracle he's still with us," said the doctor in the emergency room hours later. The driver of the pickup truck that plowed into Viktoria's dad's car at the intersection of North 27th Avenue and West Indian School Road was too drunk to even be aware of what was going on when the police officer put him in handcuffs. He had already passed out again in the back of the squad car before it left the scene.

The old Ford pickup struck the passenger side of the car at full speed, where Dylan was sitting. The solid body of Viktoria's dad's Plymouth Road Runner was most likely the reason Dylan survived.

At first, the only thing she enjoyed when wrestling was on was Dylan's enthusiasm. Looking up from the floor at her with his smile meant everything. To the rest of the world, the wide jagged scar disfiguring his face from an inch above his right eye down to his jawbone was a mere display of the damage the shattered glass of a car door window could do. To Viktoria, it was a reminder of a night when she almost lost the chance to ever see his smile again. But she hadn't, and it was never lost on her.

Also, to the rest of the world, Dylan's difficulty forming sentences, slurred speech, and constant repetition from the trauma his brain suffered was nothing more than a tragic example of the permanent damage a horrible accident could cause. Again, to Viktoria, it was a reminder of a night when she almost lost the chance to hear his voice again.

Over and over, with his eyes fixed on the TV, Dylan sat with excitement, educating Viktoria about the history and characteristics of WCCW and each wrestler — facts and statistics he had already told her a thousand times before. Again and again, as though she were watching it for the first time ever, he would update her on the current feuds and other storylines — facts she could obviously see and hear for herself, but she understood Dylan did not have the ability to comprehend that.

Dylan's incessant repetition along with his speech impediments drove other individuals crazy, especially other kids. Along with his facial scar, it was the reason he would come home from school in tears, weary from constant ridicule and harassment. They would only hear, not listen.

When it came to WCCW especially, Dylan's gift of gathering and retaining knowledge and statistics was unmatched. Viktoria quickly realized that. She listened. Her brother's excitement, his smile, the history, the storylines, the feuds, the statistics, and the wrestlers. It all hit Viktoria one day — she, too, was hooked.

From that point on, Dylan no longer spent endless hours aimlessly riding his bike throughout the neighborhood and the park trying to make friends, just to come home alone and weary with sadness. He finally had a friend: his older sister. Their secret bond? Professional wrestling.

Along with Hawk and Animal of The Road Warriors, Kerry of the Von Erich brothers in WCCW were Dylan's favorite wrestlers of all time. His dream match was to see The Road Warriors come to WCCW so his three favorite wrestlers could join forces to defeat The Fabulous Freebirds. Unfortunately, those stars never aligned.

Regardless, every time Kerry Von Erich, with his size, strength, and electrifying charisma, appeared on TV, Dylan's reaction and words were always the same. His small, painfully thin torso would twist as he turned and looked up at Viktoria with his infectious smile.

"I'm going to be like Kerry Von Erich someday, and, when I am, I'm going to join The Road Warriors."

With a nod and determined smile, Viktoria's response was always the same as well. "I know that'll be you someday, and I can't wait. I'm a huge Kerry Von Erich fan too, you know."

It was true. Kerry Von Erich captivated her, but for different reasons. With his chiseled body and face to match, charisma, radiant smile, rock god hair, and Texas drawl, she couldn't get enough of him.

As with her newfound love of professional wrestling, no one would have ever guessed a girl like Viktoria would be into a guy like him. She was, though; she craved him.

She was hooked on professional wrestling, especially WCCW. She would never admit it to anyone. Not her parents, and, above all, not Teri.

It was fine for a young boy to love wrestling. But a girl in high school? Whenever she begged Dylan to never tell anyone, he would nod with a playful grin and bring his index finger up to his lips, as if to say *this is our secret.*

The excitement between them for the next wrestling program was palpable. Walking together to 7-Eleven to purchase the most recent issue of *Pro Wrestling Illustrated* was the most anticipated event of each month. After cutting out his favorite pictures, he would hand the magazine off to Viktoria to read. The stash under her bed kept growing.

The most cut out pictures were those of Animal and Hawk. Taping their pictures to his bedroom wall, he would point to them almost every time Viktoria passed by.

"That's me one day."

"I'll be right there with you," Viktoria would say with a challenging, playful grin.

The four most recent issues of *Pro Wrestling Illustrated* at the top of her secret stash were missing something vital — they were complete. There were no longer jagged edges on certain pages where Dylan's favorite pictures were cut out.

It was the same with Viktoria's life — something vital was missing, yet, in an indescribable way, she felt complete. She missed her little brother more than anything. Somehow, though, their relationship was stronger than ever. Their bond was growing deeper.

Chapter 8

The Sportatorium in Dallas, Texas was filled with energized, screaming fans eager to hear the first bell that would start off the show. That's how it was every Saturday afternoon. The camera crew wanted to make sure everyone watching on TV across the country, like Viktoria, knew that.

Leaning forward on the couch, she was ready. It was the time of the week she lived for. Finally, she could be alone with her brother, doing what they loved.

Even after losing Dylan, their weekly routine never changed. Only the roles reversed. Her little brother could no longer be heard, but Viktoria knew how much he wanted the story to be told. She made sure he still had a voice.

It had only been a few weeks since it hit Viktoria just how much the roles truly had been reversed, and in more ways than one. It used to be Dylan who would faithfully keep his big sister, the one who looked after him and tried to protect him, updated on all the wrestling action. Now it was her keeping Dylan, who was looking over and strengthening her, updated on all the wrestling action.

Sitting alone in the living room, talking out loud to herself, anybody would've thought she was losing it. Viktoria knew better. She had a promise to keep — one she made to Dylan at his grave.

As with every other Saturday since he died, Viktoria's eyes were glued to the TV, faithfully commentating on the storylines, feuds, and statistics of the wrestlers.

After the longest commercial break, Viktoria sat up on the edge of the couch. It was the moment she had yearned for all week. Recovering from a terrible motorcycle accident, Kerry Von Erich was making his first TV appearance in four months.

Every word, smile, look, and nuance from Kerry Von Erich left her biting her lower lip, wide-eyed, and speechless. As his promo ended, Viktoria needed to shake herself back into reality to update Dylan.

His long awaited return was everything she had expected. The persistent craving had finally been satisfied.

There was still more WCCW action to go.

Come on, Viktoria. Stay focused.

Her promise to keep Dylan in the WCCW loop was going to be kept no matter what.

As soon as the main event was over with Bruiser Brody's win over Black Bart, Viktoria jumped up, turning off the TV. *Over the Edge* was about to begin, and Teri's house was a good twenty minute walk away.

In the bathroom, after exfoliating and moisturizing her face, Viktoria paused at her reflection in the mirror. She was back at that moment on June 1. The girl staring back at her was the same, though she had given up dyeing her hair jet black since May. Her hair was back to its natural blond, and it somehow served to enhance her style even more. It was also the same color as Dylan's hair.

It was striking how much they both resembled their Norwegian father — their bright blue eyes, narrow straight noses, fair skin, and slender frames. They weren't twins, but they were identical. In front of the mirror, it warmed Viktoria's heart to reflect on how similar she and Dylan were in both looks and personality. Not only was he still by her side, but he was within her as well.

Taking a deep breath, her eyes flashed with determination. She would soon step out her front door and into battle.

The enemy was in constant surprise attack position: self-doubt, fear, intimidation, belittling, failure, and the beautiful suburban monsters. It was teenage, middle America, residential guerilla warfare, and Viktoria was determined to win for Dylan and for herself.

Confidence, fearlessness, courageous convictions, standing her ground — these were the weapons needed to defeat the enemy, and it required complete self-reinvention.

Reaching into the drawer to begin her daily routine even took on a different meaning altogether. No longer was she trying to emulate her goth rock heroes. The look she had shared with Teri since perfecting it over the summer of 1982 to enter seventh grade with their own fashion statement was no longer about shock value, expressing musical taste, parental abhorrence, or open rebellion against the preppy masses. It still was for Teri, but not for Viktoria.

With the exception of her hair returning to blond, Viktoria looked the same, but everything was different. Like Animal and Hawk, there was meaning and symbolism behind every aspect of her makeup and attire to put her in the mindset for battle and undisputable victory. It was war paint.

A little sunscreen and primer preceded her favorite foundation, which was two shades lighter than her natural skin tone. Setting it with a light face powder gave her face a pale glow, symbolizing Dylan's relentless innocence and dreams of a brighter future, no matter how terrible the world was to him. It reminded Viktoria to never lose sight of her vision and promises to Dylan, no matter what the enemy said or did.

After filling her eyebrows with a light brown eye shadow for just the right color, next came the black eye shadow. Strong on her upper eyelids and crease, it gradually faded before reaching her eyebrows. The eye shadow was then used lightly on her lower eyelids.

Starting on the inside of her eyelid, moving outward, her black liquid eyeliner created a winged look extending just past the corner of her eye. Finishing off with two coats of black mascara, her eyelashes appeared even darker.

Viktoria's eye makeup was no longer a vampy goth look. It served to accent the natural features she and her brother shared. The world would have to see her brother's beauty on her since it refused to see it on him. It also ignited the challenging thrill that the war paint was on, and she was ready, if needed, for battle.

Her final application was her flawless black lipstick, symbolizing her willingness to do or say anything, even if it had to be dark or acidic, to defend herself, her family, and Dylan's honor. Also, to speak up with boldness for anything necessary in her quest to give Dylan the life he deserved — through her.

Her face mist kept it all in place, looking fresh, and her skin hydrated. It was Arizona, after all. It looked like a lot of work, but Viktoria was experienced enough to create her look in just over ten minutes.

Dressed in dark attire, which, to her, represented the color of battle, her eyes flashed again with determination, focusing on her most prized possession hanging from her black spiked dog collar: her grandmother's Norwegian silver cross.

The only thing she brought to the United States along with her son and some clothes after World War II, her grandmother gave Viktoria her cross just two weeks before she unexpectedly passed away in her sleep in April. With heavy, concerned eyes and her thick Norwegian accent, she placed the cross in Viktoria's hand.

"Your brother is special. He needs you. You need him. Always stay by his side."

After losing Dylan just one month later, her grandmother's words echoed within her, piercing her heart forever. Somehow, her grandmother must have known.

It was not a fashion statement or for enhancing her style in any way. The cross hung above Viktoria's heart to not only remind her of her grandmother's words, but also of her conviction that a day would come when she and her family, including her grandmother and Dylan, would all be together again, never having to say goodbye.

Touching her grandmother's cross held a special power. Igniting an inner strength and faith, she could speak with, feel, and even hear Dylan. Perhaps there never was a goodbye in the first place.

After one last look over in the mirror, Viktoria nodded.

"We're ready, Dylan, let's do this."

Heading toward the front door, she rehearsed in her mind how she was going to break it to Teri that she wasn't going to the party after all. There was no easy way around it.

Playing out every scenario she could possibly imagine made Viktoria feel prepared for what she anticipated. Nothing, though, could have prepared her for what awaited her that afternoon — both the good and the bad.

Chapter 9

Making it to North 74th Avenue in record time, the band's music blared from Teri's garage as Viktoria turned onto West Shangri-la Street. Catching her ear more than anything was a guitar solo being played at machine-gun speed.

Is that their new lead guitarist? Stan never played like that. That's insane!

Mismatched gravel and random wild cactus plants made Teri's front yard the eyesore of their neighborhood, so crossing over it to save a few extra steps to the front door was no issue. Viktoria especially avoided the driveway when the band was playing in the garage. The thought of them looking at her walking up alone made her self-conscious. She didn't want to look awkward or vulnerable like some sort of intrusive loner.

Familiar lines from *Over the Edge* blared from the TV as Viktoria knocked on the door.

"The door's unlocked, Viktoria!"

The overwhelming cigarette stench, as always, stung Viktoria's nostrils as her lungs burned, crying for fresh air. The movie was reaching its halfway point. Thanks to Teri, Viktoria had every scene and line memorized backward and forward.

No one was sitting on the couch, though the smoke of a lit cigarette danced into the air from an ashtray on the coffee table.

"It's about freaking time you got here!" Teri's voice shouted over the TV from the kitchen. "When are you going to get your license? You turned sixteen over a month ago!"

Viktoria shrugged as she walked into the kitchen. "What's the point? I'd end up just like you — licensed with no car."

Turning from the pot she was stirring on the stove, Teri smiled at Viktoria as her words slurred from the cigarette glowing between her lips. "Yeah, parents suck. Don't they?"

"Speak for yourself," Viktoria said as Teri turned again to the stove with her eyebrows raised and a consenting nod. "By the way, where are your parents this weekend?"

Teri shrugged as she stirred with a big wooden spoon. "Who knows and who the hell cares?"

Next to the stove stood four empty, bleeding cans of a knock-off store-brand SpaghettiOs. Viktoria's smile faded as her heart ached for Teri and Chris.

"Let me take a look in the fridge and the pantry. I'll see what I can whip up for a killer side dish."

With a sigh, Teri turned to Viktoria again, taking another drag before placing her cigarette in an ashtray on the kitchen counter. "Don't worry, Swedish Chef."

"Norwegian," Viktoria corrected with a lighthearted grin.

"Whatever. This isn't for us. We're hitting that new Mexican joint after I'm done drooling over Matt Dillon. This is for Chris and the rest of the band. Oh, and just like you, I have some tricks of my own in the kitchen as well."

Pulling store-brand saltine crackers out of the pantry, Teri crushed two heaping handfuls before adding them to the imitation SpaghettiOs. "See? I'm right up there with you."

Teri's turquoise eyes gleamed with her serene smile, one that always warmed Viktoria. It possessed a soft, maternal comfort.

Even with her makeup, Teri's face always appeared sweet and kind. Her foundation was only one shade lighter than her skin, and her eyeshadow was not as dark or pronounced as Viktoria's. Her lipstick always matched her hair, which was dark purple and a little below shoulder length.

Though she always dressed in black and anything jewel-toned like Viktoria, she appeared not as dark or morbid. In fact, there was a certain brightness and charm about her. At just barely five foot one, she was just as slender as Viktoria, so others saw her as harmless or even an easy target.

Viktoria knew better, though. She saw the silver streak that flashed in Teri's eyes when others threw names or other verbal jabs at her and Viktoria. Along with that, there was that venomous smirk in her sweet smile, one so subtle only Viktoria could see, hinting at some kind of ace up her sleeve, that said *whatever you dare try to inflict on me, I will turn it right back on you tenfold.* It was the mere thought of that smirk that made the knot in Viktoria's stomach tighter with each step to Teri's house.

"The guys can help themselves," Teri said as she placed some bowls and spoons on the counter. "They're all nervous about the gig tonight, so there's no telling when they'll take a break. Let's go finish the movie."

"Finally," said Viktoria. "If you don't turn down the TV, you're going to blow the speakers."

"How else am I going to hear the movie with the band blaring just on the other side of the wall?"

Viktoria could only shake her head and smile. "By the way, with all the noise and you being in the kitchen, how did you know it was me at the door? It's like how I approach you at the park as quietly as possible when your eyes are closed, and you suddenly open them and magically know I'm standing right there. It's kind of creepy. It's like you have some sort of sixth sense."

"I do," Teri said gravely as smoke escaped her lips. "In my bedroom every night, I light my candle. I'll never tell a soul what I do or to whom I pray following that, but that deity grants me the power to know where you, Viktoria, are and everything you're doing. Even when I appear to not be there, I see you."

The conviction in Teri's eyes and the ominous gravity of her voice was uncharacteristic of her. Caught off guard, Viktoria didn't know how to react. Following a few seconds of awkward silence, Teri lost her poker face with a snicker.

"You're such a dingbat, I swear. I saw you through the window. It's like at the park. I can hear your footsteps. The fact that you're trying to approach me as quietly as possible makes *you* the creep."

Viktoria laughed with a lighthearted smirk. "Shut up. No, it doesn't. It just became like a game to me after a while because your timing is way too good. I swear you have the ears of a wolf. Oh, and what's creepier than anything is how convincing you just were."

"Yeah, maybe I should take Drama and cut my teeth in school plays," said Teri, to which they both laughed, knowing there was not a snowball's chance in hell of that ever happening.

Teri took one last drag of her kitchen cigarette before putting it out in the ashtray. "Let's go finish the movie. My true love awaits me."

Sitting on the couch, Viktoria turned to Teri, who brought her living room cigarette back to life as her eyes fixated on the TV screen. To Viktoria's temporary reprieve, it was obvious nothing was going to break Teri's laser focus on the movie. For the next forty-five minutes, the knot in her stomach only persisted in twisting and turning.

Ugh, how do I even begin to break it to her?

It wasn't until the credits rolled that Teri put out her last cigarette and turned off the TV. "Whew! Got my Matt Dillon fill. Man, he is such a babe! I don't know about you, but I'm craving some serious Mexican food right now. Let's get out of here."

Taking hold of her grandmother's cross, Viktoria closed her eyes.

I guess there's no other way than to just say it. If you can, please help me, Dylan. You know Mom needs us.

Viktoria forced the words out as they both got up from the couch. "Wait. Before we leave, Teri, I need to tell you—"

"Just a second," Teri said, cutting Viktoria off as she glared into the kitchen. "You know, those guys can really drive me up the freaking wall sometimes."

"Why?"

"Look," Teri said with a scowl as she pointed into the kitchen. "The bowls and spoons are still next to the pot. They didn't touch my food. Can you believe that? That's it. We're leaving through the garage."

Following her through the kitchen, a gust of hot wind blasted Viktoria's face as Teri swung open the door leading into the garage.

"Chris." Teri's nagging was that of an annoyed yet concerned mother. "I told you guys over an hour ago that lunch was going to be ready in ten minutes. Well, guess what? It's all cold now."

Chris shrugged, lighting a cigarette of his own. "We were going to get to it. We're just making sure we have our chops down for tonight."

Teri folded her arms, shaking her head as she leaned against the doorframe. "Well, you're going to have to warm it up again yourselves because Viktoria and I are off. You guys better eat it. The four of you can't play on empty stomachs."

Viktoria had to laugh. Teri really did sound like a nagging mother.

"What's so funny?" Teri asked, turning to Viktoria with endearing embarrassment in her snicker. "I'm not going to stand here and allow them to go hungry, especially on their big night. Anyway, let's head out through the garage."

Following Teri through the doorway, Viktoria squinted as she looked down at her feet. Blinded by the Arizona brightness beaming into the garage, the last thing she wanted was to look like an idiot by stumbling down the two steps leading into the garage and crashing into Grant Coleman's bass guitar amplifier.

Tapping the crash cymbal on Marty De Soto's drum set as she strutted to the opposite side of the garage, Teri stopped near the front. Standing next to her was a tall lean figure with an electric guitar hanging from his shoulders. Still squinting because her eyes hadn't yet adjusted, that was all Viktoria could make out.

"Well, Viktoria? Aren't you going to introduce yourself to the one who saved the band's butt after Stan bailed on us?" Teri asked.

The more Viktoria's eyes adjusted, the less she could believe them. In shock, she reached up, gripping her grandmother's cross.

No way. No freaking way, Dylan. This would be so you, though.

And if this is your doing, I owe you — big time!

Chapter 10

Trying to keep a neutral face, she turned from his captivating smile to Teri. Covering one side of her face with her hand so only Viktoria could read her lips, Teri, with an enchanted flash in her eyes, mouthed the words, *Isn't he hot?*

Viktoria's answer to that question could only be heard in her mind.

Oh, Teri, you have no idea.

With his chiseled face, smile, and allure, as well as his long, flowing dirty-blond hair, like that of a rock god, the band's new shredding lead guitarist was a dead ringer for, of all people, Kerry Von Erich.

It was uncanny; downright freakish. For a second, Viktoria had to question whether or not she was still at home, asleep and dreaming.

Minus the sixty pounds of extra muscle, he had it all. At around six foot three, he was lean, but in a strong, rugged way. With well-worn cowboy boots, jeans, and an unbuttoned flannel shirt over a white T-shirt, it looked as though he had just come from driving cattle on a ranch that morning straight to the garage for rehearsals.

Large, pronounced veins bulged from his suntanned forearms and hands. Perhaps they came from years of blazing guitar chops, a physically exerting outdoor lifestyle, or both. It didn't matter. All Viktoria knew was, looking at those forearms and hands, along with the rest of him, she more than liked what she saw.

Not one word had been exchanged between the two of them. Still, his smile, the way his ethereal blue eyes gazed at her, his aura, even the way he stood with that guitar . . . it was undeniable. He was not only everything Viktoria wanted, but he was also everything she needed.

"Viktoria." By the slow, long pronunciation of her name, Teri might as well have waved her hand directly in front of her face, saying, *Earth to Viktoria*. "Again, aren't you going to say hi to the new lead guitarist of the band?"

Shaken back to the present moment, Viktoria's embarrassment from her stunned silence was only exasperated by the snickering from the rest of the band. She shook her head and said, "Yeah, of course. Shut up, guys. I was just about to."

With a quiet, slow breath, Viktoria braced herself as she turned again to him. She could only hope her eyes and smile didn't reveal too much. Letting out a quick sigh to come across as keeping it casual was victory enough for the confidence to push her words out. "I'm sorry. My mind just drew a blank there for some reason. Hi, I'm Viktoria."

His nod was that of a charming Southern gentleman. It complemented his wink and smile perfectly.

"No reason to apologize. I'm as scatterbrained as they come. I'm Matt. Matt Sorenson."

His warm, strong voice was too kind and reassuring for Viktoria to keep her guard up. Her lips quivered, dying to open herself to him — to tell him her hopes and dreams, even her fears and insecurities. There was something about his drawl that conveyed wisdom beyond his age and offered a soft place to land.

That drawl! I know that drawl. Do you know what I'm thinking, Dylan?

Though Viktoria wanted nothing more than for the two of them to disappear together, there were still four other individuals in the garage. She had to continue to play it cool.

"Sorensen. That makes you Scandinavian."

He smiled and winked again. "That's right. My grandfather's from Denmark."

That wink. *Way* too heart melting. A battle in the war was brewing on the internal front between her lifelong insecurities and her quest for unshakeable self-confidence. Viktoria had to strike back. Her weapon of choice? A casual nod while adding a teasing spice to her voice.

"Not bad, a quarter. My dad's from Norway."

His capitulating nod and smile to the *who's more Scandinavian* challenge oozed a lethal level of confidence. Yet just the right amount of shyness and vulnerability was mixed in — barely detectible, but enough to be adorable. He might have been totally unaware of it, but he was striking back.

With no other option but winning this battle, the Road Warrior within Viktoria had to advance. Forget overthinking and jumping to defeatist conclusions as Teri suddenly reached over, gripping his upper arm. That was what prewar Viktoria would've done, but not anymore.

Like Hawk and Animal would, she kept her eyes locked on his. The rest of the universe didn't exist. Pressing her lips together, she remembered her black lipstick and what it symbolized.

You know what you want, Viktoria. Show him what you got.

"You know, Danish is very similar to Norwegian, but you definitely don't have an accent anywhere near like my dad's. Where are *you* from?"

Matt beamed with pride. "Dallas, Texas."

With her heart pounding out of her chest, it took everything Viktoria had to keep her eyes focused on his. As nonchalantly as she could pretend, she reached up, taking a loose hold of her grandmother's cross. Just underneath her casual veneer, her mind couldn't stop racing.

Dylan! Did you hear that? Dallas, Texas. The Sportatorium! Look at him. Listen to that drawl. He's a freaking Von Erich, I swear! Still, though, look at him. This guy is obviously a rugged, outdoorsy, Texas cowboy. You know how much I love that look but look at me — I'm this suburban goth chick. What would a guy like him see or have in common with a girl like—

"Skeletal Family."

With Matt's voice, Viktoria's eyes regained their focus.

"What?"

Matt pointed at her shirt.

"Skeletal Family. I love that band. Especially the guitar sound on their *Futile Combat* album."

With her eyes like saucers and her jaw dropped, Viktoria's face had more than betrayed her thoughts. Maintaining a cool, collected facade was no longer necessary. The battle against her internal enemy was abruptly obsolete or won. Either way, she didn't care; she had discovered a powerful external ally.

"Whoa, wait. *You* like Skeletal Family?"

Matt's response couldn't have been more zealous. "Heck yeah! I *love* that scene! The Sisters of Mercy, Fields of the Nephilim, and you can't forget Bauhaus."

"Are you serious?" Viktoria was blown away. "It's like you're looking at my tape collection!"

"I'm also a huge fan of the West Coast scene," Matt continued. "Do you like Minutemen, X, or Social Distortion? And, of course, look at me. I have to love Tex & the Horseheads."

Viktoria all but jumped with excitement. "No way! I thought I was the only person who's ever heard of Tex & the Horseheads! You know, there's this killer record store just off of Indian School Road that I know you'd—"

"We need to get going." Teri's words, coming loud and clear, cut Viktoria off.

Viktoria was nowhere near finishing her conversation with Matt. "No, hold on a min—"

"Viktoria, I'm starving," Teri growled.

"Teri," Viktoria responded with her own urgency. "Can't you wait just one minute?"

"No." Teri's single-word response was dramatic and slow to get her point across. Letting go of Matt's arm, she marched up to Viktoria. "Come on. Let's go."

Viktoria could only turn to Matt with an awkward smile as Teri grabbed her wrist, pulling her out of the garage and down the driveway.

Though her encounter with Matt was all too brief, it hit Viktoria like a bolt of lightning. The two of them already had a history before they even met. They had too much in common. Sure, their common musical tastes were unique enough, but there was something deeper than that. Looking so different but being so similar, they were both not what they appeared to be. It wasn't until then that Viktoria realized what she had been missing in her life.

There was so much more to Viktoria than what the world saw, just as there was so much more to Dylan than his facial scars, impeded speech, and brain trauma from the accident. When she lost Dylan, she lost her misunderstood, misfit ally. She was alone.

From his flowing hair to his captivating smile to his strong, rugged features, Matt, to Viktoria, was everything that made a man physically attractive. Still, it was his quiet confidence, Texas gentleman charm, stunning musical talent, and their shared love of obscure bands that made him beautiful to her. It was obvious that there was so much more to Matt than the simple cowboy the rest of the world saw.

Her left wrist still in Teri's grasp as they turned onto the sidewalk, Viktoria gripped her grandmother's cross with her right hand. A smile came across her face as a vision of Dylan filled her mind's eye. He was sitting cross-legged on the floor in their living room, and just as when one of his wrestling heroes won a big match, his small torso was twisted around, looking at Viktoria with his big, beautiful smile. She got the message.

You don't know how much I love you, Dylan.

Matt. Another misunderstood, misfit ally. Perhaps Viktoria wouldn't have to stand physically alone in this war for much longer. Missing the party that night had just gone from disappointing to heartbreaking.

Chapter 11

For such a small girl who smoked like there was no tomorrow, Teri's pace was unmatched when she walked with a purpose. She must have really been starving. Viktoria found herself on the verge of jogging to keep up with her.

Having to maintain such a fast pace turned out to be a blessing in disguise for Viktoria, though. Time was running out fast for her to confess to Teri that she wasn't going to the party and concentrating on trying to keep up with her kept the knot in her stomach at bay.

It was pointless trying to bring it up anyway, as Teri wouldn't let up talking her ear off about school gossip, teachers she hated, some new TV show that came out that fall, and other things Viktoria couldn't care less about. Her mind was on Matt. She found herself wondering what was going to hurt worse: going back on her promise to Teri or that she wasn't going to see Matt again that night.

After several blocks of watching the back of Teri's chatting head, Viktoria finally caught up to her when they reached the park just down the street from her own house. As they were cutting through, Teri stopped, sitting down on a large rock under the only tree around, which was her usual spot when waiting for Viktoria on all other Saturdays.

Lighting a cigarette, she closed her eyes, enjoying the breeze as she took the longest drag. With a befuddled shrug, Viktoria raised her hands to her sides.

"Teri. What the hell?"

"What?" Teri responded with a shrug of her own.

Viktoria could only shake her head. "You know, I can't read you at all sometimes. Just a minute ago, your feet couldn't move any faster because you were so hell-bent on getting your starving little butt to the Mexican restaurant. We still have about a mile to go, but you're sitting here, smoking a cigarette."

Teri pulled the cigarette from between her lips. "So? We've been walking for, like, twenty minutes or whatever. Is it a sin for me to stop for a small breather?"

"No, it's just that *I'm* starting to get hungry. If we wait any longer, it'll be you who's trying to keep up with me the rest of the way there."

Reaching into her unbuttoned black cardigan, Teri pulled out her pack of cigarettes, holding them out to Viktoria. "Have one. Trust me, they're a great appetite suppressant."

Viktoria grimaced. "Ugh, no thanks."

Teri shrugged again. "Whatever. More for me. If you only knew how much they relax you. You know, one of these days, I'm going to finally convince you to try a cigarette."

"Don't count on it happening any time soon," Viktoria said with another grimace.

A wink and soft smile from Teri comforted Viktoria. Still, time was ticking. The weight of breaking the news that she wasn't going to the party was starting to bear down on Viktoria more and more by the second. The window was closing all too quickly.

As Teri turned her face to the breeze, taking in a long drag, the silence in the air grew unbearably thick for Viktoria. She couldn't avoid it any longer. With a surrendering sigh, she took in a deep breath before clearing her throat.

"Hey, when we're done eating, I need to stop by the video store."

"Really? What are you renting?" Teri asked.

"I'm not sure yet. Something I think both my mom and I would like," Viktoria said, warming herself up to breaking the news.

"Oh, OK," Teri said before looking at her watch. "Wait, I don't think we can do that and still get to the party on time. I told Chris we'd be there early so I could help the band get set up."

"Are you sure we can't just stop by for a video really fast?" Viktoria asked with crushing anxiety mounting in her chest. "I'll decide what to rent while we're at the restaurant."

Teri sat straight up with a jolt of excitement. "I got it! I'll crash at your house tonight. We'll stop by 7-Eleven after the party, get some ice cream, watch a movie or something, and then just sleep in and have a lazy morning. The video store opens at ten on Sundays. We'll go rent the movie and have it at your house before your mom gets home from work. She'll be none the wiser. See? It's all figured out."

Leaning on her hip, Viktoria folded her arms before resting her head in one hand. Shutting her eyes with a wince, her stomach tightened as she forced the words up from the knot and out. "Teri, I can't go to the party tonight."

After a few seconds of dead silence, Viktoria opened her eyes, lifting her head. Teri's jaw had dropped. With her pupils contracted, there was that striking silver in her turquoise eyes.

"Wait. Why? You promised."

Teri shook her head and turned away, taking another drag. The atmosphere between them became a cold thick veil. Viktoria's stomach burned as she waited for a response, *any* response, from Teri. The silence grew dark and unbearable.

Though Teri looked and truly was warm, sweet, and nurturing, she could also turn on a dime, becoming angry and ice cold to those who crossed her. Those moments were rare, but they happened often enough that Viktoria had to temporarily distance herself from Teri following her grandmother's death.

Despite being inseparable best friends since kindergarten, Viktoria knew she could not mourn her grandmother while also walking on eggshells around Teri and her potential extreme polarity. Taking a step back from their friendship had given her more time to bond with Dylan, proving to be a heartbreaking blessing in disguise with his loss just one month later.

Since Dylan's death, though, Teri had been there, spending every second she possibly could with Viktoria, lifting her up and keeping her moving forward. Listening to their favorite music again, watching the band practice in the garage, enjoying the TV shows and movies they loved — Teri initiated all of it. She was the one who laid the groundwork for recreating the bond between the two of them, which grew deeper than ever. It wasn't lost on Viktoria, and they became like sisters again.

Still, at the park, Viktoria found herself again facing Teri's incomparable distance and ice. With the meaning behind the war paint on her face, all of it, coming to mind, Viktoria mustered the strength to break the silence.

"Teri, I'm sorry. I really am. I know I promised you I was going, but something happened this morning and . . . Look, my mom needs me tonight."

To Viktoria's surprise, the expression on Teri's face when she turned to her was caring and vulnerable. She softly said, "Is your mom OK? Does it have something to do with, you know, Dylan?"

Viktoria sighed as frustration kindled within her. "It's kind of a long story. I mean, everything was fine until . . . You know, I'd rather not get into it. I just wish some people would vanish off the face of the Earth so we would never have to see or hear them ever again. They've put us through enough."

Another silver streak flashed across Teri's eyes. "Tell me what happened. Right now. Seriously."

"It's nothing, OK?" Viktoria said with almost a whisper, hoping to defuse Teri's mounting anger. "I just know that my mom deserves a lot more respect than she gets around here, that's all."

The anger in Teri's voice only increased. "Well, it'd be nice to know what happened, so I know who to be pissed off at. Honestly, Viktoria, what happened this morning? Was it about Dylan?"

"Yeah," Viktoria whispered with heavy emotion.

Her face beginning to crumble, Teri lit another cigarette, turning away. Sniffling between erratic deep breaths, her hair covered her face in the warm breeze as she wiped tears from her eyes.

For eleven years, Viktoria had concluded that Teri was immune to grief or any other form of depression. She never saw her cry — even when she crashed her bike in the fifth grade and broke her arm — until May. The first time she did, it sent a terrible chill down Viktoria's spine. Until Dylan's funeral, Teri seemed to be in complete control of all her emotions.

Following that first time in May, it touched Viktoria as Teri broke down more and more often. It was only ever for one reason: Dylan.

Chapter 12

Leaning against the rock next to Teri, Viktoria put her arm around her. While it moved her for Teri, who had the thickest skin and armor of anyone she knew, to grieve so much and often for Dylan, it hurt her as well.

Magnifying Viktoria's pain even more was the self-induced blame she bore for Teri's sorrow. After all, informing her that she couldn't keep her promise to attend the party was what led to that heavy moment.

While she knew she made the right decision, disappointing anyone weighed her down with terrible guilt, especially Teri.

Flustered and desperate to help Teri recapture her previous carefree, cheerful disposition, Viktoria's mind raced for the right words to say.

"Again, Teri, I'm sorry. Really, I am. I was just as excited about tonight as you were. I just know my mom needs me. I promise I'll make it up to you."

Wiping away a few final tears, Teri turned again to Viktoria. After a deep sigh and noticeable effort, her serene smile returned along with her usual calm demeanor.

"I understand. I do. You know, we see the band play all the time. The only difference is they'll be in a backyard instead of my garage. It'll really be nothing we haven't seen yet."

"I know," agreed Viktoria, "but I hate that I can't be there for their first show. It just makes me feel—"

With genuine sincerity in her eyes, Teri stopped Viktoria mid-sentence. "Hey, I know where you're going. Don't start feeling bad and getting all wound up. Look, it's not a big deal. There'll be other gigs. What's more important than anything is that you're there for your mom. I know how much you need each other, especially with your dad constantly on the road."

As Teri pulled out another cigarette, Viktoria, reflecting on her words, disagreed with one thing. It actually was a big deal for her to miss the gig. She wasn't going to see Matt, much less have the chance to talk to him again that night. Just the thought of that cut at her heart.

Lighting the cigarette as it dangled from her lips, Teri's words were slightly muffled. "Hell, you know how much I envy your relationship with your mom and dad. My parents couldn't care less about my brother and me." The bitterness in Teri's voice only increased as her words came out along with the smoke. "All my parents ever talk about are the places they could've traveled to and, of course, their dream house in Scottsdale they could've afforded had Chris and I not accidentally come along. Yeah, *accidentally*. What kind of rat bastards tell their kids they were accidents?"

Teri turned away and wiped something from her cheek. It might have been a tear, but it was more likely just an itch. There was no other sign of emotion when Teri turned back and continued smoking. Just in case, Viktoria tried to think of anything to say to make her feel better.

"You know, one thing I wish I had that your parents give you and Chris is absolute freedom. I mean, think about it — no chores, no curfew. Chris and the band have free reign of the garage. You both come and go as you please. As long as your grades are good, you're off your parents' radar. It's awesome."

"It's neglect," Teri responded with the silver, intense flash in her eyes. Looking away in frustration again, she turned back to Viktoria. "You don't get it. It's not freedom; it's Chris and me fending for ourselves. No rules? Sure, that might sound like a dream, but there's also no dinner as a family. There's no help with school or anything else, for that matter. Whether we eat or get our laundry done is entirely up to us. Oh, and the good grades? That's just so we get into college and out of their house. That obviously hasn't helped with Chris. Believe me, Viktoria. My parents have been and always will be about themselves. They're only into each other. Chris and me? We're just two giant hurdles between where my parents are now and where they wish to be."

Teri, always so carefree and disconnected, had never laid it out like that before for Viktoria. Even though she would sometimes complain about her parents' emotional distance from them, Teri and Chris always seemed to be all too content with living in the comforts of their house while remaining off the parental grid. Once again, Viktoria's mind raced for the right words to say.

"I'm sorry, Teri. Yes, it's been hard on you two. I was just trying to point out all the cool things. You know, the music's always coming from the garage, we always watch whatever we want, your mom and dad are always nice when I do get to see them. You and Chris both come across like you enjoy the freedom, but I know there are times when you wish your parents were there and—"

"No, I don't."

"I'm just saying, Teri, you know you can talk to me whenever you feel that way, right?"

Finishing off her cigarette, Teri turned to Viktoria, shrugging her shoulders. "Yeah. I just don't bother because I know you'd never understand."

"Try me," Viktoria challenged, offended that Teri was dismissing her as too naive to understand, even after all she had been through.

Staring out in the distance, Teri wiped her cheek again. That time, it was a tear. Viktoria's concern returned. Teri's voice was as pained and vulnerable as the expression on her face when she turned again to Viktoria.

"I'm sorry, Viktoria. I shouldn't have said that. In fact, maybe you understand even more than I do. I mean, Chris and I, at least we have each other. You know what that's like. You had Dylan, but now he's . . ." Teri looked like she might break down again, but she was able to regain her composure. "You know how I'm always wanting to be at your house? It's so I can pretend your parents are mine, especially when they talk about how they struggled for years to have kids, and how you two were miracles. They see you as blessings. Chris and I are nothing but mistakes to my parents."

Teri paused, wiping another tear from her cheek as she pulled out her pack of cigarettes. Her voice grew shakier as she continued, "I'm sorry, Viktoria. I just look at what you have, what Dylan had, and I would do anything to have that as well."

Viktoria had never seen Teri be so emotional in one day. With nothing but compassion, Viktoria reached over and embraced her. Teri wiped her cheek again with an awkward giggle. The love and appreciation expressed on her face brought a warm smile to Viktoria's.

Looking past Viktoria's shoulder toward the parking lot, a subtle, venomous smirk emerged in Teri's sweet smile. "Well, guess who decided to come play at the park today."

Viktoria turned toward the parking lot as a large white car blaring music pulled in. Once the music and car were turned off, two guys with Peoria High School letterman jackets along with three cheerleaders emerged. They proceeded to make their way toward Viktoria and Teri.

They knew who the five individuals were. They were always together. Teri just shook her head with a snort.

Viktoria, however, with her pounding heart, shivered as a cold drop of sweat rolled down her back. She had no way of harnessing the surge of adrenaline racing within her.

There was only one course of action. It was undeniable to her what Hawk and Animal would do and she had to do the same.

Gripping her grandmother's cross, she stood up and planted her feet on the ground, freezing them in place. She gritted her teeth, and every muscle tensed. Everything her makeup symbolized, *everything,* was thrust to the front of her mind. *This was war.* The enemy was advancing.

Chapter 13

A second cold bead of sweat rolled down her back. Viktoria could hardly take a deep, dry swallow. A metallic taste overwhelmed her tongue, as though she could taste blood. Her pulse pounding, a couple of knuckles cracked as her fists clenched. There was nothing she wanted more than to do what Hawk and Animal would do. Stand her ground, fight, and ruthlessly dominate.

Still, Viktoria was not naive to the harsh reality she was facing. Not only were they outnumbered, but it was also not Animal nor Hawk standing next to her. It was small, thin Teri, sitting on the rock with her knees up against her chest and her arms wrapped around her legs, smoking another cigarette as though she didn't have a care in the world.

With Teri's relentless apathy toward their bleak position, it hit Viktoria hard — she was alone in her brace for battle.

The five individuals were approaching too fast. Leading the pack, as always, was Sherry Davis. After the tense stand-off between the two moms earlier at Kelly's Frozen Yogurt, Viktoria knew Sherry's claws were out.

A rustling in the grass caused Viktoria to look down as a tennis ball rolled up next to her feet. Of the three boys who were playing some game in the outdoor racquetball courts about ten yards away, the only one she recognized came running up. Lanky with shaggy dark brown hair, he appeared to be about Dylan's age.

"Hey, could one of you do me a favor and pass me the tennis ball please?" he asked.

With Sherry and the others a mere fifty yards away, Viktoria was too focused on the oncoming threat to respond to the boy. Teri, however, hopped off the rock, smiling at him.

"No worries, Mike. I'll get it," she said with a cheerful voice as she picked up the ball and tossed it back to him.

"Thanks, Teri," he said with a big grin.

Teri responded with her sweet smile. "No problem. What are you guys playing?"

"Butts up," he said with the same big grin. "My cousins are visiting from San Diego, and we always play it when we get together."

Teri's eyes sparkled as she giggled at him. "Interesting name for a game. You'll have to show me how it's played one of these days. See you later, Mike."

The boy looked at Sherry and the others as he passed by them on his way back to the racquetball courts.

Teri giggled again. "I love Mike. He and his parents recently moved here from somewhere outside of Los Angeles. He's absolutely adorable. I wish he were a few years older. You know what I mean? Have you ever talked to him?"

"No." Viktoria's response was sharp as she turned and glared at Teri in shock and grim frustration. Their five nemeses were less than twenty feet away, yet Teri remained inexplicably tranquil and careless concerning their dire situation.

The five of them formed a half circle, cornering Viktoria and Teri against the rock. Sherry stood in the middle, staring them down. Even after a long morning of cheerleading practice in the autumn heat, her uniform appeared clean and flawless, just like the rest of her.

Tall and lean, with bronze skin and lush, long blond hair, Sherry was the school's sun goddess. It was no wonder why every cheerleader wanted to be her, and every guy clawed for her attention.

With her all-American appearance and family's prestige, it took nothing at all for Sherry to pull the wool over everyone's eyes, both young and old — except for Viktoria and Teri. They always had her number and she had despised them for that since grade school.

Unlike everyone else, Viktoria and Teri refused to be blinded by Sherry's golden glow. They saw right through her cold, piercing blue-eyed glare, stiff thin lips, and emotionless stone face.

To her right was Janine Preston, a shorter, tanned cheerleader with brunette hair and stocky, solid legs. She was always looking at other kids with disdain. Often pointing at Viktoria and Teri on campus, she would whisper in Sherry's ear, who would then smirk and shake her head in disapproval.

To Janine's right was Jeff Bryant, a large no-neck football player. Standing over six feet and well over 220 pounds, he had very thick brown hair and a low hairline. With his loud voice and obnoxious laughter, it was as though he prided himself in being an absolute meathead. His perpetual crush on Sherry couldn't have been more transparent to everyone at school. It was never reciprocated, but Sherry seemed to enjoy holding that carrot in front of his nose.

To Sherry's left was Tiffany McNamara. A couple of inches shorter, with long, teased strawberry-blond hair, she matched Sherry in looks, athleticism, and prestige. The two of them had been inseparable since grade school, and Tiffany was just as spiteful toward Viktoria and Teri.

On Tiffany's left was her boyfriend, Vince Henderson. Best friends with Jeff, he was just as tall but more muscular, lean, and reserved. Despite his receding hairline, he managed to style his blond hair like a California surfer. Though he appeared charismatic with a million-dollar smile, he was just a follower. He even appeared remorseful when the others targeted Viktoria and Teri, but he never stood up to his friends. He just stood with them in silence and laughed whenever they did. To Viktoria, he was the hardest to read.

Sherry asserted herself as the leader of the five of them, and they fell in line for her. It was bizarre to Viktoria how she was always in the direct center when they all stood together. Even more bizarre was that the four always stood on each side of her in the same order. It was as though they embraced their inferiority to Sherry and knew their individual ranks among themselves.

Sherry peered at Viktoria with a condescending half-smile that said *I got you where I want you, and there is no escape.* Basking in the moment, she remained silent.

Like Animal and Hawk would, Viktoria kept her eyes locked on Sherry. She refused to look away.

When the five of them were together, Sherry was always the first to speak. The others remained in an eerie reverent silence until then. To everyone's surprise that afternoon, Teri spoke first.

"Well, you've taken time out of your busy day of cheer-leading, cruising around in daddy's car, and valley-girl, near beer partying to come see us. We don't have all day, so what-ever you have to say, spit it out."

Viktoria turned to Teri. In the past, her initial urge would be to send a wide-eyed, desperate, nonverbal message to not say another word for sheer survival. But this wasn't a game anymore — not for Viktoria and not for Dylan.

With every muscle tensed in fierce rebellion against fear, Viktoria clenched her teeth for the mental callousness to stand by Teri's sardonic words. With a quiet deep breath to add momentum to her mounting courage, she turned again to face the five of them.

With her ice-cold glare focused on Teri, Sherry's half-smile faded. "Uh, excuse me? Why are you talking? Was I looking at you?"

Viktoria turned to Teri to gauge her reaction. With the sil-ver streak in her eyes, Teri's subtle, venomous smirk within her serene smile appeared even more acidic. Viktoria wasn't standing alone after all.

Taking a step closer, further displaying her fearlessness, Teri mimicked Sherry's arrogant body language. Folding her arms and jutting out her hip to mirror Sherry, her words came with a calm, motherly tone, which made them even more demeaning.

"I'm just trying to help you, Sherry. Your empty staring at Viktoria was getting uncomfortable for all of us. Quite frankly,

I was embarrassed for you. It was painfully obvious the two brain cells dangling off that straw in your head weren't connecting with each other to form the words you wanted to say. I just thought I could assist you in prodding them along."

For a brief moment, Viktoria couldn't tell if Sherry was angry or, perhaps, a little frightened.

Glancing side to side at the other four, Sherry reasserted her dominance with a sharp response.

"Hey, Teri. Look at the position you're in. If you had any brain cells left over after all that smoking and boozing, you'd know the best thing to do would be to shut up."

Shaking her head and snorting, Teri flashed her a belittling sneer. Sherry didn't let it get her off track.

"Besides, I'm not here because of you."

Turning again to Viktoria, Sherry's demeaning stare and half-smile returned. "I'm here because of her. This is between you and me, Viktoria."

Chapter 14

Clenching her fists even tighter, Viktoria gritted her teeth. She wanted that look in her eye — the death stare of Road Warrior Hawk toward Nakita Koloff as they squared off in the Russian chain match just two months before. Not only did she want Sherry to see it, but she also wanted her to *feel* it.

Internally focused on her grandmother's cross, her makeup, and all they stood for, every cell in Viktoria's body rumbled with adrenaline. Maintaining her death stare on Sherry, she spoke through her clenched teeth, "Yeah? Well, whatever you have to say, say it."

Sherry's smile disappeared. Though her voice was calm and cerebral, her glare and words came across as that of a scolding mother. "It's pretty sad, Viktoria. When I left for practice this morning, my mom and Jason were having breakfast and talking about the fun plans they had for the day. It was great to see my little brother finally laugh and smile again. They should've been at the movies when I got home. Instead, I found my mom upset, sitting on the sofa next to Jason, doing everything possible to stop him from crying. She told me what happened at Kelly's this morning. You know what? You and your mom are the most twisted people I know. You just can't let it go."

Taking a step forward, Viktoria's voice shook with anger and adrenaline. "If you ever say that about my mom again, I'll—"

"You'll what?" challenged Sherry, cutting her off.

Before Viktoria could respond, Teri leaned toward Sherry.

"Hey. You have no idea what Viktoria and her mom have been through. So do us all, including your four sycophants here, a favor and shut the hell up. You got that? I don't know what happened at Kelly's this morning because I wasn't there. Neither were you, Sherry. You only got your mom's side of the story."

"Viktoria was there," Sherry responded. With her eyes returning to Viktoria, she couldn't have sounded more belittling. "You can tell Teri. In fact, why don't you tell all of us what happened this morning?"

It seemed as though the four others were starting to close in on Viktoria from either side. Whether they were or not, it was still five against two.

The reality of the numbers game struck Viktoria even harder. Invading her mind were the awful words she wished she had never heard. The ones from that police officer's report regarding the conditions of Dylan's body that horrible morning in May when he was discovered by the canal just a few blocks north of their house.

The sickening vision of Dylan's bruised, bloodied, lifeless body overtook her mind. Viktoria took in a quiet, unsteady breath to resist the oncoming dizziness and nausea. Shutting her eyes tight, she opened them again to find the world around her still spinning.

Gritting her teeth in determination, she took another deep breath. Reaching up, she took hold of her grandmother's cross.

We're outnumbered, Dylan — just like you were. And all I can see is what their brothers did to you. I can't think of you that way.

That's not you anymore. I know where you are now — stronger than ever, and by my side. I need your strength.

"We're waiting," Sherry demanded with urgency.

Viktoria's lips snarled with angry determination. "You want the truth? You got it. The truth is—"

"Hey!" Teri's loud, forceful voice startled Viktoria, sending everything around her spinning again. Shutting her eyes tight and opening them again, she gripped her grandmother's cross even harder as Teri continued, "How about the five of you just drive your car off a cliff so you can feed the vultures with your rotting carcasses. Having to see and deal with you at school is punishment enough. The least you can do is give us the weekend off."

Dropping her calm, collected veneer, Sherry turned and snapped at Teri, "OK. First, don't tell us what to do! You got that, Bride of Dracula? Second, why the hell am I even hearing your voice? This conversation has absolutely nothing to do with you."

Teri returned with a sneer. "Oh, that's where you're wrong. Anything that has to do with Viktoria, or her family, has absolutely everything to do with me."

Sherry turned again to Viktoria, regaining her calm, demeaning composure. "Is that true, Viktoria? Does Teri have a hand in everything that goes on within your family? Is she just as guilty?"

"Guilty of what?" Teri asked with a demanding voice.

Sherry's eyes remained locked on Viktoria's. "Teri's dying to know. Are you going to tell her?"

Still trying to fight off the dizziness, Viktoria pressed her hand against her stomach, hoping it would help settle the increasing nausea from everything spinning around her. Within her chest, something indescribable yet vital was being stretched beyond its limits and was about to snap in two.

"Man, look at her," Jeff blurted out with his toothy grin. "She looks like she's about to heave or pass out."

Teri jumped in again. "Do you want your vocal cords severed, knuckle dragger?"

"Teri, I got this," Viktoria said with her voice strained, still buckled over as the queasiness intensified.

She closed her eyes for a moment and the dizziness started to subside. As Viktoria took in another deep breath to regain her strength, Sherry shook her head in disgust.

"I don't have time for this. You know what? If she won't say it, then I will." Sherry's eyes remained locked on Viktoria's. "Like I said, it's pretty sad, Viktoria. The denial you and your parents live in is astonishing. You're standing by Teri, who's saying that I don't know what happened at Kelly's this morning because I wasn't there. Yet, somehow, you and your parents know exactly what happened at that stupid junior high school dance, even though the three of you were miles away at some restaurant at the time. Somehow, my mom — a successful, intelligent woman — can't accurately recall something that happened directly to her just this morning. Yet a small group of dumb, prepubescent kids can precisely recall some fight they saw outside of the junior high gym, in the dark, last May." Sherry then gestured to the other four. "That's why we're here. I'm putting an end to this now."

"How?" Viktoria asked, feeling stronger and clenching her fists. "If you think ganging up on us will make it all go away, you're wrong."

A disparaging snort escaped Sherry before she continued, "We're not the bullies here, Viktoria. You and your parents are. Try to actually think about it for once. Jason and Dylan got into a fight over a stupid girl. It happens all the time with boys. Tiffany, Jeff, and Janine's little brothers are Jason's best friends. When they saw him in a fight, of course they ran over to help him. They didn't care who was winning or losing. They just wanted to get Jason out of a bad situation. That's what friends do." Sherry's voice lowered to a condescending whisper. "A fight. That's all it was. Kids get into them every day and then go on with their lives. Whatever made Dylan put a gun to his head over by the canal and pull the trigger that night is something we'll never know, but it sure takes a lot more than a school dance scuffle to drive someone to the point of taking his own life."

"I swear, Sherry," Teri snarled, her voice shaking with fury. "One more word, and I'll—"

"I said I got this, Teri," Viktoria interjected, lifting her left arm to her side as if to block Teri from the five of them. Her voice shaking with anger as well, Viktoria's eyes never veered from Sherry's as she spoke through her teeth, "Do you really want to put an end to this, Sherry? I'll tell you how. You, Jeff, Tiffany, and Janine get back in your car and go pick up your little brothers. Drive them to the cemetery, have them take a long, hard look at Dylan's tombstone, and just do your best to comfort them as they surrender to this harsh reality — my little brother's horrific death will always be the single most defining moment in their lives, and there is *nothing* they can do about it."

Viktoria's words caused all of them, except Vince, to close in on her. Their anger was palpable. Grossly outnumbered by angry, vengeful enemies, just as Dylan was, the image of his beaten lifeless body recaptured Viktoria's mind as she found herself up against the rock, frozen in fear as Sherry snapped at her, "Who the hell are you to say that about our little brothers, you psycho zombie? You heard what the judge said. Suicides are contemplated for months or even years. They're not knee-jerk reactions. What proof is there that the fight led to Dylan's suicide? None! That's why he dismissed the case. You're obviously too brain-dead to remember that!"

Sherry's glare grew even more bone-chilling. Following a quick inhale through her nose, her words came through her gritted teeth with a wrath powerful enough to hit Viktoria physically. "Our little brothers are not what your dad called them in the courthouse: murderers. You better always remember that. And you and your mom better stay away from them from now on. Do you understand me? Don't look at them. Don't look at our parents. Nothing. Let them finally move past this."

Sherry's half-smile returned along with her calm cerebral voice. "Our brothers aren't murderers. In fact, it's the other way around. You heard me. Dylan chose to end his life a long time ago. He just chose that night because of the fight. He knew what he was doing. He knew our brothers' lives would never be the same. He wanted it to be too much for them to handle so they would eventually follow in his footsteps. In his head, he was initiating his own twisted suicide pact."

Her pulse racing, Viktoria's eyes darted back and forth between Sherry and the other four. Her diaphragm was frozen. The words to defend Dylan wouldn't come out.

Sherry seized on her silence. "That's the real truth and you know it. Dylan's the murderer and he has you and your parents trying to finish what he started. Hell, with such a messed up family, he never had a chance. He's way better off dead."

"Hey!" Teri shouted, stepping in between Viktoria and Sherry.

Over Teri's shoulder, the shock on all five faces, especially Sherry's, surprised yet somehow comforted Viktoria. Even the three boys at the racquetball courts had stopped playing their game to see what was happening.

Viktoria had seen Teri angry before, but it was never as intense as at that moment. A thick dark silence filled the air.

Startled, Sherry turned to Tiffany.

"Look at me!" Teri shouted. As Sherry's cold angry eyes shot back at Teri, they were also softened by shock and a certain level of fear.

"That's right, Whore Barbie. Look at me and listen," Teri demanded, her voice shaking with rage. "You just crossed the line. When you do that with me, there's no coming back. Trust me, you *don't* want that."

Teri took another step forward. Her face almost touching Sherry's, her voice grew more tense and chilling. "You have no idea what I'm capable of. If you think my look is dark, then you don't want to see my heart. This is your last chance — don't push me. Take those two oversized meathead jockstraps and the two other pom-pom-shaking sluts, get back in your daddy's car, turn on whatever Thompson Twins or Howard Jones crap music you were just blasting, and get the hell out of my park. If you don't, you *will* regret it — all five of you."

Losing the intense stare down with Teri that followed, Sherry shook her head with a smirk as she started to back off. "We're obviously getting nowhere here. Let's go, guys. We have better things to do."

As the five of them made their way toward the parking lot, Sherry, at a safe distance, turned around. "You and your mom are the ones who crossed the line, Viktoria. Enjoy the rest of the weekend with Teri. Just remember, she can't always be by your side. I know when you're alone. That's when we will finish this. That's not a threat; that's a promise. It's going to happen when you least expect it."

Chapter 15

Sherry slammed her car door with such force that Viktoria felt the vibration in her chest. With music blaring, the car skidded out of the parking lot and out of sight.

Viktoria turned to Teri, who was sitting on the rock again, pulling out another cigarette as though nothing had happened. Taking a drag, she pulled it from her lips, giving Viktoria a comforting smile with a slight, childlike shrug.

"That's how you deal with them, Viktoria. They're just bullies. Once they realize you don't fear them, and you're also willing to take it to the next level, they'll always back off like the cowards they are."

Viktoria couldn't believe how fast Teri had relaxed. It was as though their intense standoff with Sherry and the four others never happened. Teri smoked her cigarette with an entertained grin, laughing at the three boys who continued their game at the racquetball courts.

"Hey, Viktoria, check it out. Now I know why Mike calls it 'Butts Up.' I guess the little cousin lost, so he's bent over, on his knees, facing the wall with his butt in the air. Mike and the older cousin are throwing the tennis ball as hard as they can, trying to hit him. That's freaking hilarious."

Viktoria couldn't help but look at Teri with admiration for taking such a ferocious and fearless stand for her and her family. Still, it wasn't Teri staring at the girl in the mirror on June 1 with resolve to win this war — it was her.

Closing her eyes, she took hold of her grandmother's cross.

What happened, Dylan? We were surrounded and outnumbered just like you were, and all I could see was what happened to you. It was too much. Everything was closing in on me. I could barely stand, I almost threw up, and Teri was able to jump in before I could rip into Sherry after what she said about you. Why did Teri do that before giving me the chance? We can't win the war like this. That should be me sitting on the rock, basking in the triumph of defending our family and making three stuck-up cheerleaders and two football players back down. Me, not Teri.

Viktoria opened her eyes to a frustrated concern on Teri's face. Taking one last drag, Teri put out her cigarette on the side of the rock and looked up at her.

"Viktoria, screw Sherry and those losers. Don't let what she said get to you. She's always been a rich spoiled hag who only gets off on demeaning others, which she only does to hide her own messed up issues and insecurities."

"It's not that," Viktoria replied, folding her arms and looking away.

"Then what is it?"

Viktoria turned back to face Teri. "Thanks for sticking up for me and my family. You didn't have to, and it means a lot to me. You know I could've handled it myself, though, right?"

Teri shrugged. "Yeah, of course. You saw how easy it was. Even her highness, Sherry Davis, backed off as soon as she realized I wasn't going to play her little game. Like I said, they're cowards. I could see it from a mile away. Hell, look at how small I am, and even those two oversized Neanderthals backed off."

Teri's response made Viktoria realize she was seeking validation that, with or without Teri, she could have won that battle with just as much fearlessness and ferocity, and with the same dominating results, just like a Road Warrior. It didn't go down that way, though.

Another stark reality came from Sherry's last words to her — another battle was on the horizon, but where and when was unknown. To be ready, though, Viktoria knew she would have to confront another harsh fact unveiled to her during the intense standoff with Sherry — one about herself; one she hated.

The police officer who discovered Dylan's body by the canal that early morning in May didn't hold back on even the slightest detail in his report. It was too graphic, too heartless, but also too accurate.

It had been too much for Viktoria in May, and it had just proven to still be too much. When Sherry, Tiffany, Jeff, and Janine closed in on her with such anger, all she could see was the damage their little brothers inflicted on Dylan. Girls could be just as vicious as boys. As much as it hurt, the truth was, at that moment, Viktoria was frightened.

The morticians, with all their makeup, effort, and secrets of their trade, still could not adequately cover up the extensive trauma done to Dylan's body for his wake. When Viktoria looked at Dylan's body for the last time, it was ghastly. Was she going to be next?

The silent fear had invaded and taken deep root. Its power was too debilitating, and for Viktoria to win this war, this enemy needed to be destroyed. There was only one way.

To turn the tide back in her favor, the next step was unde- niable and vital. Viktoria needed to look at the girl in the mir- ror again, recapture her vision and mission, and exorcise that fear. Another June 1; a re-declaration of war.

Teri stood up from the rock, giving Viktoria a smile and a reassuring hug she received, but didn't need.

"Don't worry about all that crap. You're going to be fine, all right? Let's hit that Mexican joint. Now I'm really starving. After that, we'll go rent a video for you and your mom."

Teri had walked about ten feet before turning around. Vik- toria hadn't taken a single step. "Come on, Viktoria, let's go. Don't let those idiots ruin our weekend."

Viktoria did not respond to Teri. Instead, she started to walk in the direction of her house with determined steps.

"Viktoria!" Teri yelled as she ran up and stood in front of her, pointing in the opposite direction. "The Mexican restau- rant's *that* way."

"Go on without me," Viktoria said. "I need to go home right now."

"Are you serious?" Teri asked with her brow furrowed in confusion. "Don't let Sherry get you all wrapped around the axle. That's what she wants. Screw her. Let's go get something to eat. I thought you were hungry."

"I am," Viktoria said with conviction, "but not for food any- more."

Teri shook her head as though what Viktoria had said didn't make any sense. Still, her voice grew soft. "Well, what about the video for you and your mom?"

"Oh, the movie," Viktoria said with a sigh. "Don't worry about it. My mom and I can pick it up later."

Teri's voice remained quiet. "Are you sure? You know you can talk to me, right?"

"I know," Viktoria said. "There's just something I need to go home and do, and I need to do it to be the person my mom needs tonight."

Teri looked down for a moment before turning again to Viktoria with deep concern in her eyes. "I get it. This isn't about Sherry, it's about Dylan."

Viktoria nodded with a whisper. "Yeah."

Lighting another cigarette, Teri gave Viktoria one of her serene smiles. "I understand. Are you coming over to my house tomorrow morning as usual?"

"Definitely," Viktoria said with a smile as she hugged Teri. "Thanks for understanding, Teri."

Teri placed her hands on Viktoria's cheeks, shaking her head back and forth to lighten the mood. Smiling again, she talked with the cigarette hanging from the side of her mouth. "That's what sisters do."

As Teri made her way in the direction of the restaurant, Viktoria turned again toward her house. With just two blocks to walk, each step she took on North 53rd Avenue increased the resolve within her.

Another battle was inevitable and on the horizon. Where and when, she didn't know. It was going to be sooner rather than later, though, and she was going to be ready — ready to win, no matter what.

Chapter 16

After locking both the handle and the deadbolt, Viktoria turned around, resting her back against the front door. She glanced at the TV, the couch, and the clock on the wall. The kitchen table was in the distance. The dark living room was brighter than the Arizona sun outside.

Taking a deep breath to focus on her mission, Viktoria formed tight fists as she gritted her teeth. The clock on the wall read twenty minutes past five — her mom would be home any minute.

Time was ticking, igniting Viktoria with the urgency to make her way toward the bathroom. The girl in the mirror was waiting for her.

With the bathroom door just a few steps away to her left, she found herself frozen in place about halfway down the hallway. To her right, between the living room and her bedroom, was Dylan's bedroom. She had not seen the door open since May. As she had done many other times alone that summer, Viktoria placed her trembling hand on the doorknob.

The mission she was so focused on fled as she placed her left hand over her pounding heart, daring her right hand to turn the doorknob. Her hand wouldn't budge, though. Just like every time before, she pulled it away.

Clasping her hands together, she rested her head on them. Shutting her eyes, she cringed at the vision in her mind of what she feared most if she opened the door. She didn't know why, but the thought of seeing Dylan's clothes, both hanging and folded, terrified her. The idea of them being lifeless and empty, knowing his body would never fill or give life to them again, was dark and haunting. She knew then she made the right decision to not give in to the temptation of opening his bedroom door.

Opening her eyes, Viktoria looked up, and took a deep breath. Straight ahead, her bedroom door was open. With the blinds open, the brightness outside illuminated her bedroom, giving her heart a much-needed positive lift. It brought her back to the present, reminding her of why she was there.

Viktoria walked into her room with purpose and then got on her knees. Reaching under her bed, she pulled out the May 1986 issue of *Pro Wrestling Illustrated*. Standing back up, she took a long, hard look at the magazine's cover. Just as earlier that morning, Hawk and Animal stared back, challenging her.

Are you one of us, Viktoria? You better believe you are! You can't see your tag team partner; does that mean he's not there? Hell no! Your brother's right by your side. Redo your makeup. Winning this war is your only option!

The bathroom door was across from Dylan's bedroom. Viktoria reached over to turn on the light as she walked in. Setting the magazine on the counter, she looked into the eyes of Animal and Hawk, accepting their challenge before turning to her reflection.

Staring at the girl in the mirror for a minute, she reached in the drawer and pulled out her eye-makeup remover. Starting with that, she proceeded to wash away the makeup she had put on earlier that afternoon.

After drying her face, she looked in the mirror again. It was refreshing, as though a part of what happened at the park was washed down the drain to never return. It was the moment she needed; her true self was staring back at her in the mirror. There was no war paint, and no outside influence. It was June 1 all over again.

With determination in her eyes, she took a deep breath. Gazing at the reflection of her most valued possession, she lifted her hand to the dog collar around her neck, gripping her grandmother's cross.

Visions of Dylan filled her mind. It was beyond her control, just as it was during her confrontation with Sherry and the others at the park. But this time, they weren't the visions of Dylan's ravaged, lifeless body. They were of him, as he had dreamed of becoming. He was bigger, stronger, fearless, and powerful — another Road Warrior.

A chill swept through Viktoria. Her grip on the cross tightened even more.

It's not just Animal and Hawk anymore. Now you're challenging me. Is that what you want, little brother? Well, you got it!

With her teeth clenched, Viktoria looked into the mirror again. The wicked flash in her eyes brought a warm, righteous smile to her face and heart. June 1 had returned stronger than ever.

After exfoliating and moisturizing her face, she applied her sunscreen and primer, followed by her foundation. With the pale glow of her face, Dylan's innocence and visions of a brighter future were brought back to life.

She brushed on the light brown and black eye shadows, followed by the black liquid eyeliner. As the winged look gently extended past the corner of her eye, she finished off with the two coats of black mascara, making her eyelashes appear even darker.

With the natural features she and Dylan shared accented through her makeup, another smile crossed her face. After her black lipstick was applied, followed by her face mist, she gripped her grandmother's cross before closing her eyes.

Here we are, Dylan. Another new beginning — a re-declaration of war. We have to win. It's the only option we have. Are you with me? I need to know. Are you really with me?

Viktoria let go of her grip, pressing her grandmother's cross between the palm of her hand and her upper chest. Covering the cross then with both hands, she found peace in the serene atmosphere surrounding her. Wanting to do nothing to break the silence, her words remained in her heart.

Are we going to win, Dylan?

A burning, heart-pounding sensation overwhelmed her. It expanded from her chest, electrifying every part of her body with a bright energy she could not hold back. Her mind was cleared, and her bones and muscles had never felt stronger. The individual she dreamed of transforming herself into had never appeared more attainable.

The girl staring back at her in the mirror had never looked stronger and more determined. With an unfounded energy and intensity, the wicked flash returned in her bright blue eyes. The righteous, warm smile on her face and in her heart followed as before, but with an underlying edge.

Animal and Hawk were right; Dylan was still there, right by Viktoria's side. The girl staring back at her in the mirror knew the war was just heating up. She was going to have to prove she had what it took to win. Not only would she have to prove it to herself, but to her mom, Teri, Dylan, and everybody else.

Above all, at that moment, she knew she was going to have to prove it to Sherry. That would be sooner rather than later.

Chapter 17

Just as Olivia's car pulled into the garage, there was a knock at the front door, which was unusual for that time on a Saturday evening. Viktoria figured that Teri was already at the party, helping the band get set up for the gig. The only other individuals who ever stopped by anymore were a few caring leaders from the church. They never stopped by on a weekend evening, though.

Opening the front door, she found that nobody was there. Viktoria figured the O'Flannery boys, two brothers a little younger than Dylan, were up to their usual shenanigans and doorbell ditching the neighbors.

"Hey," Olivia called out as she came in from the garage. "Is that Teri at the front door? Tell her she's welcome to stay if she wants. I decided to order a large instead of our usual medium at Angelo's so there's a few extra slices if she wants to claim them."

"No, I'm sure it's . . ." Viktoria happened to glance down as she started to close the front door. Resting on the doormat was a VHS cassette tape from Superstar Video. Picking it up, she realized it was Neil Diamond's *The Jazz Singer*. Only one other person in town knew it was her mom's favorite movie: Teri.

A warm smile formed on Viktoria's face. Somewhere between the Mexican restaurant and heading to the party to help the band get set up, Teri went out of her way to make sure Olivia could get lost in both her daughter's company and her favorite movie that night. She wouldn't have done that for any other mom. Teri's words from earlier at the park hit Viktoria: *That's what sisters do.*

Looking down at the VHS tape, Viktoria continued smiling as she closed the door.

"I'm sorry, Viktoria, I didn't hear you. Was that Teri?" Olivia asked, walking into the living room after setting the pizza and other groceries on the kitchen table.

"Yeah, it was." Viktoria's response was nonchalant, though she beamed ear to ear.

"Oh, OK," Olivia said with a concerned look. "It's going to be dark soon. Is she going to be all right walking home alone? Are you sure she didn't want to take any food with her? Sometimes I look at her and hope she's getting enough to eat. You too, quite frankly. I swear if I turned you both sideways, I wouldn't be able to see you two. That's why I ordered the large this time. I worry about you girls."

Worry was the last word Viktoria wanted to hear her mom say that night.

"Mom, she's fine. I'm fine. We're both fine. You don't have to worry about us all the time."

Olivia stood there with folded arms, tilted head, and raised eyebrows, and Viktoria realized she might have been a little sharp in her response. Knowing that would sabotage her efforts to keep the mood light for their night together, she was quick to retract it.

"Ooh, Mom, I'm sorry. I didn't mean it like that. What I meant to say was that tonight's *your* night. After your crazy workweek, I'm just anxious to make sure that you don't have to worry about anything but getting your fill of fun and relaxation tonight. You're always looking out for me, so it's my turn to look out for you. I really mean that."

Looking at Viktoria for a few seconds, Olivia shook her head with a smile.

"Good save."

"No, I really mean that," Viktoria persisted. "Teri's off to the party. She'll get all the food she wants there. And for us, it's Saturday night. As always, it's just the two of us, the girls. Oh, and guess what I happen to have in my hands."

"What?" Olivia asked, snatching the tape from her in a playful manner.

Viktoria snickered as Olivia's jaw dropped. Her wide, green eyes sparkled as she looked up again.

"No way! This is amazing! It's been so long since I've seen this. You know this is my favorite movie of all time."

"Of course, Mom. All you ever listen to in the car is the soundtrack. You know, there are other singers and bands out there, right?"

"Hey," Olivia responded with a playful shove. "You know there are other musicians I like, and they're just as cool as those crazy bands you listen to. When you were born, I let your dad name you. When your brother was born, your dad let me name him. And who did I name your brother after? That's right — *Bob Dylan*. See? Rock 'n roll was around even when we were kids. We're not as out of touch as you think."

Looking back down at the cassette, Olivia beamed again before giving Viktoria a tight embrace. "You and Teri are the best. I've been at Superstar Video a million times looking for this. How did you find it?"

"You'll have to ask Teri, she's the one who found it."

With pizza on paper plates and Pepsi in plastic cups to avoid washing dishes later, the two of them sank into the couch. As the movie was about to start, Olivia suddenly turned off the TV.

"Wait, not yet — there's something we need to discuss before we watch the movie."

Viktoria's empty stomach twisted. Nervously gripping the cushion underneath her, she considered the possibilities of where Olivia was going with the conversation she was initiating. Did she somehow catch wind of what happened at the park that day?

Regardless, the words "there's something we need to discuss" meant all too often that something was wrong, or someone was in trouble. That was definitely not the direction Viktoria had hoped their evening together would go.

"Seriously, Mom, can it wait? Let's just forget all our worries and enjoy the movie. That's what this night is all about. Besides, I'm starving."

"It won't take long, Viktoria. You're not in trouble or anything. I just know I won't be able to truly relax and enjoy our evening unless I get out what I need to say, OK?"

"OK," Viktoria responded with caution.

Setting her plate and cup on the coffee table, Olivia took a deep breath. Viktoria clutched the cushion even tighter.

Ugh. Where is she going?

"First, thank you for being here. I know that party meant a lot to you and setting that aside to be here means so much to me."

"There was no decision to make, Mom. It was the right thing to do."

"Still," Olivia continued, "it means everything to me. It made me realize that I'm not so alone after all."

Viktoria smiled. That was how she wanted her to feel. Olivia responded with a wistful smile.

"I'm going to be honest. I'm also relieved that you're home tonight and not at the party. What happened this morning with Linda Davis and, you know, seeing her son and everything, it really rattled me. All day, I couldn't shake it. It just brought it all back." She reached out and took Viktoria's hand. "Look, I don't know if I'll ever be able to forgive myself for pushing Dylan to go to that dance. It's the one thing in my life I wish I could take back, and I'm frightened of making that same mistake again."

Running her fingers through her hair, Viktoria took a deep breath to ease the knot forming in her stomach. "Please, Mom, can we not go there? I see what it's doing to you. It's too heavy. Can't we just put it aside for now and enjoy our time together?"

Olivia was quick to respond. "Of course. Don't worry, I'm almost done."

With her eyes shut tight, it seemed as though Olivia was gathering her thoughts before she looked back at Viktoria and continued, "I love seeing you and Teri having so much fun together, and believe it or not, I actually think it's fun that you two share such a, well, unique style. I also know that you two, like Dylan, have been targeted by the kids at school in the past for being different, and, as much as I hate it, it's continued into this schoolyear. Because of that, when it comes to parties, dances, and other activities where these other kids can be, I'm just not ready for you to attend those events right now. Not after what happened to Dylan."

Viktoria pulled her hand away. "That's not fair, Mom. Teri and I are not Dylan. We have each other. We're older. We also shouldn't be punished for what those little pricks did to my brother. If we are, then they won!"

Putting her hands up, Olivia kept her voice soft. "I get it, and you're right — it's not fair. You're sixteen and should be out having fun and enjoying these years. Honestly, what would hurt me more than anything is letting my fears cause you to miss out on what life has to offer you at this time. I can't do that to you. Because of that — and here's where I'm going with this — I decided today that I'm going to get help. You know, professional help."

Viktoria's frustration was replaced with deep empathy. She had found much needed help and guidance from Mr. Tailor, the school counselor. Realizing how much it did for her to visit Mr. Tailor in his office during lunch every Tuesday, she knew it would help Olivia to find someone to see as well.

Viktoria also found relief in Olivia's words. After everything her family had been through, she never heard her parents mention going to anyone for any form of counseling. In fact, nobody she knew ever talked about it. Consequently, she never told Olivia or even Teri about going to Mr. Tailor.

Besides, her conversations with him were ones she valued and kept between herself and Dylan.

Knowing Olivia wanted to find her own therapist took a weight off Viktoria's shoulders that she hadn't even realized she was carrying. She didn't feel so alone anymore. Perhaps it would be a new bond for them to share.

"I think that's great, Mom," Viktoria said with encouragement.

"You really mean that?"

"Definitely. I think it'll help you out more than you know."

Olivia sighed with relief. "Thanks, you don't know how much your support means to me. I promise I'm going to find someone good who'll help me get through this. So, just for now, keep doing fun things with Teri, but if you would stay away from parties, dances, football games, and other gatherings where those other kids could be, it would mean a lot to me."

To extinguish the rekindling resentment of Olivia once again asking her to take on the social life of an eleven-year-old, Viktoria took hold of her grandmother's cross.

It sad to say, Dylan, but what is Mom really asking me to do that's different from the usual? All I ever do is hang out with Teri. All the other stuff she's asking me to stay away from are things I can't stand anyways. Football games? Dances? Is she serious? Tonight's about Mom. Let's keep it that way. Let's finish this conversation the right way.

Viktoria formed a sarcastic grin on her face. "That's it, Mom? Seriously?"

Oliva shrugged. "Well, yeah. Can you do that for me? Like I said, it's only temporary. Once I find someone really good who can help me, then watch out, Viktoria! I'll be right there helping you plan and get ready for all those high school festivities that make for the best memories. You know, like your dad and me — from our sophomore year on, we never missed a dance or football game. You know, it was watching your dad fix his flat tire on the way to our senior prom that it hit me like a bolt of lightning. I truly knew then that he and I were . . ." Olivia paused with an inquisitive look. "What's so funny?"

Viktoria couldn't stop snickering. "Really, Mom?"

"What?"

"When have I ever wanted to go to a dance, football game, or any other stupid rah-rah high school activity? Never. You didn't see Teri and me going off to get fitted for dresses for next week's homecoming dance, did you? I mean, look at us. Just thinking about it makes me want to throw up. Oh, and the parties? Yeah, don't expect us to get invited to any big bashes at some cheerleader's house anytime soon. Even if we did, we still wouldn't go — we hate that fake crap. We like doing what we've been doing."

To help remove the shocked look from Olivia's face, Viktoria sighed before continuing with a softer voice, "Mom, you have nothing to worry about, and I'm starving. Let's press *Play* and start digging in, OK? The party tonight was a fluke, and we were only going to support the band. It's their first gig, and they had a hard enough time just getting that one. I seriously doubt they're going to get lucky again anytime soon. And if, somehow, they do, I won't go, I promise."

Chapter 18

With no memory of seeing the end of the movie, Viktoria woke up in the most comfortable position on the couch, nestled under a blanket Olivia had obviously covered her with before she had gone to bed. It was her favorite way to wake up on Sunday morning.

The thick curtains kept the sunlight out of the living room, but the kitchen was brighter than Viktoria cared for. The clock on the wall opened her eyes a little wider. It was almost ten o'clock. She couldn't believe she didn't wake up earlier, as with every other Sunday, to the smell of coffee and the usual commotion of Olivia getting ready and leaving for work.

Sitting up, Viktoria's entire body ached. With her elbows on her knees, she rested her head in the palms of her hands. Everything that happened the previous day had taken its heavy toll, leaving her exhausted to the bone. It was no wonder she didn't hear Olivia that morning.

Turning on the TV for mere background noise, some random Sunday morning news program played in the background as she stumbled into the kitchen. The coffee pot was still half full and warm. Along with a couple pieces of toast, it was enough to get her day started.

Thumbing through her grandmother's old Norwegian cookbook — which she could read because her grandmother had taught her the language — she found a picture of *krumkaker*, her grandmother's favorite pastry, which brought a bright, wistful smile to Viktoria's face.

Just as Teri was her best friend and Dylan would always be her little brother, a special place in Viktoria's heart would forever be filled by Grandma Margit. Not only did she teach Viktoria how to speak and read Norwegian, but their endless hours in the kitchen was also where she taught her the secret to becoming "The Master Chef."

Grandma Margit's secret? It was a trick she taught herself when it was just her and her son alone in Norway during World War II — how to make something filling and delicious out of almost nothing. She then combined it with American diversity and abundance when they moved to the United States.

From decadent cakes and pastries to filling stews and other dishes, Grandma Margit's secret was how she was able to raise Viktoria's dad on her own. She made a living selling her products around the Phoenix area while also running the kitchen at the truck stop where Viktoria's dad would eventually find work as a trucker after high school.

Going to the truck stop on the weekends and during the summer since she was twelve to help out and make some money on the side, Viktoria, over time, was able to learn all the secrets and tricks from her grandmother in the kitchen. Everyone there saw her as carrying on Grandma Margit's stellar work after she had passed away in April. When her grandmother was no longer there to pick her up and take her in the mornings, though, Viktoria no longer saw any point in going.

Viktoria turned her eyes to her grandmother's cross attached to her dog collar, which she'd left on the counter the night before.

I should've known that Grandma giving me her cross was her way of saying goodbye. I should've heard it in her words concerning us, Dylan. I mean, she knew somehow. It was all too sudden.

Taking a deep breath to muster a little more emotional strength, Viktoria continued to thumb through the cookbook. With her parent's wedding anniversary just two weeks away, she was already planning what dishes she was going to prepare for them. It was her way of showing faith that her dad would be home for that day.

There was too much Viktoria had missed since her dad switched from local to interstate trucking in late June. From their daddy-daughter dates to the Phoenix International Raceway and the Arizona Theater Company to their amusing conversations in Norwegian that drove Olivia crazy because she couldn't understand what they were saying, what she missed most was him coming home every night from work.

More money was her dad's reason for switching from local to interstate trucking for the company. Viktoria could understand that, but they seemed to be doing just fine before that, which made her wonder — was that really the reason or was it his way of escaping from all the darkness in their lives surrounding her grandmother's and Dylan's deaths? Viktoria could understand that too. She would also escape if she could. Still, though, he was also leaving Viktoria and her mom to deal with all the trouble and grief alone.

Setting the cookbook down, Viktoria took her dog collar from the counter and put it around her neck.

More money has to be the reason, Dylan. Why else would he just up and leave us behind to deal with this nightmare of a situation alone?

Before pouring herself a second cup of coffee, Viktoria went to her bedroom, reached under her bed, and pulled out the May 1986 edition of *Pro Wrestling Illustrated*. With a new day, she needed Animal and Hawk on the front cover staring back at her, challenging her to do what they do best — donning their warpaint and facing the enemy with fearless aggression and conviction.

The band practiced in Teri's garage like clockwork every Sunday afternoon. Viktoria could only hope the previous night's gig didn't disrupt their routine. Gazing at a picture of Kerry Von Erich in the magazine while nursing her coffee, she was dying to see Matt again.

The sudden ringing of the rotary phone on the kitchen counter caused her to jump. Hating how loud it was, she ran over to answer it.

"Hello."

Teri's voice came in loud and clear. "Hey! Where are you? You're usually here by now."

"Yeah, I'm sorry," Viktoria said. "I was wiped out last night, so I totally slept in. I didn't even hear my mom leave for work this morning."

"Fine, but hurry up and get here," Teri said in a demanding voice. "The day's almost half gone."

"I just need to straighten up the kitchen, get ready, and then I'll be on my way. Hey, I have a quick question—"

Viktoria wanted to know if the band was going to be there, but Teri cut her off.

"Good deal. Look, I have a pot of water on the stove that's about to boil over, so I have to go. I'll see you in a bit, OK? Bye."

Hanging up, Viktoria took a short pause to groan. She was so close to knowing if Matt was going to be there, but she couldn't get an answer.

She cleaned the kitchen as fast as possible, and then she raced to her bedroom, placing the *Pro Wrestling Illustrated* magazine well underneath her bed. Dressed in almost all black as usual, a surge of energy rushing through her reflected in her eyes as she looked at the girl in the bathroom mirror. She was ready to prepare for war.

After putting on her makeup, she took a step back, smiling at the cross hanging from her dog collar. Black, white, gold, and silver from head to toe with her war paint flawlessly applied, she wasn't only ready for war, she was ready for Matt.

On her way to Teri's house, Viktoria was walking down West Desert Cove Avenue when the roar of a loud engine rattled her frame. Coming up fast from behind, she didn't think much of it, with muscle cars and trucks being so common in suburban Phoenix. The loud horn, though, sent her pulse racing.

A massive pickup truck, which she recognized because it stood out for its size in the high school's student parking lot, passed her. Viktoria grabbed her chest as an empty beer bottle smashed on the sidewalk no more than three feet in front of her.

"Aw, man! I was *this* close!" a teenage boy's voice cracked from the other side of the truck as he wiggled himself back in through the open passenger window.

Appearing through the rear window of the truck were two guys with crew cuts sitting on each side of a girl with a brunette ponytail. It was easy to recognize who they were, and Viktoria was well aware of who they associated themselves with. It was a lot easier to spot the enemy because they all wore the same letterman jackets and cheerleading uniforms.

Just ahead, the truck was slowing down to make a stop at the intersection with North 63rd Avenue. Taking hold of her grandmother's cross, Viktoria gritted her teeth. Giving anger the permission to burn through her veins, the image of the girl standing in front of her in the bathroom mirror that morning was all her mind could see. Her war paint was on, she was ready for battle, and the enemy had just advanced.

No, Dylan, not like yesterday — not this time. This is the battle to turn the tide back in our favor. We will win this one, no matter what. Are you with me? I know you are!

Like a large percentage of front yards in the Phoenix suburbs, the one to her left had no grass; it was all rocks.

Reaching down, Viktoria picked up just the right river rock. It was smooth and the perfect size — light enough for a strong throw, heavy enough to inflict damage.

Chapter 19

It had been a while since Viktoria had played catch with her dad and Dylan, but the adrenaline rushing through her more than made up for lost time. The rock struck the driver's side of the bed, just above the back tire, with a loud ding, leaving a large dent with the white paint stripped at the point of impact.

The truck remained still at the intersection for a few seconds before the driver hit reverse, backing up and stopping in the middle of the street parallel to where Viktoria was standing on the sidewalk. Like the day before at the park, Viktoria stood her ground, refusing to budge.

Cody Rutherford, a teammate and friend of Jeff and Vince, exited the driver's side, slamming the door. His face was beet-red as he examined the dent on his truck. "What the hell? What the hell!"

Racing around from the passenger side was Brett Robinson, another teammate. "Man, look at that. I can't believe she did that."

Rocking the truck as he shoved the bed in frustration, Cody turned to Viktoria. She still refused to budge as he marched toward her.

"Look what you did, vamp tramp! What the hell is wrong with you?"

"What the hell is wrong with Brett?" Viktoria shot back. "He's the one who threw that beer bottle at me. Blame him. What makes you think I wasn't going to do anything about it?"

Looking back at his truck, Cody turned again to Viktoria. "You're paying for that. You got that?"

Clenching her fists, Viktoria snarled through her teeth. "The hell I am. Make me!"

"Hey, Cody," Brett called out as he stood next to the dent. "We better get this fixed before your dad sees it."

Cody kept his eyes on Viktoria. "He's not going to be mad at me. He'll be pissed at this psycho blond ditz once I tell him what happened. He knows her little brother wasn't the only one in the family who's all screwed up."

"Hey!" Viktoria shouted as her closed fists shoved Cody hard enough to knock the wind out of him, causing him to stumble off the sidewalk and back onto the street. "You bastard! Don't ever talk about my brother! You got that? Say one more thing about him and I swear I'll kill you!"

Breathing heavier to catch his breath, Cody stepped back onto the sidewalk. "You're so lucky you're not a guy. Believe me, if you were, I'd be beating the living crap out of you right now."

"Pretend I am, then," Viktoria challenged.

As Brett approached from behind Cody, a thought pierced Viktoria: *You know what Animal or Hawk would do right now.*

She looked down and next to her feet was the neck of the shattered beer bottle, still intact with jagged, sharp edges. Picking it up, she glared over Cody's shoulder at Brett.

"What about you? Do you have the balls to make a move, or are you also going to use the fact that I'm a girl as an excuse to back down?"

Viktoria refused to be intimidated as the two of them, shoulder to shoulder, towered over her with faces twisted in anger. After what Cody said about Dylan, this battle was hers to win. It didn't matter what it took.

"Come on, boys," Viktoria's voice shook with adrenaline. "There's nothing but your fear between us. Make your move. Don't be afraid of a little blood."

"You're right — we're boys," Cody said, his face still red. "That's why you're saying all that. You know we won't give you the beating you deserve. Trust me, if we were girls, that'd be a different story."

Viktoria looked over their shoulders at the cab of the truck. Still inside, looking toward the three of them, was Cody's girlfriend, Nicole Zielinski.

"What about your mall maggot girlfriend?" Viktoria responded to Cody, more than loud enough for Nicole to hear. "She's a girl. Let's have her get out of the truck and come beat the crap out of me."

Viktoria turned again to Nicole, whose jaw was dropped, and her eyes were wide open as she remained in the cab with the door closed.

"The window's open, Nicole! I know you can hear me! Do you have what it takes to come over here and finish the job your boyfriend's not man enough to do? You're not afraid of getting your cheerleading uniform a little dirty, are you?"

Nicole turned away and didn't respond.

Viktoria turned again to Cody and Brett. "That's what I thought. I guess the three of you all have something in common — you're too scared to gang up on a freak girl who's half your size. Pathetic."

At that moment, a huge tractor trailer roared up right behind Cody's truck, blowing its loud horn. The door opened and out stepped a massive man with curly, long blond hair and a beard to match.

"Hey, you little pricks! Why the hell is your truck stopped in the middle of the street? Move it now or I'll move it for you! You've got five seconds — just try me!"

Viktoria shouted her last words at Cody and Brett as they raced back to Cody's truck. "Dylan's got one thing over you two — he fought back! He wasn't a coward like you!"

As Cody's truck sped away, the big trucker looked at Viktoria, shaking his head while the tractor trailer roared forward. Viktoria didn't know what he thought of her, as he wasn't aware of what was happening. Regardless, unbeknownst to him, he proved to be a powerful ally and the cause of the enemy's rapid retreat.

Wanting the big trucker to share in the triumph, Viktoria gave him a big smile and a wave. With his large, muscular arm hanging out the window, he shook his head again, smiled, and waved back as he made his way to the intersection and went on with his day.

With the smile on her face persisting, Viktoria took hold of her grandmother's cross.

Did you see the size of that man, Dylan? He could've been a Road Warrior! I'll tell you who really were Road Warriors just now: We were. We won, Dylan. The war has just turned in our favor, and you know we're going to win.

Viktoria's march all the way to the corner of North 74th Avenue and West Shangri-la Street remained fearless and strong. She could only imagine what Teri's reaction was going to be when she told her what had just happened between her and Cody Rutherford, Brett Robinson, and Nicole Zielinski. They were three individuals Teri couldn't stand.

Just as the day before, a fast, piercing guitar solo stood out above the blaring music from the garage as Viktoria walked into Teri's neighborhood. Even after playing their first gig the night before, the band hadn't strayed from their Sunday afternoon rehearsal. They were there after all, and more importantly, Matt was there.

Biting down on her lower lip, Viktoria smiled. The warm breeze on her face made her think about her makeup. From her foundation to her eye shadow to her lipstick, her war paint was on, and she had proven herself worthy of everything it symbolized.

Instead of wild and racing butterflies, her stomach tightened with determination. Matt was in Teri's garage. Forget making her way through Teri's yard and straight to the front door. Just as she stood her ground against Cody, Brett, and Nicole, she was going to do exactly what Animal and Hawk would do.

Walking straight up the driveway to the open garage, she saw the four members of the band concentrating on getting through a song. She was going to make sure one of them knew she was there. How? By strutting into the garage like she owned the place and commanding his attention, just like a Road Warrior.

Chapter 20

The positioning of the band made the garage itself look like a stage with the rest of the street as the audience, whether the neighbors liked it or not. Slightly stage left and center was Mike De Soto bashing away at the drum set. To his right was the bass player, Grant Coleman. Slightly right of center stage, behind the mic stand, singing and playing rhythm guitar, was Teri's brother, Chris Allardyce. On the far right, last but definitely not least, was their new lead guitarist, Matt Sorensen.

With the exception of Chris giving her a quick nod, the rest of the band kept playing, paying her no attention as she stepped into the garage. The fact that Mike and Grant didn't acknowledge her didn't bother her in the slightest, but she was going to get Matt's attention.

Walking past him, Viktoria leaned in, nudging him a little. After taking a couple of steps, she turned around just in time to see his long, thick, dirty-blond locks flip back as he lifted his head. In the sunlit garage, his ocean blue eyes sparkled. His perfect bright teeth only added to his rugged features as he smiled.

He looked like a tall rock god, and Viktoria was smitten. Still, she was going to prove that she could play at his level. With all the courage and game she could muster, she locked eyes with him, flashing her best flirtatious grin with a quick eyebrow raise.

Turning his attention again to his guitar, Matt's smile grew even wider as he shook his head. Not knowing what to make of his reaction, Viktoria could sense her internal enemy advancing.

Matt was two years older than her, living away from home, and studying to become an electrician. He was an adult doing adult things. Viktoria was a high school junior. She couldn't help but wonder what he would see in her.

As Viktoria passed the drum set, Mike was looking in Matt's direction, almost laughing. Was Matt looking back at him, doing the same?

Keeping her eye on the door leading into the house, Viktoria tightened her stomach. Self-doubt, the internal enemy, was gaining too much of an advantage. In her mind's eye, she gave this enemy the form of a man, and pictured herself slaying him with a mighty swing of a sword.

With the enemy gone for the time being, Viktoria placed her hand over her grandmother's cross.

Do you want Matt? Then show him you got what it takes, and you know it.

Viktoria opened the door with a determined grin. If Matt was looking in her direction, he was going to watch her walk into the house with no need for his feedback. What could be more confident than that?

Entering the house through the kitchen, she saw unwashed pots, pans, and other dishes filling the sink as usual. Junk mail and other piles of paper monopolized the dining room table. Also, as usual, Teri's parents were nowhere to be seen.

Viktoria couldn't find Teri, but she was home for sure. The dusty TV in the living room, like the day before, was on at a deafening volume. Both ashtrays, the one on the kitchen counter and the one on the coffee table in the living room had lit, half-finished cigarettes in them.

As always, Viktoria made herself at home, grabbing the *1986 Fall Preview Special Edition TV Guide* to thumb through while watching TV as she sat on the couch. Hoping to find a new series to interest her, she got caught up in the articles while *Popeye the Sailor* blared from the TV. As if Teri was even watching it. Unless it was a Matt Dillon flick or some bloody horror movie, TV was only there to give Teri company and drown out the band's noise in the garage.

Despite her intense focus on an article about a new series called *LA Law* while the sound of Popeye giving Bluto a spinach-induced pounding filled the room, Viktoria still managed to hear the toilet flush, and the bathroom door open in the hallway.

"Teri! Seriously, can we turn down the TV?"

With a slight embarrassment in her grin, Teri raced over, almost completely turning down the volume.

"I was wondering where you were," Viktoria said, looking up from the *TV Guide*. "I was beginning to think that I should maybe go to the store and put your picture on milk cartons if I had to wait any longer."

"Look, I'm sorry, OK? It's not like you were getting here in a flash so I decided to give the bathroom some much needed cleaning since I was already in it." Teri reached down for the cigarette on the coffee table. Taking a drag, she looked at Viktoria and shrugged. "What?"

"Nothing," Viktoria said with a shrug and a smile. "But two ashtrays at once again? Your addiction has really gotten out of control. Your lungs are going to look like charred steaks."

Teri sneered with sarcasm. "Oh, OK, Mom. I guess I missed that *Afterschool Special*."

Viktoria could only shake her head and snicker. "So, speaking of your mom, where are your parents today?"

Teri shrugged, taking another drag. "Who knows and who cares? Golfing in Scottsdale. Boating on Lake Pleasant. In Vegas for the weekend. Gone to hell." Teri placed the cigarette back in the ashtray. "Hey, come in the kitchen with me. The band's almost done practicing and I have lunch made for us and Chris."

Teri was no homemaker or chef by any stretch of the imagination, but so very maternal when it came to taking care of her older brother. She would always do his laundry and prepare his meals.

"Sorry the TV was so loud," Teri said as Viktoria followed her into the kitchen. "The band kept playing Led Zeppelin's 'Black Dog' over and over and over again and I couldn't take it anymore. I love my brother, but he's no Robert Plant."

Teri placed three plates on the kitchen counter, proceeding to fill them with chicken-flavored Top Ramen noodles. Next came two boiled hot dogs placed on the noodles of each plate. Then, out came the forks and three cans of Pepsi.

"Voila!" she exclaimed, gesturing like she had just created a work of art. "See? I'm a Master Chef, just like you. Oh, wait." Reaching into the pantry, Teri pulled out a bottle of Flintstones vitamins, placing a tablet next to each plate. "Look — I even make sure my cuisine is healthy."

They both laughed. With an endearing smile, Viktoria shook her head. "I have so much to teach you, Grasshopper."

"Hey, it's a start, right?" Teri said with a smile. "Someday, I'm going to blow your mind."

Viktoria almost leaped from her counter stool. "Oh! I've got something to tell you that will blow *your* mind. On my way here, I was on West Desert Cove when that big freaking truck from school—"

"Wait," Teri interrupted. "Hold that thought. I have even bigger news."

A slight sting of annoyance caused Viktoria to persist. "No, wait — you've got to hear this. Trust me, you'll love this."

"No, trust *me*!"

Teri's second interruption only served to cut Viktoria even deeper. Still, she knew the back and forth game wouldn't help her at all as Teri looked as though she was about to jump out of her own skin. With an expressionless face to get her annoyance across, she let Teri continue, "Here's something that'll make your day. I found out this morning from Chris that—"

Swoosh! A gust of hot air hit Viktoria's face before the strong central air-conditioning evaporated it. The door between the kitchen and the garage swung wide open, but it wasn't Chris as usual.

Whatever Teri was going to say, what happened with Cody, Brett, Nicole, and the big trucker, the hurt of Teri not giving Viktoria the chance to tell her — it was all gone and long forgotten.

Viktoria opened her mouth, but no words came out. The band had stopped playing, and of the four of them who could enter the kitchen from the garage, it was Matt.

Biting down on her lower lip, as though she could taste him, Viktoria's eyes were fixed on him. The Road Warrior within her was growing restless.

Viktoria knew he saw her make her way through the garage as though she owned the place. She was not going to let Matt leave the kitchen without her owning him.

Chapter 21

Taking in a slow, deep breath through her nose, Viktoria's eyes followed Matt from the door to the refrigerator. Biting down even harder on her lower lip, her fists clenched under the counter as he leaned into the refrigerator, reaching for a cold can of Pepsi.

"Whew! Man! Don't get me wrong, it's hotter than hell in Dallas, but it's a whole other ballgame in that garage. It's so hot and dry outside, the bushes are following the dogs around."

Viktoria didn't know where Matt got that saying from, but it made her want to burst out in laughter. Instead, only a hearty snicker escaped her as she continued to gaze at him. From underneath the counter, her hand came up, taking hold of her grandmother's cross.

That drawl, that smile, everything about him — this is a different kind of battle in the war, Dylan. Still, it's one I am going to win.

"Gross, Matt! That's disgusting."

Teri's rebuke toward Matt was out of character, especially with her usual dark and twisted sense of humor. In shock, Viktoria turned to her. Washing dishes with a scowl on her face as her eyes darted between Viktoria's eyes and her grandmother's cross, Teri shrugged with a sharp response, "What?"

With a bewildered smile, Viktoria shook her head. "What's going on with you, Teri? That was hilarious!"

Teri kept her eyes locked on Viktoria as she continued to reprimand Matt, "No, it wasn't. Freaking cowboys . . .

you know, Matt, there are classier ways of telling two girls it's hot outside. Try stepping outside the ranch and being a gentleman for once. Oh, and by the way, unless you're Chris, you need to knock before you come in. This isn't *your* house."

Mortified and confused, Viktoria could only look at Teri. Up until then, all Teri ever did was sing praises about his guitar playing and talk about how cool and hot he was. Suddenly, she was being a completely different person toward him.

With a kind, humble smile as he cracked open his Pepsi, Matt apologized, "I'm sorry, Teri. For what it's worth, Chris said I could just let myself in to grab a drink."

"Yeah? Well, I live here too, you know," Teri said with quiet sharpness toward Matt as she continued to keep her eyes on Viktoria.

Matt being a true gentleman while Teri was being so rude toward him cut Viktoria even deeper than Teri's interruptions before he walked in. Yes, Teri was her best friend, but what she was doing was wrong and embarrassing. Matt was in the right, and Viktoria was going to stand up for him.

"Are you serious, Teri? The other guys in the band and I barge in without knocking all the time and you don't even bat an eye. What's with the double standard?"

After an awkward moment of silence, Matt looked up from his can of Pepsi at Teri with his kind, charismatic smile. "Well, hey, here's another one we say in Texas: It's hot enough outside to sunburn a horned toad."

"Whatever that means," Teri mumbled as she turned off the faucet with irritated force.

"*Both* are hilarious, Matt," Viktoria said, reaching over the counter and placing her hand where Teri was looking down to get her attention. "Are you OK?" she mouthed as Teri looked up. The look on Teri's face was one of shock and disappointment — even betrayal. It was a *how dare you disagree with me and side with him* look.

Taking hold of her grandmother's cross to harness a deeper level of courage, Viktoria's voice was soft but focused as she shrugged and smiled at Teri. "Why are you so grossed out by what Matt said? I've heard you say *way* worse. I've also watched you laugh hard at things Matt Dillon said in his movies that are much more vulgar."

Leaning over the counter, Teri's questioning eyes were fixed on Viktoria's hand holding the cross. Her response was in a loud whisper — more than loud enough for Matt to hear. "Well, that's Matt *Dillon*, not Matt *my brother's guitar player*."

Viktoria couldn't believe Teri's belittling words toward Matt. Teri was always so considerate and caring. To her brother and the rest of the band, *she* was the mother of that house. It took a lot — a level that very few besides Sherry and her friends could reach — for her to be so derisive and harsh. What did Matt ever do to her?

Viktoria turned to Matt with her most apologetic facial expression. Just finishing his first gulp of Pepsi, he looked down at the can with his smile and an adorable look of satisfaction. He didn't even care what Teri said. He was totally impervious. Could he be any more appealing?

"Viktoria, over here." Teri intercepted Viktoria's attention with both index fingers pointing at her own face. "Before we were interrupted, I had some big news that will blow your mind. I found out from Chris this morning that the band got another gig."

Viktoria's face lit up as she turned to Matt. "Really? Already? No way!"

Teri's voice grew louder as, again, her index fingers pointed at her face. "*Viktoria*, again, over here. They sure did. It's a party at a house not too far from the high school, and it's on Friday. Your mom always works the closing shift at the store on Fridays, so nothing is standing in your way this time. We're going."

Viktoria looked down at her plate with a silent groan. Her stomach twisted as her mind went right back to the previous night. She wanted to support her mom in getting help. In fact, she needed to.

No gigs, no parties — she had promised Olivia. Again, she grabbed her grandmother's cross.

You've got to be kidding me, Dylan. After years of stagnation in the garage, the band gets one gig. One random, chance gig at a churchgoing high school kid's birthday party. Now, within the last twenty-four hours, this band, who couldn't get arrested if they tried, are booked for another gig just five days from now? What's next? A freaking world tour opening for AC/DC? Is Teri going to make me promise to follow them to every city too?

It was irrational, and she knew it, but Viktoria was annoyed at Teri for bringing it up and throwing a wrench in their light-hearted afternoon, especially in front of Matt. Why couldn't the one and only big news of the day be her triumph over Cody, Brett, and Nicole? That never even came up.

Viktoria realized how deep in thought she was over this new dilemma when Teri's hand waved rapidly back and forth between her eyes and her plate.

"Earth to Viktoria."

Raising her head, she cringed at the quizzical look on Teri's face as she took a drag from her kitchen cigarette. Teri then gave her a soft, somehow adorable, punch to the arm.

"Hey, you're getting that far-off, distant look in your eyes again, and I know you didn't hear a word I just said. Are you OK?"

"Yeah, of course. I'm fine," Viktoria said as she shook her head, blinking her eyes.

Teri replied with a skeptical look, "OK. Well, start eating. I don't want your food to get cold."

Viktoria smiled. Sometimes, Teri sounded just like Olivia. *Mom.*

Teri *wanted* her to go to the party. Her mom *needed* her to not go.

What was right was too obvious to not choose. She had to place her mom's needs over Teri's wants. That's what her grandmother, Dad, and, of course, Dylan would want.

"Viktoria." A strong, rugged left hand with calloused fingertips placed a half-filled Pepsi can next to her plate. Thrust back into the present with her heart skipping a beat, Viktoria lifted her head. Matt's smile and clear blue eyes were as stunning as they were sincere.

"It would mean the world to me if you came to see us play on Friday."

It would mean the world to him? Come on, Viktoria, own him!

Lost in his presence and her desire, every thought and quandary beforehand vanished from Viktoria's mind. "Absolutely — you can count on me being there, front and center, my eyes on you."

Matt's smile grew even wider and more breathtaking. "I'll definitely bring my A game, then. I can't wait. I'll talk to you later."

Reality returned to Viktoria as Matt swaggered back to the door and disappeared into the garage. Gripping her grandmother's cross, she shut her eyes.

Oh, Dylan. What did I do? What am I going to do?

Viktoria opened her eyes. Teri, with another questioning glance at Viktoria's grandmother's cross, took a drag from the kitchen cigarette. "See? He interrupted us again. Can you believe that? He knew you were going to go to the party on Friday. He didn't have to intervene for you to say yes."

Teri put out the cigarette and walked over to the other side of the counter. Sitting next to Viktoria, she put her arm around her with her usual comforting smile.

"Forget him. Friday night, it'll be you and me hanging out at the party, just the two of us. Maybe I'll crash at your house that night."

Ugh.

* * * *

The sun was setting as Viktoria walked under the weeping willow in her front yard. Walking from Teri's front door to her own, she tried to think of someway — any way — she could somehow resolve the messy predicament she had gotten herself into. Nothing at all came to her.

She walked into the house to find Olivia standing in the living room with her arms folded and a look of disdain on her face.

"Mom, are you OK?"

No response.

"Mom?"

Still no answer.

Oh no. Did Teri call for some reason while I was walking home and mention that I was going with her to the party? Did I forget to do something important? What's going on?

"Mom, you're worrying me. What's wrong?"

Without saying a word, Olivia walked past her, slamming the front door on her way out.

Standing alone in the living room, her mind raced with confusion.

A tall, lean figure emerged from the hall into the living room: Henrik, her father.

Chapter 22

Smiling from ear to ear, Viktoria wiped tears from her face. She rushed over and embraced him as tightly as she could and, reaching up, kissed his cheek.

"Hey, did you get any of that black lipstick on me?"

Viktoria snickered, rubbing his cheek. "Oh my gosh, Dad, I've missed you so much!"

"I've missed you too, Viktoria. More than you'll ever know."

She placed her hands on his perpetually clean-shaven face. His short, thick, straight blond hair shined like a halo in the light.

"Seriously, Dad, I can't believe you're here. I didn't see your tractor trailer outside."

"It's being serviced at the station. Your mother picked me up."

She buried her face in his chest, and Henrik's lean, strong arms pulled her against him, comforting her with a security she had not felt in over three months. His strong hands took each side of Viktoria's face, gently lifting it. He then kissed her on the forehead. With a quivering smile, tears filled his eyes as he looked at her.

Clearing his throat, he quickly wiped a tear from his cheek and flashed her a playful, loving grin.

"Look at you, with your beautiful smile, sparkling eyes, black fingernails, and that spiked dog collar around your neck." Henrik stepped back, slowly reading what was on her shirt in his Norwegian accent, "Siouxsie and the Banshees."

Viktoria laughed as he smiled at her. "Come on, Dad. You know you love my style."

"Absolutely. Anything looks beautiful on you, angel — I truly mean that."

From the garage, the sound of the car door slamming turned Viktoria's attention to Olivia.

"Is Mom OK? What's going on?"

Henrik sighed. "Viktoria, I know I've been gone for a long time. I just drove into Phoenix, and I am so happy to see you. I wish so badly that I could stay, but I have to get on the road again tonight."

With her heart sinking, Viktoria grabbed Henrik's arms, not wanting to let him go. "Dad, we haven't seen you since the end of June."

"Well, we're shipping goods all over the United States and Canada. We are low on drivers right now, so we're constantly on the road. Look, the pay is very good, much more than my last position. I'm taking care of you and your mother, the house is almost paid off, and I'm putting a lot more away for your college education. Believe me, this is a good thing."

Viktoria gripped Henrik's arms even tighter.

"We were doing just fine when you were driving locally. And you were home every night." Viktoria hadn't even talked on the phone with him since he'd been on the road. She could see why Olivia was so upset. "Mom . . . she needs—"

Henrik put his hands on her shoulders. "Don't worry about what's going on between your mother and me. Just focus on school and being a kid. You have your mom. You'll be fine."

"I know, Dad, but I don't have Dylan and I don't—"

A cold chill fell over Viktoria as Henrik took his hands off her shoulders, closed his eyes, and turned away. On a razor's edge between not wanting to further upset him and knowing he needed to understand the toll his absence was taking on her and Olivia, her voice grew soft and slow, "Dad, I need you. Mom needs you."

He ran his fingers through his hair with a heavy sigh, and frustration flashed in his eyes. Viktoria's stomach twisted.

"I am doing what a father does. I'm providing for you, putting a roof over your head, and food on the table. What more do you want from me?"

Trying to keep her voice soft and calm, Viktoria could not hold back the strain of her anxiety. "I need *you*, Dad. *You. Here.* Look at us. Look at Mom. Can't you see how tired she is? Yes, I'm here, but she's alone. And lonely. So am I."

The sudden concern in her father's eyes warmed and relieved Viktoria's heart. His unconditional love, attention, and care were solely on her, undivided. After more than three long months, she found herself in the moment she had yearned for. She could finally be heard — truly heard.

The relief was too strong. Allowing herself a moment of weakness, the pain surfaced along with her words. Holding her hands to her chest to somehow find the strength to conceal her emotions, her voice shook as she forced her words out. "You know, Dylan wasn't the only one having a hard time at school. You know those boys who beat him up made his life a living hell. Well, guess what? They have older brothers and sisters at the high school who are just as horrible and, unlike me, they have lots of friends who are just as bad. All I have is Teri, and since kindergarten, we've been alienated, called names, and laughed at. Just like Dylan. And it's only gotten worse since everything happened, and we pressed charges."

"Worse?" Henrik asked with the same concerned look. "What do you mean by 'worse'?"

Viktoria continued, resisting the urge to break down emotionally, "It's not just name calling and laughing anymore. Just this weekend alone, five of them surrounded and threatened us at the park, and I had a beer bottle thrown at me walking to Teri's earlier today. Even mom was confronted by Linda Davis when we were out. What's next? Are they going to gather in our front yard with torches? I don't feel safe anywhere. We need you home, Dad — every day."

Taking hold of her upper arms, Henrik looked in her eyes. The concerned frustration in his voice was sincere.

"I wish I knew what to do, Viktoria, I do. I, too, want to be home. There are simply not enough truck drivers, and they need us out there on the road, nonstop, to meet the demand. There is nothing at all that I can do about it. Trust me, I hate it."

"Yeah? Well, I hate it too," Viktoria said, wiping a tear from her cheek. "It's not right that you're always on the road, leaving us abandoned and scared."

Letting go of her upper arms with a sudden cold glare, her father was farther away than at any other time since June. Her heart sinking, Viktoria wished more than anything that she could take back the last three words she said.

"Scared?" Henrik echoed with sharpness before turning away, muttering words under his breath in Norwegian. Running his fingers through his hair again, he shook his head in frustration before turning to face Viktoria again.

The love and concern in his eyes were gone, replaced by that of anger and trauma. Viktoria had never seen that look in Henrik's eyes until they lost her grandmother and then Dylan just a month later. In the small amount of time between the two terrible events and Henrik's sudden transition from local to long-distance trucking, she saw it all too often.

Viktoria placed her hands over her heart again, hoping she could somehow hold it together to keep it from breaking. She knew where Henrik was going, and she braced herself, hoping it would not be too much for her to hear.

"You're scared, Viktoria? Let me tell you what it really means to be scared. Scared is being born during the war in German-occupied Norway. Scared is being only a year old when my father was killed in the resistance movement. For four years, it was just my mother and me, a toddler, living alone, hiding from war-hardened enemy soldiers. My earliest memories were of them busting through our door, searching the house, and taking anything they wanted."

Viktoria closed her eyes. "Dad."

"There were no checks being mailed to us. No father to stop by for a couple of hours, taking a break from the war. It was just fear, cold small potatoes, and soup. Oh, and the only man in our house was an occasional enemy soldier with a gun pointed at us should we make any wrong moves."

"Dad, please stop. I know."

"Do you? You *think* you do but you don't! You have a comfortable house, air-conditioning, plenty of food, television, you name it. Above all, you have freedom. I was five when the war ended. We were put in a displacement camp because our house was destroyed. We had nothing — nothing at all. If your great aunt didn't have an extra room at her house in Peoria, who knows where we would've ended up, or if we would have even survived. Your grandmother and me had to build our lives from scratch. Just the two of us, alone. So don't tell me about fear, loneliness, and hard times."

Keeping her eyes on Henrik, Viktoria took hold of her grandmother's cross.

He didn't mention you, Dylan. He didn't acknowledge my pain of losing you and grandma, or even try to understand what Mom and I am going through. Am I invisible?

The frustration burning within Viktoria was instantly evaporated, replaced with shame as Henrik took another step closer to her with even more intensity, speaking through his teeth, "And never say that I abandoned you. Never. Do you understand me? Unlike my father, I'm still alive. He shouldn't have died. He shouldn't have abandoned us, prioritizing his want for revenge over his own family, but he did. So don't stand there and accuse me of doing so. You got that?"

Viktoria tried to open her mouth to explain and defend her words, but the pain was too strong. Henrik had never lashed out at her like that before. It was something she thought he would never do.

Grief, frustration, shock, and shame all struck Viktoria at once. Overwhelmed and crushed, her stomach and throat tightened as her chest convulsed. All she could do was bury her face in her hands.

Henrik raced to embrace her, pressing her face against his chest. "I'm sorry, Viktoria. I shouldn't have been so cross with you. I feel absolutely terrible. You didn't deserve that at all. I will never do that again, I promise."

Lifting her face with his hands, his smile and voice had the love and softness Viktoria was used to from him. "Viktoria, you are safe and loved. I promise. I may not be here physically, but I am here in my heart, always."

Holding her face even tighter, Viktoria recognized the affectionate, sly smile on his face from when he shared with her exciting news or a fun secret.

"Do you remember how your mother and I used to go out in the desert to the shooting range on the weekends? You were always amazed at how good your mom was with the shotgun, remember?"

She nodded, forcing a smile.

"Well, that's one of the many reasons why I fell in love with her. She grew up on that shooting range. With her, if something were to happen and I couldn't be around, I knew my home and children would be safe and protected. World War II and Norway were finally in the past. I know I've been gone too long. I can, though, because I know her; I know what she's capable of."

As he wiped tears from her cheeks, the sincerity in Henrik's eyes comforted her. "Trust me. With your mother here, you are very safe. Our home is protected. Do you understand me?"

Viktoria nodded again.

He pulled her in for another tight embrace, kissing her forehead.

"Your mother's in the garage. I have to go. I love you more than anything. I miss you every day. The company is hiring more drivers soon, so I'll be home more often. Until then, I'll do all I can to be stronger for you, OK?"

Henrik hugged and kissed her again. As always, they expressed their love for one another in Norwegian.

"Jeg elsker deg, min engel."

"Jeg elsker deg, pappa."

Viktoria watched as her father left. Sitting on the couch, she wiped her tears away, trying to hold on to the sensation of her father holding her as she waited for her mom to come home.

Chapter 23

The blurred sight of her sandwich came back into focus as Teri's sharp voice yanked Viktoria from the night before into the present.

"Hey, Earth to Viktoria."

Shaking her head as if to wake herself from a dream, Viktoria looked up.

Teri took a bite of her own sandwich with concerned curiosity in her eyes. "Are you OK?"

"Yeah, why?"

"Well, you barely spoke to me the whole way to school, and you didn't say a word to me in third period. It's now lunch and you're still giving me the silent treatment. What's wrong?"

Viktoria sighed as if to prepare herself for a long, detailed explanation. "When I got home last night, my dad was there."

Under the tree where they spent their lunchbreaks, Teri jumped up from the grass they sat on. "No way! Viktoria, that's exciting! He's been gone way too long. Look, I have detention after school, but I'll go straight to your house right after."

"He's already gone."

"Already? Why?"

Teri appeared disappointed and deflated after Viktoria told her about her conversation with her dad the night before.

"Ugh, that sucks. I miss your dad so much. I wish I could've seen him."

Viktoria couldn't hide the frustration in her voice, "Yeah? Well, I wish I could've seen more of him. It was no more than thirty minutes from the time I got home, and my mom was already taking him back to his truck. I knew from the moment I walked in the house that she was livid. She didn't get home until around eleven o'clock and didn't say a word. She just went straight to her room. She didn't care that I was still up on a school night watching TV. She had already left for work when I got up this morning. She always leaves a note for me on the refrigerator. Today, there was nothing."

Teri moved next to Viktoria, placing her hand on her shoulder. "I'm sorry, it will get better."

The frustration in Viktoria's voice grew sharp. "Will it? It's not fair — my dad pressed charges against those boys who beat up Dylan, raised all sorts of hell with them *and* their families, and then he hit the road, leaving my mom and me to deal with the mess he created."

"It's only temporary. Besides, can you blame him?" Teri asked as she looked in the distance.

Viktoria pulled her shoulder from Teri's hand. "Wait, what do you mean?"

Teri shrugged. "Nothing. I'm just saying, look at what he's been through this last year. If that happened to me, I'd want to skip town too."

Viktoria glared back. "Really? And leave your family behind?"

"No, I didn't mean it that way. All I'm saying is that after all he's been through—"

"Why are you defending him?" Viktoria shot back.

"I'm not."

"Well, then don't, OK?"

"OK," Teri answered back defensively, shrugging her shoulders.

The awkward silence returned. The guilt of snapping at Teri started to gnaw at Viktoria. Reaching up, she pressed her grandmother's cross with her fingertips.

Ugh. What's wrong with me, Dylan? She was only trying to help.

Viktoria turned again to Teri with a sigh. "I'm sorry, Teri. I shouldn't have gotten upset with you like that."

"No, I understand," Teri said with a gentle smile. "I'm sorry too. I should have worded that better."

Weary of her heavy emotions, Viktoria searched for a way to end their lunch break on a lighthearted note. "So, you have detention after school, huh?"

Teri sighed and shook her head. "Yes, I got it in English this morning."

"What happened?"

"Marie Cooper made a comment about my hair, so I threatened to find her after school, tie her down, and shave her head. To make a long story short, after Ms. Cavanaugh called me up to her desk and lectured me, she heard me tell her to go to hell under my breath."

Viktoria cringed. "Ooh. I guess that means I'll be walking home alone today."

Teri shrugged again. "I'm afraid so. Well, I need to stop by my locker before lunch is over. I promised Mr. Gaskin that I'd be in class early so he could help me with my math homework, so I better get going."

"Let me guess — when you think you're using the right formula to solve the problem but you're not sure, Mr. Gaskin will tell you to 'follow your heart.'"

"Yeah, he missed his calling as a shrink," Teri said with a laugh before giving Viktoria a hug and her warm, sweet smile. "Like I said earlier, things will get better. In the meantime, you have your mom, and you definitely have me. You know that, right?"

"Always," Viktoria said with a smile. "Why don't you come over to my house when you get out of detention? I know my mom could use a fun evening with the girls. The three of us will do something together. She'll love it."

"Tell her I'll go there straight from school," Teri said, flashing an excited grin as she began to make her way to her locker.

* * * *

Staring at her feet as she walked home from school, the rest of the world seemed millions of miles away as Viktoria brainstormed ideas for a fun evening with Olivia and Teri. Movies, restaurants, and their favorite card games raced through her mind.

She knew Olivia would be home by the time she got there. Monday nights were always uneventful at their house, so she couldn't wait to surprise Olivia with her two favorite words after a stressful day at work: girl's night.

Two blocks from home, a younger girl on a bicycle passed by her on the street.

Viktoria happened to glance up in time to see the long blond hair and the side of her face. Her heart stopped. "Hey!"

When the girl turned around to see it was Viktoria calling for her, a startled look struck her face as she pedaled faster and turned into the park.

"Wait! I need to talk to you!"

Viktoria ran after her. When she got to the park just a few seconds later, the girl was out of sight. There was only one place she could hide.

Rushing to the first outdoor racquetball court, Viktoria looked in. Sure enough, the girl was standing against the back wall. Holding her bicycle in front of her like some sort of shield, her whole body trembled.

Catching her breath, Viktoria lifted her hand with her palm out, trying to communicate to her to not be afraid. Viktoria had desperately wanted to talk to her since May.

The frightened girl barricaded between the back wall of the racquetball court and her bicycle was Candace Armstrong, the junior high cheerleader who Dylan had a crush on and danced with the whole night before he died. The fight had been apparently over her. If anybody could tell Viktoria the real truth about what happened that horrible night, she could.

Chapter 24

Candace jerked her bicycle even closer to herself. Viktoria stopped halfway inside the racquetball court, not wanting to alarm the girl any more than she already had.

"Candace? Look, I know who you are. There's no reason to be scared, I just need to ask you some questions."

"My parents and my sister told me to stay away from you," Candace responded in a panic. "Please go away and leave me alone."

As Viktoria stepped closer, Candace continued to gasp for air as she sniffled, wiping tears from her face. "I'm not the reason why your brother died — my parents and sister told me so."

Her straightforward words caught Viktoria off guard. Still, she was able to maintain her focus on subsiding whatever fear Candace had of her. "I'm not accusing you of that, I promise. Look, if it helps, I knew Dylan liked you. I was the one who encouraged him to ask you to dance with him."

Candace stopped trembling, though her face was still red and alarmed as she remained looking toward, but no longer directly at, Viktoria. Taking a few more steps closer, Viktoria went even further to reassure Candace that she had no ill will toward her. "In fact, I want to thank you for making my little brother feel special. Just for once, he had the chance to be the man he dreamed of becoming before he left this life, and it was you who gave him that last gift. You will never know how much that means to me."

Candace then looked into Viktoria's eyes. Her face grew even redder as though she were about to burst into tears. She didn't move as Viktoria walked up to her, got down on one knee, and put her hands on the bicycle. To maintain the peace she had achieved between them, Viktoria continued to speak in a soft voice, "The reason why I wanted to talk to you is because I have heard everyone else's version of what happened at the dance, and they are all focused on, you know, the tragedy. I've always known that, with you, I would get what I have wanted most — the real truth. Most important of all, though, I would hear about how my brother was able to finally live a dream that night because of you."

Holding her breath, Candace lowered her head, beginning to sob. Viktoria placed her hands on her shoulders.

"Don't cry. What you did for Dylan that night was priceless. Of everyone that was involved in what happened, you're the one who should never feel any guilt at all. You are the one good thing that happened."

Through her sobs, Candace began to force out her words, "I did it. It's my fault. I killed Dylan."

Viktoria tried to lift her face. "Don't say that. You were only trying to be nice to my brother — I understand that. What those boys did to Dylan was their choice, not yours. *They* are the ones who have to live with their guilt, not you."

Candace jerked her head up. "You don't understand!" Her eyes had a striking, terrible flash. They alarmed Viktoria as she removed her hands from her shoulders.

"Jason Davis was my boyfriend. He was such a jerk to me, so I dumped him the day before the dance. He tried to call me a bunch of times, but I wouldn't talk to him. He came to the dance and followed me around, trying to win me back. I knew he hated your brother — all his friends did. They always said he was an annoying little dweeb. When Dylan asked me to dance, I thought, 'What better way to get back at Jason than by showing him that Dylan, this small guy he hated, was better than him?'"

Every word jabbed into Viktoria's heart as Candace continued. "I danced and danced with Dylan, and it worked — I had never seen Jason so mad. When I saw him approaching us with his friends, I topped it off by quickly kissing Dylan on the lips. Jason grabbed my arm so hard it scared me. Dylan grabbed his shirt and told him to let go. That's when Jason and his friends grabbed Dylan and forced him outside. Other kids followed to see what was going to happen, but I didn't care. I got what I wanted. Did you hear what I just said? *I got what I wanted. I didn't care.* And now I have to live with that every single day."

Candace pulled her bicycle from between the two of them and started to get on it as she continued to sob. "I'm sorry, OK? I wish I could tell you something different, but I can't. I used Dylan to get back at Jason and he died because of it. I hate myself for what happened, and I will never forgive myself. That's *one* thing you can feel good about, that I will never forgive myself. Please let me go and leave me alone!"

Viktoria could still hear Candace's sobs as she rode away. Still staring at the back wall of the racquetball court where Candace had been standing, she couldn't tell if she was numb with shock, heartbroken, or both.

Slowly turning around, she leaned her back against the wall and sat down. With her legs against her chest, she rested her elbows on her knees, and her face in her hands. Feeling tears leak though her fingers, she kept her face buried in her palms as she sniffled.

I'm the one who will never forgive myself. I should've never encouraged you, Dylan. You were too good for her. You were too good for any of us.

Resting the back of her head against the wall, Viktoria looked up at the cloudless desert sky. She wished she could go back and not do what she had wanted to do more than anything — talk to Candace Armstrong.

Chained down by a newfound, debilitating guilt, standing up and walking home felt insurmountable. She could only take hold of her grandmother's cross.

I don't know what to do, Dylan. Will you ever forgive me?

Her stomach twisted as her chest started to tighten. She couldn't fight the panic building inside her.

Why did I do it? Why did I talk to her? More than that, why did I encourage you to dance with her when all she wanted was to use you? I'm afraid you blame me for what happened.

The dinging of a bicycle bell pierced Viktoria's ears, breaking her train of thought. In front of her, just outside the racquetball court, a boy around eleven years old was riding a red bicycle — one identical to Dylan's.

The boy was slightly built with thick blond hair. The more Viktoria watched him ride around the park, the more she saw Dylan. Serenity warmed her heart and eased her mind.

An adoring smile graced her face as she realized the fear and guilt had disappeared.

Dylan, is that you?

At that moment, out of nowhere, the boy turned and looked at Viktoria, giving her the widest, most genuine smile. It was the same smile Dylan beamed when his professional wrestling heroes prevailed on TV.

The boy then rode off and disappeared, but seeing him was enough for Viktoria. Her smile broadened as she laughed with nostalgia and emotion.

She also couldn't help but notice the boy's T-shirt. It said *Love and Peace* with a large peace sign on the back. It made her think of the one person she knew who could truly help her move past what had happened with Candace: Mr. Tailor. The next day was Tuesday, and as always, Viktoria would be meeting with him during lunch. The timing couldn't have been more perfect.

Thank you, Dylan. You knew I needed that too.

Chapter 25

Her eyes had been locked on the clock for the entire last half of third period, so Viktoria grabbed her books and jumped up from her desk as soon as the bell rang. But before she could take her first step toward the door, a hand grabbed her left sleeve.

"Hey, what's with the big rush?" Teri asked. "You've been squirreling around in your seat during the entire class. If you're really *that* excited for lunch, then I want some of whatever you made."

Viktoria's response was rapid, "Hey Teri, I'll meet you under the tree in about twenty minutes, OK?"

Teri tugged at her sleeve again. "Whoa, whoa, wait. Hold up."

"What?" a flustered Viktoria asked.

"Easy. Don't get all wrapped around the axle. I'm just wondering where you're going, that's all."

After an exasperated sigh with her eyes closed, Viktoria looked back at Teri. "I need to go to the office to see if—"

"Mr. Tailor's there?" a visibly irritated Teri interjected.

Viktoria sighed again. "Yes, OK?"

With folded arms, Teri rolled her eyes. "Again? How did that hippie burnout become your personal shaman? He's a high school counselor, not a shrink. He's no more qualified than I am to give you sound advice on life."

"Well, obviously, you don't know him as well as I do. He's been able to help me so much because he's been where I am."

"Yeah?" Teri replied with increased frustration. "Well, I've known you much longer than that bohemian flowerchild, and I also know more about where you are because I've been *with* you through it all."

"Teri," Viktoria said, trying to get her to stop. Still, Teri wouldn't let it go.

"You're taking all your problems to Mr. Tailor instead of to me. Something's wrong with that picture."

"Teri," Viktoria said in almost a whisper, trying to diffuse the tension. "You're right. You've been with me through all of this, and you've suffered too. Why don't you come see Mr. Tailor with me? I think that'd be good for both of us."

"No, thanks," Teri grumbled as she grabbed her books, making her way to the door. "I hope you get what you need out of that tree-hugging dope-head. I better see you under our tree in twenty minutes."

"Fine," Viktoria muttered under her breath as she followed her out the door, and then headed in the opposite direction.

Racing to Mr. Tailor's office to make up for the lost time, she was relieved to see his light was still on. It took a few loud knocks on the already open door before Mr. Tailor looked up, removing his headphones.

"Viktoria Vikstad! Please, come in and take a load off."

His voice was deep and strong, like a radio DJ. He reminded her of Dr. Johnny Fever from the TV show *WKRP in Cincinnati*, except Mr. Tailor's hair was long, thick, and jet black, as was his beard.

Viktoria sat down. As always, she looked at a picture of a younger Mr. Tailor on his desk. The long black hair was there, but he was clean-shaven. Sitting next to him on a rock beside a small waterfall was a stunning girl with long, straight light brown hair. Both were adorned in leather and beads. Mr. Tailor evidently followed Viktoria's eyes.

"You know, my wife and I met at Woodstock."

"Yeah, I know. You tell me every time I come in here."

Mr. Tailor snickered and smiled. "Yeah, I guess I do. How are you, Viktoria? How was this last weekend?"

The entire previous weekend, the good and the bad moments, rushed through her mind within a second. The time and energy simply weren't there to even scratch the surface, so she went right to the one she knew he would understand the most. After all, it still did trouble her. "I put my hand on Dylan's bedroom door, but I still couldn't open it."

"That's OK," Mr. Tailor said with an understanding smile. "It's still OK. Like I've said before, it's been eighteen years since I lost my twin brother in Vietnam. To this day, I've never entered the bedroom we grew up in. I've never touched or even looked at the toys or books we shared — nothing. Just like you, though, that doesn't make me crazy, cold, or weirdly superstitious. Through all my research and reflection, I've come to realize something: Yes, it is natural for people to hold on to physical objects and keepsakes of a loved one who has passed on so they could remember them in a personal way. Do you know what's just as natural and healthy? Instead of holding on to objects and keepsakes, there are those, like you and me, who would rather just hold that loved one in our hearts. The reason why we do so is because we are blessed to know something that too many people don't."

Mr. Tailor then lifted his hand, holding his thumb and index finger about an inch from each other. "We know that our loved one is only this far away. Objects and keepsakes, to us, are just things of the past. Our relationship with that individual, though, is still present and has a forever future."

Mr. Tailor's words pierced Viktoria's heart with a peaceful warmth. After a few quiet seconds, he added a nod to his smile. "It's true."

With an understanding half-smile, Viktoria took hold of her grandmother's cross.

I needed to hear that, Dylan. You are right next to me. I just wish I didn't chase after Candace yesterday. You didn't deserve to hear what she said about you.

"Something else is bothering you, Viktoria. How can I help you?"

With a soft, quiet sigh, Viktoria could not help the vulnerability expressed in her eyes. "Something happened on the way home from school yesterday."

The comforting smile and understanding in Mr. Tailor's eyes gave Viktoria permission to completely open up about what had happened with Candace, how it made her feel, and why she knew she needed to come to him for help.

As always, Viktoria knew she had Mr. Tailor's undivided attention. He remained quiet until Viktoria was finished. He then looked down with a serious expression for several seconds before looking back up with a smile. "Dylan was really into that girl, wasn't he?"

"She was his one and only crush since the fourth grade. She was everything to him. He didn't want to go to that stupid dance, but my mom was making him. I was just trying to be the cool big sister and give him your typical 'girl advice' so he could at least take away something special from that night. Candace always seemed to be nice to him. I should've known better. Now I feel like . . ." The words wouldn't come to Viktoria.

"Do you feel like Dylan is angry with you because you encouraged him and coached him on how to approach Candace at the dance?" Mr. Tailor asked in his gentle way, somehow knowing the words Viktoria wanted to say but couldn't express.

"Yes," Viktoria could barely answer. "I want to take it all back. I'm afraid this is all my fault. I'm afraid Dylan will never forgive me."

Mr. Tailor leaned forward in his chair. With his intense but caring stare, his smile became just a little more pronounced. "I want you to do something, Viktoria. Let's take a moment and have you reverse roles with Dylan. What if it was Dylan who gave *you* advice on approaching your crush at the dance, and the tragedy that night happened to you? If he was sitting in your chair right now, afraid that you were angry with him, what would you want to tell him?"

The very thought broke Viktoria's heart. After clearing her throat, her voice shook with emotion, "I would want to tell him to not be afraid. I love him and would always love him. I would never leave his side. I would tell him that I know that all he wanted to do was — after all that I had suffered — help me have one special moment to remember, for me to live one of my dreams. And, in spite of all that happened, I did.

Because of him, I lived that dream. And, because of all he did for me in my life, I would always stand by him, create special moments with him, and help make his dreams come true."

Viktoria sniffled, wiped a tear from her cheek, and could only shrug. "He would always be my little brother. No matter what."

Mr. Tailor smiled wider and, lifting his hands to his sides, nodded. "Well, now you know how Dylan feels."

A quick laugh of great emotional relief escaped Viktoria. "Perhaps I got my answer when that boy with the hippie T-shirt smiled at me like Dylan."

Mr. Tailor laughed a little. "Your brother knows how to talk to you."

Viktoria smiled as she stood up. "As always, thank you, Mr. Tailor. You're the best, I really mean that. Well, I guess I better catch up with Teri before she starts putting my face on milk cartons."

Mr. Tailor nodded again and smiled. "My door is always open. By the way, let Teri know I'm excited for her brother and his band for getting their second gig this Friday."

Viktoria paused. "What? How do you know about that?"

Mr. Tailor shrugged. "Hey, I may be knocking on forty, but I still know what's going on in the local music scene."

"Are you serious?" Viktoria asked. "*That* local? They just barely made it out of the garage."

"Well, I'll admit, Teri told me about it," Mr. Tailor said.

"*Teri* told you?" Viktoria could only think of all the derogatory comments Teri made whenever Mr. Tailor came up in conversation.

"Yeah," Mr. Tailor said. "Teri stops by my office quite a bit, like you. You're very lucky to have her as a best friend. She's just a very thoughtful, nurturing individual — bringing me cookies, asking about my wife and son. She is always very kind to me."

Viktoria could barely hold in her snickering as she left Mr. Tailor's office. She couldn't wait to find Teri under the tree and tell her what she had just found out.

* * * *

It had definitely been more than twenty minutes. The only vision in Viktoria's mind was Teri sitting alone under the tree, stewing as she looked at her watch every ten seconds. Rushing to her locker, she gritted her teeth in frustration, getting her combination wrong twice before getting it open to grab her lunch.

As always, she quickly made her way to the gymnasium. Cutting through was the quickest way from her locker to the tree. Racing toward the gym entrance, her mind went back to the end of her conversation with Mr. Tailor.

I can't believe that. After all the grief Teri gave me for seeing Mr. Tailor? After all her criticisms of him, she's been going to his office this whole time? I can't wait to—

Viktoria gasped. Turning the corner and entering the gym, her race to the tree came to a startling halt. Just a few feet in front of her stood Sherry Davis. To each side of her were Janine Preston and Tiffany McNamara. As always, they stood in their cheerleading uniforms, attached at the hip.

Her whole body trembling with adrenaline, Viktoria clenched her fists, looking her enemy dead in the eye. "Is this what you were talking about Saturday as you were retreating back to your car? Fine, Sherry, I'm here and I'm alone. What happens now?"

With her condescending half-smile, Sherry kept her eyes on Viktoria as she gestured behind her with a nod. "Shut the doors. Make sure no one else comes in."

Chapter 26

Shoes squeaked behind Viktoria on the basketball court. She whipped around as Jeff Bryant and Vince Henderson closed the gymnasium doors. The lights were on inside, but it seemed much darker.

Viktoria's stomach tightened as she clenched her teeth. In her mind was the girl staring back at her in the bathroom mirror that morning, applying her war paint. It was the same girl who, just two days before, stood her ground with fearlessness against Cody Rutherford, Brett Robinson, and Nicole Zielinski. She was the girl Animal and Hawk would've been proud to call one of their own, and she was determined to do it again.

"It's about time," Sherry said with her arms folded. "You know, you try to look all deep, dark, and mysterious, but you are so pathetically predictable. You come this way every day to meet up with Teri. Thanks to you taking so long today, lunch break is shot for the rest of us. It is well worth it, though."

Channeling all the anger she'd been harboring since May, Viktoria dropped her lunch, tensing every muscle in her body. Her lips moved with a resentful quiver as the words came through her clenched teeth, "You got what you wanted, Sherry. You're here and I'm here, and I am not backing down. If you want a fight, then stop talking and start doing."

Sherry glared back. "Easy there, Morticia. Teri's not here to back you up this time."

"What makes you think I need her?" Viktoria shot back. "This is just between us, right? Unless you're going to cower behind your friends as usual. Are you going to do that, or do you actually have what it takes to face me by yourself?"

"That's for another day," Sherry answered before turning to her right, calling beyond Tiffany. "Bridgette, this is the one you wanted to talk to, right?"

Viktoria's chest pounded even harder as a fourth glaring cheerleader marched in their direction from the locker room entrance next to the bleachers. Redheaded and slightly stocky, it was Bridgette Armstrong, Candace's older sister, and her claws were out.

"Who the hell do you think you are? What makes you think you can get away with chasing down my little sister and scaring the hell out of her?"

"That wasn't what I was trying to do," Viktoria called out in her direction with her palms out, trying to reason with her. "I just wanted to know what really happened that night. I didn't think—"

"Yeah, obviously you *didn't* think," Bridgette continued. "You didn't think about what cornering and forcing Candace to rehash everything would do to her. You didn't think about how much you would scare her and how upset she would get."

In between Sherry and Tiffany, Bridgette stomped up to Viktoria. "You also didn't think about how messing with my little sister would make me want to tear your clown-painted face off!"

Tiffany placed her hands on Bridgette's shoulders. "Trust me, Bridgette, she's not worth losing your position on the squad. I mean, look at her."

"Yeah?" Bridgette snapped back. "Well, I'm not the only one who's pissed at her."

Over Bridgette's shoulder, behind Sherry and Tiffany, appeared Nicole from Sunday's battle. Squeaks of tennis shoes behind Viktoria caused her to turn around. Cody and Brett had lined up with Jeff and Vince.

The enemy, with its largest army ever, had Viktoria surrounded, and she stood alone. With adrenaline at war with fear within her, her whole body was tense and trembling. Two or three drops of cold sweat raced down her back. Touching her grandmother's cross for strength, she froze her feet solid to the ground, refusing to budge.

"You've pissed a lot of people off these last few days," Sherry said with her eyebrows raised. "You know we're all tight, right? You didn't think we'd all find out what you've been doing, with or without your mom and Teri?"

"So, what now?" Viktoria asked, clenching her fists. "Are you all going to gang up on me and beat me up? What is that going to accomplish? How is that going to make you feel better? It's not going to change what happened."

"We're all here for only one reason," Sherry responded. "Look around you — there's nothing you can do about it. This is your final warning; it's over."

"Not to me, it isn't," Bridgette snarled. "Not after what she did to my little sister."

"Oh yeah? Well, what about what Candace did to Dylan?" Viktoria shot back. "She used him, and he died because of it."

Bridgette, with a vengeful glare, took a step closer, but Viktoria refused to lose her ground.

"That's right, Bridgette. I heard it directly from Candace. If she's turning into one of you, then Dylan was way too good for her."

Bridgette raised her hand to hit Viktoria, but before she could, Viktoria pushed her hard enough for her to stumble behind Sherry and Tiffany. As Tiffany held Bridgette back from retaliating, two of the football players did the same to Viktoria. With both arms locked in strong grasps, Viktoria was defenseless as Sherry and the other girls closed in.

Vince stepped in between Viktoria and the approaching girls. "All right, it's over. That's enough."

"Screw it," Jeff called out, letting go of Viktoria's left arm. "If the girls want to fight, let them."

"Is that what you want? A fight?" Sherry yelled in Viktoria's face as the five cheerleaders had her backed up against the wall. "Be careful what you wish for, Viktoria!"

Viktoria's eyes darted back and forth. Five cheerleaders and four football players had her trapped. The numbers game between her and the enemy was not in her favor, and it was much worse than on Saturday at the park.

Bridgette broke through Sherry and Janine, grabbing Viktoria by the shirt. Her other arm was held back by Tiffany.

"Let go of me!" Viktoria shouted as she grabbed Bridgette by the neck. Bridgette attempted to pull her head back, gasping for air as Viktoria started to squeeze.

Sherry then thrusted an unbalanced Viktoria against the wall. The back of her head hit the hardest, and Viktoria closed her eyes, wincing. As she opened them, she didn't see Sherry pinning her shoulders against the wall — it was Sherry's little brother, Jason. Surrounding her were all the other young boys who had ganged up on Dylan the night of the dance.

Shutting her eyes, she clenched her teeth as she gripped what she thought was Jason's shirt with both hands. It was all caving in on her again: the police report, Dylan's beaten, lifeless body, and the awful damage the mortuary couldn't hide.

With nausea overwhelming her, Viktoria opened her eyes, taking in a deep breath. Jason, still pinning her against the wall, and his friends spun all around her. She closed her eyes again.

No, Dylan! Not again! We have to win!

Reaching over Jason's arms, she found his neck, and started squeezing.

"Stop!" It wasn't Jason's voice. It was Sherry's. "I said stop!"

Viktoria opened her eyes. It was Sherry, not Jason, pinning her against the wall and it was *Sherry's* friends looking on. With crippling nausea and unsteadiness still overtaking her, Viktoria's attempt to push Sherry away was weak.

Bridgette pushed Sherry to the side, grabbing Viktoria by the shirt again and shoving her against the wall. With all the strength and balance she could muster, Viktoria fought back, punching Bridgette in the mouth. A trickle of blood ran down Bridgette's chin as Tiffany and Janine pulled her away. Exhausted from giving all she had into the one punch, Viktoria still tried to grab hold of Bridgette, refusing to give up.

"I said stop!" Sherry yelled again, grabbing Viktoria by the shirt. "It's over!"

"No," Viktoria struggled to say loudly, determined but drained from the nausea and dizziness. "Not yet."

Grabbing Sherry by her cheerleading uniform's top with both hands, Viktoria, with all her strength, tried to maintain her balance and keep fighting.

"Let go of me, you freak!" Sherry shouted as she grabbed Viktoria by the shoulders, thrusting her to the floor.

On her hands and knees, Viktoria lifted her face from where it had struck the floor. Blood dripped from her nose onto the hardwood of the basketball court, which continued to spin. Holding her breath was all she could do to keep from vomiting. Everything seemed to be moving in slow motion and the voices around her were barely audible.

"You don't want this to be over?" Sherry's voice was loud but muffled with almost an echo. "Fine! We'll keep this going, and believe me, you're going to regret it!"

The dizziness only increased and everything around Viktoria grew even more slow and numb as a sharp tugging came from behind her neck, yanking her head up. She gasped for air as though she were being strangled. The pressure on the front of her neck became unbearable before total relief came in an instant, allowing her to fall to the floor and catch her breath.

The nausea and dizziness started to subside as her breathing returned to normal and she could hear the others walking away. The last muffled echoing words came from Sherry followed by a few laughs, "This actually looks nice. I think I'll keep it on my hope chest."

Blood stopped dripping from Viktoria's nose as the gym fell silent. The bell ringing for fourth period startled her.

Getting off her hands, yet still on her knees, Viktoria looked around. The room had stopped spinning, and the nausea had faded. She glanced down at the blood on the floor and felt like something was missing. Remembering the tugging and gasping for air, her hands rose to her neck — only skin was there.

Her heart shattered. Viktoria buried her face in her hands. Sherry had taken her grandmother's cross. Though she couldn't stop the tears, her teeth clenched while tight fists formed over her face.

The war isn't over, Dylan. It is only beginning.

Chapter 27

Viktoria refused to get up from the couch. Sitting forward, her face was buried in her hands. Her palms covering her eyes created a comforting darkness, as though it held the power to make her invisible from the world. She just needed time — time to recover and regroup.

On the other side of the front door, in between the relentless knocking, Teri's voice grew louder. "Open the door, Viktoria! I know you're in there. Where else would you be? Come on, let me in."

Viktoria wished she had four hands so she could cover her ears as well and remain in her own little private world. After a couple of minutes, the jingling of keys made her regret going behind her mom's back and giving Teri a spare key to the house. Their fun secret had backfired.

As the front door swung open, Viktoria had no other choice but to look up. Out of breath, as though she had just sprinted four blocks, Teri's mouth hung open with deep concern in her eyes.

"What the hell, Viktoria? Why didn't you come to the door?"

At that moment, silence was all Viktoria wanted. It was numbing, a powerful shield that would also help strengthen her.

"Viktoria." Teri softened her voice. The frustrated concern, though, was still there. "I waited under the tree for the entire lunchbreak. I didn't see you in the hall between fifth and sixth period, and you weren't at your locker after school. Are you OK?"

Weary and emotionally drained, Viktoria maintained her silence.

Teri turned away, running her fingers through her hair before folding her arms. After a couple of deep breaths, she sniffled. Turning back around to face Viktoria, her whole frame appeared weighed down with deep anxiety. Her eyes expressed it more than anything else.

"Are you mad at me?"

Viktoria knew the least she could do was relieve Teri of that worry, so she did the one and only thing she could — forcing a slight smile, she shook her head.

After a deep sigh, Teri turned away, wiping under her eyes. She then walked over and sat down next to her. Rubbing Viktoria's back before placing her hand on her shoulder, Teri's voice returned to its usual serene and nurturing manner. "Please talk to me. You know I'll understand, no matter what. Whatever it is, I'll help you through it."

It wasn't more than a few seconds later when the garage door opened and Olivia's car pulled in. With a frustrated sigh, Viktoria buried her face back in her hands.

Please, everyone and everything, just go away. I just want to be left alone for once.

All too quickly, the car door shut. Still donning her cashier's getup, Olivia walked in, setting a couple of grocery bags on the kitchen table.

"Hey girls, what are you two up to?"

After a few seconds of silence, Viktoria, out of the corner of her eye, could see Olivia sit next to her.

"What's wrong?"

"I don't know," Teri answered. "She won't tell me."

Viktoria pressed her hands even tighter against her face.

Please, just go away and leave me alone.

Sandwiched between Teri and Olivia, with both of them rubbing their hands on her back and asking what was wrong — it was too much.

Jumping up from the couch, annoyed and frustrated, Viktoria walked to the middle of the living room before turning around. Facing them, she pointed to her neck. "Look."

From the quizzical look on their faces, it was clear Olivia and Teri didn't know what they were supposed to be looking for. Them not noticing that something so vital to her was missing made Viktoria even more frustrated. "They took my grandmother's cross!"

"Who?!" they demanded to know in unison.

"You know who," Viktoria said, looking straight at Teri.

"Pretend I don't," Olivia demanded.

Having to just say her name and admit what had happened brought Viktoria's pain to the surface.

"Sherry Davis — she took it right off my neck. She and her friends surrounded me. I got into a fight with Bridgette Armstrong, and they all got involved. I was outnumbered and all I could see was what happened to Dylan. Then something within me . . . I don't want to talk about it, OK?"

"Oh no," Olivia said as she stood up, pacing back and forth like a caged tiger. "No, no, no, no, no." She then turned to

Viktoria, pointing her finger at her. "I'm giving you a day off tomorrow. I'm calling out of work and you're not going to school. But we will go and meet with your principal. This ends tomorrow — I'm going to take care of this."

"Mom!" Viktoria exclaimed, pushing the palms of her clenched fists against her forehead in frustration. "No!"

Marching down the hallway and slamming the bathroom door behind her, Viktoria turned on the sink's faucet. With no regard to whatever Olivia and Teri might be discussing in the living room, she removed her makeup and washed her face.

Forcing Sherry Davis out of her mind and returning with laser focus to June 1, the girl in the mirror gritted her teeth as her eyes flashed with vengeful determination. Like Animal and Hawk, it was time again to apply her war paint and prepare for battle.

After sunscreen and primer, the white foundation was applied along with the face powder. A pure, bright silver lining pierced through the cloud hovering over her. The eye shadow and makeup followed, accentuating the piercing conviction in her eyes. Her black lips stiffened with conviction.

Ignoring the muffled voices down the hallway, Viktoria looked herself over in the mirror. The makeup was fresh and flawless — war paint.

Viktoria closed her eyes and placed her right hand over her upper chest.

You're still there, Dylan. Right next to me.

She opened her eyes to a determined girl in the mirror, and a burning, exhilarating sensation streaked through her heart. It appeared as though her eyes were on fire; her entire soul was electrified.

Like I said, Dylan, the war is only beginning.

Marching from the bathroom back into the living room, Olivia and Teri fell silent. They both flashed her a surprised second look. Whether it was the fresh makeup, her sudden surge of determination, or both, she didn't care.

"No day off tomorrow, Mom. I'm going to school."

"Viktoria," Olivia said, trying to intervene.

"No, Mom. You can't fight this battle for me. This is mine alone to fight and it goes much deeper than Sherry Davis and her friends. I will not live my life in fear. It's not what I want. It's not what Dylan wants. I know that, and I refuse to let him down."

As Olivia stood in surprised silence, Viktoria took another step toward her, maintaining their intense eye contact.

"Chris's band is playing again Friday night. Nothing crazy — it's just at another high school kid's house. I want to go. You always say you want me to live my best life, but I can't do that being afraid. I want to go to school, and I want to go with Teri to the party. You also know that's what Dylan wants; he doesn't want our lives to end because his did."

The room was silent as Olivia paced back and forth, looking down with her arms folded. It was about a minute before she turned to Viktoria and said with a quiet voice, "Go to school tomorrow, and go to the party with Teri Friday night. You two stick together, OK? If there's even an ounce of uneasiness, you come straight home."

Turning to Teri, whose eyes glittered as her face beamed, Viktoria maintained her intense, unrelenting demeanor. At that moment, going to the party wasn't about fun — it was about taking a stand.

With concern in her eyes, Olivia looked at Viktoria for several seconds before returning to the kitchen, grabbing the two grocery bags off the table, and carrying them to the counter. From the kitchen, her voice returned to its usual, spirited manner, "Are you staying for dinner, Teri?"

"I'll take a raincheck, Mrs. Vikstad," Teri said as she darted to the front door. "I have a ton of homework to do."

Viktoria stopped Teri at the door. "Are you sure you don't want to stay?"

"I can't. Like I said, I have a ton of homework."

"Since when have you started prioritizing homework over my mom's cooking?"

The lighthearted relenting Viktoria expected from Teri didn't come. Instead, she looked dead in Viktoria's eyes. "Look, there's just something I need to get done, OK?"

"Sure," Viktoria said, taken aback.

Closing her eyes, Teri sighed. "I'm sorry, I didn't mean to come across that way. It's not you, it's me. I'm just very angry with myself. I should've been there for you. Trust me, I'm going to fix this."

"Don't worry about it," Viktoria said. "You were right on Saturday. The only way to fix this is to show Sherry that I'm willing to take it to the next level, and that's what I'm going to do. This is my battle, not yours."

Opening the front door and stepping outside, Teri turned back around. "No, Viktoria, your battle is my battle. And your mom's right — this ends tomorrow."

Chapter 28

Viktoria tossed and turned throughout the night, wrestling between grief and anger.

A recurring dream of putting on her dog collar and then looking at her grandmother's cross in the bathroom mirror jolted her awake over and over again. The pain only worsened each time she sat up in bed, feeling her neck, only to realize that it was truly gone.

Between her iron resolve to attend school the next day and her unyielding restlessness throughout the night until her exhausted body finally gave out, she had neglected to set her alarm. Olivia was an opening cashier that morning, so she wasn't there to wake her up.

Her heavy eyes opened to a very bright bedroom and her radio alarm clock read a shocking 8:39 a.m. She gasped, jumping out of bed.

No, no, no. Crap! Wednesday of all mornings! Where is my head? I can't miss the test in third period. Ten percent of my grade?! Teri would never let me live it down, and Mom would kill me if she found out!

First and second period were a wash — no big deal. Third period, though, was a must, and she had just enough time to get ready and get there on time.

Thank you, God. Thank you so much.

Racing down the hallway into the kitchen, she inhaled a bagel and downed a large cup of coffee. Dressed and in front of the bathroom mirror in record time, she then paced herself to apply her makeup.

Just like the day before, suburban warfare could very well be awaiting her with the enemy entrenched in the school halls and buildings. This time, she had to be ready for anything. Her war paint was more vital that morning than ever. Her concentration was not only on applying it to her physical face, but to her spiritual face as well.

Looking herself over in the mirror, she took a moment to place both hands over her upper chest where her grandmother's cross once hung — not for further grief, but for a renewed determination: never again.

Walking as fast as possible when she could no longer run, Viktoria made it to third period with just enough time to fly into the classroom two minutes after the tardy bell rang. The air-conditioning gripped her sweaty face and back, sending an intense chill down her spine. Mr. Crawford, the most insanely passionate history teacher ever, liked to keep the classroom ice cold to keep the students awake.

The classroom was silent as the entire class, with the test already in front of them, looked at Viktoria as she walked up to Mr. Crawford's desk. With a stern, punitive look in his eye, he stopped just a few inches of officially handing Viktoria her copy of the test to get his point across. "God must really love you, Ms. Vikstad. This test is ten percent of your grade. A few more seconds and not only would I have not let you take the test, resulting in an F, but you would've also had detention as well. You're lucky I'm in a good mood this morning. Here's the test — you have about fifty minutes to complete it, young lady."

With a sincere smile of relief, Viktoria took hold of the test and crept her way to her desk. Feeling the stare of everyone in the classroom, she only looked at the seat next to her, where Teri was shaking her head with a smile and a silent sigh of relief for Viktoria's sake.

Not only did she finish the test before everyone else, but Viktoria also knew she aced it. For the sake of the slower test takers, the remaining few minutes of class were spent in silence. As soon as the bell rang, Teri, reaching down to grab her book bag, looked at Viktoria. "Where were you this morning? I thought you decided to skip school after all."

"No," Viktoria said, shaking her head in embarrassment. "I forgot to set my alarm and I overslept."

"That late?" Teri asked with a look of shock. "With today's test? You should've just had your mom call you in sick. Mr. Crawford would've had to let you take it on another day. You lucked out."

"My mom was already at work. Besides, you knew I was coming to school today no matter what."

"I know," Teri said after a few seconds of silence. "Look, I can't spend lunch with you. I'm really falling behind in math, and Mr. Gaskin said he'd spend lunch in his classroom so he could help me get caught up with the rest of the class."

"What? Again? I guess it's payback for me making you spend lunch alone yesterday. Hopefully today's lunch won't be like yesterday's for me — if not, though, I'm ready."

Teri leaned toward her with her comforting, reassuring smile. "Trust me, Viktoria. You have nothing to worry about *at all*. Go put your stuff in your locker and enjoy a quiet, peaceful lunch under the tree. I'll meet you there after school, OK?"

Viktoria left the classroom with more caution than Teri. She looked in every direction as she entered the hallway.

With her late start that morning, lunch was going to have to come from the cafeteria. At least her locker was on the way there.

Rounding the corner, just a few feet from her locker, her feet stopped, frozen to the ground. Dropping her books with a surge of anger, she found herself face to face with Sherry. Unlike the day before, nobody was with her.

The girl in the bathroom mirror that morning, donning her war paint, appeared in Viktoria's mind, stronger than ever. She glared at Sherry with her fists clenched.

"It's just you and me, Sherry. If you want this to end, then let's end it right now."

No jutting out her hip with her arms folded, no belittling, cold glare, no smirk, no rude response — instead, Sherry appeared startled and shocked. With the exception of her cheerleading uniform, she was almost unrecognizable. Hunched over while holding her books to her chest with crossed arms like a shield, Sherry's eyes grew wide with fear. The color had drained from her face.

"Where's my cross?" Viktoria demanded through her teeth.

Sherry opened her mouth as if to answer, but no words came. Instead, she turned around and walked in the opposite direction.

"Hey!" Viktoria shouted as she ran up to Sherry, grabbing her uniform top with such force it tore as she turned her around. "You have no idea what that cross means to me.

Either tell me where it is or, I swear, I will beat it out of you right here and now!"

Without saying a word, Sherry yanked herself away from Viktoria's grasp and ran down the hallway.

"This isn't over! I'm going to find you!" Viktoria yelled as Sherry continued to retreat.

Taking several seconds to clear her head and take a step back from what had just happened, Viktoria picked up her books and approached her locker. Before she even reached the second combination number, a strong, vascular hand appeared on her locker door, as if to stop her from opening it.

"Hey, wait."

Viktoria turned, following the arm and voice. Her pulse raced as she recognized Vince Henderson, the silent one of Sherry's group. He may have never jumped in with the verbal assaults and bullying, but he still stood by and let it happen, so he was just as guilty in her eyes.

"What do you want?" Viktoria snarled, not holding back her disdain.

"Don't be upset with me," Vince said with his hands up and palms out. "I know you and my friends clashed, but I wish that didn't happen."

Viktoria's response came with a sneer. "You're with them, though, every time. Sure, you never say anything — sometimes it looks like you even feel bad."

"I do."

"But you never do anything about it. Just like yesterday when I got ganged up on and Sherry took my grandmother's cross — you just stood there and let it happen."

Vince shrugged. "I'm sorry. Look, what can I do? Tiffany's my girlfriend. Jeff's my best friend."

"Yeah?" Viktoria responded. "Well, here's what you can do: Find yourself some new friends. Good friends. Until then, 'sorry' doesn't cut it."

Before Viktoria could turn and open her locker, Vince put his hand on it again to keep her attention.

"Wait, I just need to tell you something."

"Make it quick," Viktoria snapped back.

Looking away for a second, Vince turned again to her. "I don't know how else to put it: Congratulations, you won."

"What do you mean?" Viktoria asked, annoyed and puzzled.

"You'll see," Vince said. "I don't think Sherry will ever give you trouble again. I think that's good, personally. You've been through enough." Vince looked away again, as if to gather his thoughts, before meeting her eyes. "Look, you got what you wanted. I just want to give you, I don't know, some friendly advice."

"Friendly?" Viktoria echoed with cynicism. "That'd be a first. Go ahead, give it to me."

The genuine concern in Vince's eyes and voice caught Viktoria off guard. "I know Teri's a really good friend to you but be careful around her — she's really sick."

"What?"

"Look, that's all I'm going to say," Vince said with his hands up and palms out again.

"Teri's been by my side through everything — *everything* — so don't stand there and call my best friend 'sick.' You got that?"

"I said what I needed to say," Vince responded as he backed up. "I'm just trying to look out for you, that's all."

Not paying Vince any more attention as he walked away, Viktoria turned around, shaking her head in frustration as she raced through the combination on her lock.

She swung open her locker door, and what she saw froze her in place. Dropping her books on the ground again, Viktoria placed both hands on her chest.

Resting on her Algebra II textbook was her dog collar with her grandmother's cross still securely attached. Gently picking it up, she held it closer to her face to examine it in case her eyes were fooling her.

Oh, thank you, God. Thank you, thank you, thank you.

Reattaching the dog collar around her neck in triumph and lowering her hand, she gripped her grandmother's cross. Its reflection glowed along with her smile in the tinted classroom window next to her locker.

It wasn't long before her smile in the window's reflection slowly faded in puzzled thought. Teri — who sometimes needed a place to hide her cigarettes quickly when teachers started getting suspicious — was the only other person who knew Viktoria's locker combination.

How did she do it, Dylan?

It was her second thought, though, that caused her stomach to twist with a dark feeling that she couldn't shake for the remainder of the school day: *What does Vince know that I don't?*

Chapter 29

For the rest of the day, Viktoria couldn't let go of her soft grip on her grandmother's cross. She still couldn't believe it once again hung above her heart.

She also couldn't let go of Vince's words. The genuine, concerned look in his eyes grew to be just as haunting as his words.

I know Teri's a really good friend to you but be careful around her — she's really sick.

Exacerbating her anxiety was how Teri had said she needed to miss lunch break to get help from Mr. Gaskin. Viktoria's sixth period class was Algebra II, and there was a substitute teacher that day, so Mr. Gaskin was out sick.

Her concerns were temporarily extinguished, though, at her first sight of Teri after school. To Viktoria, waiting for her under their tree wasn't a troubled girl with some dark secret. It was her best friend who not only had stood by her through everything but had also done the extraordinary for her. Whatever it took and risked, she saw to it that Viktoria's most valued treasure, so wrongfully taken from her, was back in her possession.

Viktoria couldn't help but run up to Teri, embracing her as tightly as possible. Even Teri's eyes welled with tears as Viktoria profusely thanked her. At that moment, it didn't matter to Viktoria *how* Teri got her dog collar with her grandmother's cross back; all that mattered was that she *did* it.

The seed of concern was once again planted in Viktoria's heart, though, as they were about to walk off campus. Mr. Tailor, walking in their direction, stopped in front of them.

"Hey, girls! Just two more days before your brother's next big gig, Teri. I've always loved their name, The Forgotten Ones."

"Uh-huh," Teri responded with reservation, looking at Viktoria and then him, as though he was from outer space.

"Anyway, you girls have fun. You both deserve it," Mr. Tailor continued. "Oh, and Teri, thanks for another good visit at lunch. I'm taking some of that pumpkin bread home for my wife to try — I know she'll love it. My office door is always open to you two."

The mortified expression on Teri's face was undeniable as she turned and walked away. It was as though she could literally see the questions and wheels spinning in Viktoria's head.

The walk home from school was going by too fast. The silence between the two of them grew thicker as Teri managed to maintain a three foot lead in front of Viktoria.

As they approached Teri's neighborhood, the silence, questions, and anxiety Viktoria carried had grown unbearable. Desperate to get to the bottom of everything before they split in their different directions, Viktoria ran to catch up with Teri.

"Hey, wait up." She stepped in front of Teri, stopping her in her tracks. "Why the hell are you walking so fast? I can't keep up."

"I just don't feel like talking," Teri said tersely.

"What's wrong?"

Teri didn't answer. Instead, while avoiding eye contact, she pulled out and lit a cigarette.

"I know Mr. Gaskin wasn't there today," Viktoria said, breaking the silence. "You went and saw Mr. Tailor at lunch. So what? I get it. I go to see him all the time — you know that. So, what's the big deal?"

"I'm embarrassed, OK?" Teri finally said through her cigarette with raised eyebrows.

"Why?" Viktoria asked. "Because you need help? Why is that embarrassing? I do too. You know I would've understood and done whatever I could to support you. I mean, you didn't have to lie and go behind my back to see Mr. Tailor too."

Teri pulled her cigarette from her lips, pointing at Viktoria with a flash of anger in her eyes. "I am not a liar, and I don't need help."

Shocked by her unexpectedly intense reaction, Viktoria stood in silence as Teri stepped away, taking another drag of her cigarette. She turned to Viktoria again. "Fine. So I feel bad for the hippie burnout. Everybody else sees Mr. Tailor for who he is: a pothead sixties relic who'll always be nothing more than a high school counselor. You're the only one who ever sees him, so I just wanted to be nice for once."

"For once?" Viktoria echoed with boldness. "Teri, he told me you stop by his office quite a bit."

Smoke and exasperation exhaled through Teri's lips. "Can't we just let this go? Please?" Her usual sweet smile and caring eyes returned as she reached up, taking a gentle hold of Viktoria's grandmother's cross. "Look, you got this back. This is what really matters today. In fact, let's celebrate. Your mom should be home from work. Let's go to your house and the three of us do something fun."

Teri was right — her grandmother's cross again above Viktoria's heart was what mattered more than anything that day. Still, Vince's words were too unsettling to just ignore.

"Teri, how did you get my dog collar and cross back?"

With her serene smile, Teri took another drag, shrugged, and winked. "Don't worry about it. I knew it meant the world to you, so I reasoned with Sherry, and she decided to give it back."

Folding her arms and raising her eyebrows as Olivia would, Viktoria wanted to get through to Teri that she knew more without mentioning Vince and what he'd said.

"Look, I know Sherry — she's not a *reasonable* person. Also, I saw her at lunch today. She backed down and took off way too fast."

"Viktoria," Teri shot back. "What are you trying to say?"

"Nothing. I just want to know what happened, that's all."

With folded arms and a smoke-filled sigh, Teri's intense eyes locked on Viktoria's. "Fine, so you saw Sherry today, right?"

"Yeah," Viktoria answered right back before Teri continued.

"Was she alone or with her minions?"

"She was alone."

"Did she leave you alone?"

Reflecting on her encounter with Sherry, Viktoria shook her head in confusion. "Yeah, I actually tried to force her to tell me what she did with my grandmother's cross, but she just freaked out and ran off."

Teri smirked. "Well, there's your answer. How many times have I said Sherry is your classic bully? She's only bold and strong when she's with her friends. The trick is finding her when she's alone. Do you remember on Saturday when I showed her that I wasn't going to put up with her crap? She backed down even then in front of her four toadies. I knew that if I found her and stood up to her, especially when she was alone, she would show her true colors and fold like the coward she is. I had your dog collar in my hands within five minutes of finding her."

Teri took another drag as she looked at Viktoria. "That's all that happened, OK? Can we move on and enjoy the afternoon?"

Even though it still didn't sit right with Viktoria, she knew she wouldn't get anything more from Teri. Deciding to let it go for the sake of a well-deserved fun afternoon for them and Olivia, she smiled and shrugged.

"Sure," Viktoria said as she reached up, touching her grandmother's cross. "But first, thank you, Teri, for this."

They smiled and hugged each other. The cigarette between her lips muffled Teri's voice as she said, "That's what sisters do. Let's go see what your mom wants to do."

The two of them were just two blocks from Viktoria's house when a blue Jeep skidded onto the sidewalk, cutting off their path by about twenty feet.

They stopped dead in their tracks, and Teri held her arm across Viktoria's chest as if to shield her from any possible danger the Jeep could cause. The driver's door swung open and out came Jeff Bryant.

"Oh, you don't have to worry about your friend," Jeff bellowed with his eyes on Teri as he made his way around the front of the Jeep. "This is between you and me!"

With her pulse racing, Viktoria turned to Teri, who showed not even an ounce of fear or alarm. Her eyes were kind yet piercing. Her smile, serene yet chilling.

Chapter 30

The back passenger-side door was the second to open. Vince jumped out with just enough time to grab the right shoulder of Jeff's letterman jacket.

"Hey, come on, Jeff. You heard me — leave her alone. Do we actually know what happened?"

"Don't touch me, man," Jeff growled as he lifted his arm to loosen Vince's grip.

"Let it go," Vince said, trying again to reason with Jeff. "Don't lose your cool and jump to conclusions. How many times has Coach Mathis lectured you about this?"

Jeff stopped, turning to Vince with his voice tense and his finger in his face. "I said don't touch me, Vince. Believe me, I know enough."

"He does, Vince," Janine said, leaving the front passenger-side door open as she got out. "Sherry told me everything and then I told him."

"Why?" Vince asked Janine with a quizzical, frustrated expression. "What good could come from that?"

"Who cares about that?" Janine asked with her own quizzical look, gesturing toward Teri. "You know how protective Jeff is of Sherry. Watching him fly off the handle like this is too entertaining to miss. Besides, she needs to be taught a lesson and scared straight."

"Jeff?" Teri scoffed. "What lesson is he going to teach me?"

Seeing the rage in Jeff's eyes, Viktoria took Teri's arm. "Come on, Teri. It's not worth it."

"What?" Teri asked, still smirking as she pulled her arm away. "Seriously, he's our age and he still drools like a teething six-month-old."

Viktoria didn't know what to make of Teri's fearlessness. Was it uncommon courage or something in the realm of suicidal tendencies? Whichever one it was, this enemy was large, angry, and focused, and Teri didn't seem to care. Still, Viktoria stood by her only ally. That's what Animal and Hawk would do for each other, no matter what.

Tiffany had gotten out from the back driver's side of the jeep and, with the condescending half-smile she and Sherry shared, pulled her boyfriend away from Jeff, locking hands with him. "Quit always trying to be Jeff's guardian, Vince. He's a big boy. He knows what he's doing."

"Thank you!" Jeff exclaimed in Tiffany's direction with dramatic relief before turning his attention again to Teri. Marching up, he stopped within a foot of her personal space. "Up until now, we've tolerated you and, especially, your friend here, but now you've crossed the line."

Impervious to Jeff's large frame and attempt to portray a menacing presence, Teri snorted, then snickered. "I think you got that wrong, Jeff. It's the two of us who've been tolerating you guys. Oh, and—"

"No, *you're* wrong!" Jeff roared, cutting Teri off while keeping his eyes on her as he pointed at Viktoria. "She and her family started all of this."

"No, they didn't," Teri countered. "You guys have all been pricks to us for as long as I can remember."

Lifting his hands to his sides, a flash of excitement lit Jeff's eyes as though he had just conceived of one of the greatest, cleverest comebacks ever. "I won't lie — it's never been our goal to have Vampira and Lily Munster as friends."

"Brilliant," Teri jabbed.

"I mean, it's obvious the two of you will never be normal. So, yeah, we're not going to go out of our way to be friends with you."

"Sure, you haven't gone out of your way to be friends with us," Teri agreed, "but you have gone out of your way to harass, demean, and gang up on us. Just like you are now."

"Hey, we didn't start this," Jeff argued, pointing at Viktoria. "Again, it was this walking zombie here and her family. Taking our little brothers to court over a stupid fight, dragging our families' reputations through the mud, and then continuing to harass them. Just like on Saturday — you heard how she and her mom tracked down Sherry's mom and her brother at Kelly's."

"What?!" Viktoria shouted in disbelief.

Jeff turned to Viktoria. "Yeah, that's right. And don't try to deny it. Sherry told us all about it. But that wasn't enough. Now you had to bring your Grady Twin into it and make it even worse. Sherry was just trying to teach you a lesson for harassing Jason and Bridgett's little sister. She was going to give that stupid dog collar back to you eventually. How insane do you have to be to send Teri to take it back from her at *knifepoint*?"

The shock on Teri's face matched Viktoria's when they turned to each other. Teri placed both hands over her chest.

"What?! Are you serious? There's no way in hell I would *ever* do something like that! Viktoria, are you hearing this? You know there's no way I would ever do something that crazy."

"Don't lie, Teri," Janine interjected. "I told Jeff everything Sherry told me. Even how she discovered this morning that the light bulb from her front porch was missing. Sound familiar?"

"You better believe I heard everything," Jeff barked. "How it was pitch black in her front yard when Sherry got home last night. Halfway between her car and the front door, she felt the knife's blade against her throat. You grabbed her hair, pulling her down as you told her to get on her knees."

"What?!" Teri exclaimed with her brow furrowed in absolute shock.

"Oh, she knew it was you," Jeff continued. "She told Janine it was clearly your voice. She could even smell the cigarette stench on your clothes. We all knew there was something off about you, but we didn't know you were *that* sick."

Shaking her head, Teri smiled with a soft laughter of disbelief. "You know what? This is such—"

"It's a good thing Sherry had that dog collar in her book bag," Jeff interrupted. "Who knows what you would have done if she couldn't reach over, open it, and give that stupid thing to you."

With arms folded and her eyes locked on Jeff's, Teri's face and voice grew serious and sincere, "Jeff, I promise you, I did meet Sherry at her house, but all I did was explain to her how important that dog collar was to Viktoria because it had her grandmother's cross. She felt bad about what she did, reached in her book bag, and handed it over to me. That's all, I swear. I don't know why Sherry fabricated this crazy story. Maybe she was afraid to expose that she actually has a heart after all. Regardless, what she said simply isn't true. Even if it were, she would have absolutely no proof."

Jeff grinned with excitement. "Yeah? Well, that's where I got you. You told Sherry you always carry that knife with you, and she would pay the 'ultimate price' if she ever said or did anything to Viktoria again. Seeing how she was this morning, you must've been pretty freaking convincing."

"What?" Teri appeared even more confused than before. "I never carry a knife with me — ever. Ask Viktoria, I don't even have one."

"Why would Sherry lie?" Jeff asked. "Face it, you've been caught. That's why I pulled over. I know you have that knife on you. There's no way I'm going to let you get away with what you did. Hand it over!"

Reaching toward her, Teri pushed Jeff's hand away. "Don't touch me."

Again, Vince put his hand on Jeff's shoulder. "Come on, Jeff. Leave her alone. You know this isn't right."

Turning toward Vince, Jeff grabbed a handful of his T-shirt. "Back off!"

Tiffany placed a hand on each of them, dissolving the sudden explosive tension. Jeff turned his attention to Teri again, placing his hand on her shoulder like a condescending adult would to a child.

"Just give me the knife, Teri. Admit what you did, and we'll leave you alone."

184 · *The Cross I Bear*

Teri slapped his hand away.

"Leave her alone, Jeff," Viktoria intervened, stepping closer to Teri's side.

"Not until she gives me the freaking knife," Jeff barked as he reached for Teri's shoulder again.

Thrusting her shoulder back, she pushed his hand away again. "I said *don't touch me.*"

Unrelenting, Jeff finally succeeded in grabbing Teri's shirt just above her left collarbone. Before he could react, she hit him in the mouth with such force, blood sprayed in all directions.

"Don't touch me!"

In stunned silence, everyone looked at Teri with wide eyes and dropped jaws. Viktoria was awestruck at the power of her punch. Blood spatter was spread from the sidewalk onto the street.

Jeff looked down at his shirt. A combination of drool and blood dripped from his mouth onto it. He looked back at Teri, visibly shaken.

For a reason only known to him, he stepped toward Teri again, and she landed another devastating punch on him. This time, the blood spattered onto his letterman jacket and Janine's cheerleading uniform.

Viktoria looked at the others. Vince was shaking his head. Janine, staring at the blood on her uniform, held her mouth as though she might vomit. Tiffany, holding onto Vince's sleeve, was pale, appearing to be on the verge of fainting.

"What the hell?" Jeff finally said after wiping blood from his chin, looking at his trembling hand. His face turned red, and anger started to replace his shock. "What's your problem, freak? You're a girl; I wasn't going to hit you. All I wanted was your knife. You're lucky you're not a guy."

The sound of a siren squawking for just a second caused everyone to turn as a squad car pulled up with its lights flashing. A police officer wearing a hat and sunglasses emerged from the car. Viktoria shook her head, letting out an exasperated sigh.

Officer Blanchard, of course — who else would it be?

The officer surveyed the scene, keeping his silence as though he were trying to further intimidate the kids. He looked at Jeff and grinned. "You're number 24 on the Peoria High football team. Great defense. I also played for them a number of years ago. Did that little girl do that to your face?"

Jeff looked at the officer but didn't say anything. He wiped underneath his nose, looking at his hand and his shirt again. Blood continued to drip from his chin onto the ground. He looked at Vince, then back at the officer.

Visibly embarrassed for Jeff, the officer smirked, shaking his head. "I know that little girl did that to your face. I saw the whole thing. Judging by what I saw, I'm definitely putting my money on Cactus High for Friday night's homecoming game."

Officer Blanchard then laughed at his own joke.

"I wasn't trying to fight her, officer," Jeff said. "I know she's carrying a knife. She threatened my friend with it, and I was trying to talk her into giving it to me."

"Is that true, Miss Allardyce?" Officer Blanchard asked, turning to Teri.

"For the millionth time, no!" Teri shot back.

"Well, let's just be sure," Officer Blanchard said as he approached her. "Turn around and put your hands up on that fence behind you."

After a thorough search, Officer Blanchard turned again to Jeff. "Except for this pack of cigarettes I'm confiscating because she's underage, she's clean."

"See?" Teri said, glaring at Jeff. "I told you, jock strap, I would never do anything that insane. Sherry and I only talked — that's all."

"Get out of here, boys," Officer Blanchard told Jeff and Vince. "Take your two cheerleaders with you."

Vince, Jeff, Tiffany, and Janine all got in the Jeep and took off. Officer Blanchard then turned to Teri and Viktoria.

"Do me a favor, Miss Allardyce. Go ahead and walk home. Miss Vikstad, you're coming with me. I'm driving you home."

Again?

"Officer Blanchard, my house is only two blocks away," Viktoria said.

"Well, you'd be surprised what could happen in two blocks," Officer Blanchard said with a grin. "I've learned that in law enforcement. I also just want to check in and make sure your mom is OK with your dad still gone."

This creep is relentless!

As Teri started walking, Viktoria was put in the back of the squad car. Officer Blanchard's big, victorious grin appeared in the rearview mirror.

Chapter 31

The front door swung open wide and fast. The concerned fury in Olivia's eyes made it evident to Viktoria that she'd looked through the peephole before answering the knock on the door.

"Are you alright, Viktoria?" Olivia was still in her Safeway cashier getup since she'd just gotten home from work. Her glaring green eyes remained locked on Officer Blanchard, even though her question had been directed at her daughter.

"Yeah," Viktoria answered, not knowing how else to respond in the tense, uneasy moment.

Olivia's attention refused to veer from Officer Blanchard. "This is absolutely insane, Dwight. This is the fourth time since July that I've found you knocking on my door with my daughter standing next to you. What happened this time? Did you bust her for loitering because she happened to stop to retie her shoe in front of a 7-Eleven?"

Officer Blanchard's response was formal and robotic, as though his actions were nothing but professional. "I happened to be turning left from West Cholla Street onto 53rd Avenue and saw Viktoria and Teri Allardyce in the middle of a confrontation with two football players and two cheerleaders from the high school."

"Again, Viktoria?" Olivia sighed with exasperation. "The same kids as yesterday?"

After Viktoria nodded, Olivia seemed even more agitated. "Are you serious? When is this going to stop?"

"It wasn't our fault, Mom," Viktoria said. "We were just walking home, and they drove up and confronted us."

"Let me guess," Olivia said as her glare returned to Officer Blanchard. "It was Sherry Davis and a few others."

"Sherry Davis was not present," Officer Blanchard said. "I would assume, though, the four individuals are, at least, acquainted with her through football and cheerleading."

"Oh, I'm sure they are," Olivia said with a quiet, tense tone. "In fact, I'd put all my money on the table that among them were Tiffany McNamara, Janine Preston, and Jeff Bryant."

"You're right, Olivia," Officer Blanchard said with a nod. "It was the three of them plus another young man."

"Vince Henderson," Viktoria interjected.

Olivia gave Officer Blanchard a stare that looked harsh enough to annihilate him. "Were those boys a physical threat to Viktoria and Teri?"

"I'd venture to say it was the opposite." Officer Blanchard chuckled. "Jeff said or did something to Teri that apparently crossed a line with her. I saw him approach her, and she laid in a couple of punches that split him right open. I never knew such a small girl could pack such a powerful punch. The blood on the sidewalk under Mr. Bryant's feet made it look like he had just stomped on a tomato."

Officer Blanchard chuckled again. Olivia, not sharing in his humor, folded her arms as her glare at Officer Blanchard intensified. "So, four individuals, two cheerleaders and two *football players*, encountered two girls, Viktoria, and Teri, and pushed them to the point where they needed to physically defend themselves." She paused for a second, as though she wanted the thought to sink in for Officer Blanchard before she continued, "Four on two, Dwight. Two girls, outnumbered and outsized, confronted and forced to the point of a physical fight. You know how bad that could've turned out. What did you do to the four others? How did you enforce the law?"

Officer Blanchard cleared his throat. "Well, I didn't actually see how it all started. I couldn't just assume the four were the true aggressors in this situation. There are two sides to every story, so I did what I had to do: I broke it up and sent them on their way."

"You sent them on their way," Olivia echoed. "That's it. I'm sure you also sent Teri on her way, *alone.* Six kids were involved and, yet, once again, here you are on my front porch with Viktoria."

Officer Blanchard then changed his tone to that of a proper gentleman. "Well, Olivia, with your husband not around anymore, I like to stop by and make sure you're being taken care of. That's what a man does. What better way is there to show how much I care than by bringing your daughter home to you safely?"

Viktoria shuddered at the tenseness on Olivia's face. Her silence was deafening before she finally turned to Viktoria.

"Viktoria, come inside, go to your room, and shut the door. For once, I actually want you to play your music so loud you're waking up the dead. Stay there until I knock on your door."

Even though she didn't dare look as she walked into the house, Viktoria could feel the weight of Olivia's stare on Officer Blanchard. With a strong hunch that their conversation would have nothing to do with her, Viktoria marched straight to her bedroom, laser focused on obeying her mom.

Shutting her door loud enough for Olivia to hear, she opened a shoebox full of cassettes. Finally finding herself alone, she took a moment to close her eyes and take hold of her grandmother's cross hanging, once again, over her heart.

I can't believe it, Dylan. I thought it was gone forever, but it's back. It feels like you're back.

"I want to hear music, Viktoria!" Olivia's demand coming loud and clear from the front door thrust Viktoria back to the present. Returning to her shoebox, she fixated on a borrowed tape from Chris. Picking up the case and reading the cover, a devious smile crossed her face. It was Megadeth's album *Killing Is My Business... and Business Is Good!*

Concerned for Olivia, Viktoria wanted nothing more than to eavesdrop on the conversation. It wasn't an option, though, so she was going to use the music to make the creep at their doorstep disappear quickly.

Viktoria put the tape in her stereo, turned the volume all the way up, and pressed *Play*. The heavy speed and aggression of the music, especially at such an earsplitting volume, was too much for even her. Still, sitting on the floor with the back of her head resting against the side of her bed, she closed her eyes and let the music work its magic.

Just under the minute mark of the third track, the pounding on her bedroom door was barely noticeable over the unyielding rapid-fire guitar and drums.

Before Viktoria could get up to open the door, Olivia swung it open. Racing over to the stereo, her index finger shook in a frantic search before pressing *Stop*.

"Good gosh, Viktoria! What the hell was that?!"

Viktoria's devious smile returned as Olivia continued, "I mean, I know rock music has gotten even louder since The Beatles and The Rolling Stones, especially the stuff you listen to, but that was a whole other animal."

Viktoria shrugged her shoulders. "Well, it got Officer Blanchard off the front porch. That's what you wanted, right?"

Sitting on the floor next to Viktoria and resting the back of her head against the side of the bed as well, Olivia turned to her with a polite, reserved smile. "To be honest, Officer Blanchard and I needed to have a little talk and come to an understanding. It was a conversation that I didn't care for you to hear. I just want you to focus on being a kid."

Viktoria turned to her with an annoyed, perplexed look. "Are you serious, Mom? I'm sixteen, not six. It's also not like I've spent my whole life on some deserted island being raised by nuns and monks. I'm sure my innocent ears can handle whatever it was the two of you were discussing. Besides, four times now, Officer Blanchard has found some lame excuse to drive me home in his squad car and walk me up to the front door. I see our neighbors looking through their curtains. Do you know how embarrassing that is? I think I deserve at least some sort of explanation."

Olivia turned to the bedroom window, then back to Viktoria. "OK, fair enough. Officer Blanchard wasn't always trying to be some gunslinging, intimidating cop. Dwight was actually a really sweet guy in high school. Anyway, I guess he had a huge crush on me and, according to my friends, he was pretty devastated when your dad and I started dating. He never got married and, after your dad switched from local to interstate trucking, Dwight got the wrong impression. He figured that, after everything with Dylan, your dad was gone for good."

Closing her eyes for an extended blink, a soft snicker escaped Olivia as her eyes and slight smile revealed a degree of long lost teenage blushing. "Basically, he thought he was given a second chance. What better way is there to win a woman's heart than by being a knight in shining armor? After bringing my only daughter home safely with unequaled care and attention, I guess he thought we'd ride off together into the sunset."

The shock and disgust Viktoria felt must have been transparent, as Olivia's smile broadened and her eyebrows rose in agreement. "I don't think you'll have to worry about any further encounters with Officer Blanchard. We had the talk we needed and, well, I set him straight."

"OK," Viktoria responded, almost in the form of a question.

"And that's all you need to know. All right?"

"All right," Viktoria echoed, knowing she wasn't going to get any further information.

With a comforting smile, Olivia put her arm around her. "Are you OK?"

"I'm fine," Viktoria answered to assure her. "I'm just worried about Teri."

"Me too," Olivia said. "Before our personal discussion, Dwight, as an officer, owed it to me to at least tell me what happened. I can't believe a big football player would do that — you know, get in such a small girl's face and try to scare her, poor little thing. Dwight said she split him open pretty good, though. Wow! I was blown away. I never would've guessed our little Teri had that in her. What can I say? Good for her."

"Yeah, well, Jeff had it coming," Viktoria said as she took hold of her grandmother's cross. "Look at what I got back."

Olivia gasped. "Oh my gosh! How did you get it back?"

"Teri," Viktoria answered. "She found Sherry and talked to her, letting her know it was my grandmother's cross. Apparently, Sherry has a heart after all. I confronted her about it at lunch today. She more than left me alone — she ran off as quickly as she could."

Olivia shrugged. "Hmm. Maybe the impossible happened."

"I doubt it," Viktoria said. "You wouldn't believe what her friends accused Teri of. They said she threatened Sherry with—"

"A knife?" Olivia interjected.

"Wait. How did you know that?"

"Dwight told me about that too," Olivia said. "Unbelievable — he said he even searched her. Teri would *never* do anything like that."

"They're manipulators, Mom. They always twist things around so they're seen as the victims, the good guys. Just like on Saturday with Sherry's mom and Jason. They made it sound like we were stalking them. You know how they are."

Olivia closed her eyes with a taxing sigh. With a smile, she took Viktoria's hand. "You know what? Forget all of this. What are you feeling? The movies or Carlos O'Brian?"

"Mexican food," Viktoria said, smiling back. "I'm starving."

Olivia's voice grew even softer. "Yeah, me too. Let's take Teri too. I know she could use a good dinner."

Viktoria nodded. "She deserves it too. Can I ask you one more thing?"

"Sure."

"I know you're not working tomorrow. Can I take you up on that day off from school?"

Placing the back of her hand on Viktoria's forehead, Olivia snickered. "Yeah, you are feeling a little hot. I'll call the school office in the morning."

Getting up off the floor, Olivia grabbed both of Viktoria's hands and pulled her to her feet. She then reached up to Viktoria's dog collar, taking hold of the cross with gleaming eyes and a proud smile.

"Give Teri a call. Tell her to get ready for us to pick her up. We need to look out for her. I don't know why, but I can see she really needs our help right now."

Viktoria, reflecting on their walk from the school to their conversation just outside of Teri's neighborhood, nodded. "You're right, Mom, I think she needs us more than we realize."

Chapter 32

Viktoria's determination was indisputable. Thursday wasn't going to be a typical day of skipping school. No sleeping in and vegging all day in front of the TV or having Olivia taxi Viktoria to all the places only she wanted to go. There would be zero selfish desires for that day. It was going to be a day of playing hooky with a mission: Viktoria wanted to completely dedicate it to Olivia.

The electricity started to build within her the night before. The long forgotten girl who, before May, raced around the truck stop's diner and the kitchen in her house as "The Master Chef," with a giving heart and a genuine smile, was suddenly reclaiming her life, but with more focus and determination than before.

Beating Olivia to the punch, her alarm went off at 5:30. Soon she was up and dressed and itching to start the day. Her grandmother's cross shined brighter in the bathroom mirror than ever before. She was winning the war.

Seeing the absolute, jaw-dropping shock on Olivia's face as she stumbled into the kitchen a little over an hour later, Viktoria couldn't hold back her laughter. The kitchen table was already set. Freshly cooked Norwegian crepes along with homemade hot chocolate, topped with extra thick whipped cream and shavings from a Hershey chocolate bar, were already served. Olivia could only fold her arms, smile, and shake her head.

"Wow, Viktoria. I have missed this so much. This looks amazing!"

Viktoria beamed. "Thanks, Mom. You know what, though? I think I've actually missed this more than you. Believe it or not, I had to hold myself back from making some of your other favorites. I knew I had to keep it light after our giant plates at Carlos O'Brian last night."

"This is absolutely perfect," Oliva said with an embrace. "It's amazing how you can take crepes and hot chocolate and turn them into pieces of art. It's almost heartbreaking to start eating and see the beauty disappear."

After a modest laugh, Viktoria sat down. "I also realized that you were right Saturday morning. I have been given a gift and it's been too long since I've used it. I think the time has come for 'The Master Chef' to make her comeback. Not only here at home, but at the diner too."

Olivia's face beamed with pride. "I would absolutely love to see that. And, yes, you have been given an incredible gift. I'm sure you know what I'm about to say."

"Of course, Mom, go ahead — fingerprints."

"Fingerprints," Olivia echoed with a nod. "Just like our fingerprints, God gives us gifts that are unique to each of us so we can touch and help others in ways nobody else could. When we use those gifts only to serve and lift others, we know we are heading in the right direction in life."

It was the millionth time Viktoria heard Olivia's fingerprints/gifts analogy. For the first time, though, she didn't just hear the words — they pierced her. Finally, what had eluded Viktoria since losing Dylan was made clear. Fearlessness, determination, confidence, and faith in using whatever gifts she could discover within her were going to make that life happen. The one she and Dylan would both rightfully claim. With quiet excitement, Viktoria placed her hand over her grandmother's cross.

It finally makes sense, Dylan. You know. That fingerprints/ gifts analogy Mom's been preaching ad nauseum. She's actually right. What perfect timing too — tomorrow night's the gig, and Matt's going to be there. It's time to start seizing opportunities, and he's the first one. Let's see what I've got!

"A penny for your thoughts." Olivia's voice pulled Viktoria back to the kitchen table.

"What?"

"A penny for your thoughts," she said again. "You're holding your grandmother's cross with your head clearly in the clouds. Wherever you are, it looks nice. Maybe I'd like to go there too."

Looking down with an awkward smile and blushing, the thought of bringing her mom along on her imaginary romantic journey with Matt mortified her. "It's nothing, Mom. Just thinking about our day together, that's all."

"Really?" Olivia asked, raising her eyebrows. "No girl bites down on her lower lip, casting her eyes dreamily to the heavens when she thinks about spending the day with her mom. Is there something I need to know? Should I really be letting you go to that party tomorrow night?"

Seriously, Dylan, am I that transparent? She's relentless! I need to play it cool.

"It's nothing, Mom, I promise. You know me — my mind is always all over the place. And you can't get all my thoughts for a penny. Do you have fifty bucks in your purse?"

Following a few seconds of silence, Olivia looked down and laughed. "Yep, you definitely take after me. I swear I can think a million thoughts per second while your dad can focus on one thing for four hours. I just remember being a teenage girl myself. I had that same look in my eye when I would think of your dad. You just stay glued to Teri's side tomorrow night."

"OK!" Viktoria snapped back. "Can you please just drop it?"

Eating their crepes in silence, Viktoria, with annoyed gratitude for Olivia's genuine concern for her, sighed in regret for snapping at her.

We were off to such a good start this morning. This day is for Mom, Dylan, not me. Look at her — I swear she's gotten even thinner throughout this week. The store is working her to death. She needs this day more than I do. I need to turn this around. I owe it to her.

"Mom?"

With worried eyes but a hopeful smile, Olivia looked up. "Yes?"

Viktoria bit her lower lip as her smile grew into a wide, devious grin. "When you told me to just stay glued to Teri's side at the party, what other options did you have in mind? Any details?"

With shock and embarrassment, Olivia's eyes grew wide. "Are you serious?"

"You better believe I am. A penny for *your* thoughts. If you need, I have twenty bucks in my room."

Olivia could only look down at her plate with a stunned grin and a quiet, uncomfortable laugh. Shaking her head as though she were trying to gather and make sense of her own thoughts, her lips quivered, forcing out words that came to her on the spot. "OK, you really have me wondering what's going on in that head of yours."

"Do you really want to know?" Viktoria asked. "I can give you all the forbidden details."

"Absolutely not," Olivia answered.

Resting her arms on the table, Viktoria leaned toward Olivia. "Fine. Here's the deal, then. Forget the party. Forget school and work. Forget everything. When it comes to today, we are the only two people on this planet. Well, us and the restaurant staff when we stop for lunch. Pick the locations, Mom. I'll have the dishes done in ten minutes and then we're off. This is *your* special day."

Olivia's choices for the perfect day off proved to be exhausting for Viktoria. She forgot how athletic and outdoorsy Olivia was. Still, knowing that she could spend the day alone with her mom, she soldiered through with all smiles.

After hiking Camelback Mountain, it was off to Durant's Steakhouse for lunch. Viktoria knew Olivia was being nice to her when she chose going to the Desert Botanical Garden over the shooting range, but still, it was a lot of walking.

Though the physical activity that day was immense, Olivia, sporting a black form-fitting tank top with her thick, strawberry blond hair pulled back, looked healthier and more vibrant than she had since before May, even at the end of the day. Viktoria, on the other hand, with smeared makeup, aching feet, and sore legs, collapsed on the couch as soon as they got home.

With Olivia in the shower, Viktoria's weary body remained motionless, nestled too comfortably, sinking into the soft cushions. Staring up at the ceiling, her anxious, restless mind refused to join her body in exhaustion.

After keeping Olivia blissfully unaware of the third wheel occupying her mind throughout their entire day together, Viktoria could finally completely concentrate on Matt.

I think I'll wear my Tex & The Horseheads T-shirt tomorrow night. I know he absolutely loves that band. Wait — maybe I should go with the New York Dolls. I'll definitely wear my cross-pleated, short black skirt. Mom will already be at work, so she can't stop me from wearing it. Footwear? Definitely those black leather, double buckle boots. Now, how to get him alone? Maybe after they're done playing I can—

Sudden, relentless knocking on the front door startled Viktoria. Getting up from the couch was a stark reminder of her sore muscles and fatigue. Stumbling on her aching feet toward the door, the knocking grew even louder and more rapid, as though the person on the other side was in the middle of a terrible crisis and needed urgent help. Her heart beginning to race, Viktoria placed her hands on the door, looking through the peephole.

She breathed a sigh of relief at seeing Teri, but the curiosity still remained and even intensified. Teri never came over when she knew Viktoria and Olivia were spending the day together. Just outside the front door, though, she stood out of breath with perspiration glistening on her face as she continued to bang on the door.

"Viktoria! Are you home?"

Chapter 33

Viktoria swung the front door wide open. "Teri, is everything OK?"

Her wincing in pain didn't stop Teri's jarring, tight hug after racing in. "Oh, I missed you like crazy today!"

"Easy," Viktoria said, trying to loosen Teri's tight embrace. "You have no idea how sore I am. I feel like my body's about to break in half."

Teri backed off a couple of steps, laughing a little. "I'm sorry. Look, I know today's all about you and your mom, but I was way too excited. I had to come see you."

Viktoria was a little irritated about the unnecessary panic the pounding on the front door caused her, and she gave Teri a puzzled look. "Why? Did Matt Dillon miraculously knock on your door today and ask you to run off with him and start a new life together? Did you go to school and find yourself being worshipped by all the kids who hate Jeff?"

"What?" Teri asked. "Is it wrong for your best friend to just simply stop by and be excited to see you?"

"OK," Viktoria said, shaking her head in confusion. "Still, you had me freaking out by the way you were pounding on the door. I was afraid something bad had happened. I was already nervous about you going to school today after what happened with Jeff yesterday."

"Oh, no worries there, I ditched."

"You ditched school? Why?"

"Forget about it," Teri said, throwing her hands in the air as if to push the subject into outer space. Her words came out so fast Viktoria could barely keep up. "Look, tomorrow night's the party. Let's just focus on that. I have it all planned out. We'll come here after school tomorrow. Your mom will already be at work. Hold it! Rewind. We'll stop for some Mexican food first. *Then* we'll come here, watch some TV, and then go to the party. There's more! At that point, our weekend's just beginning—"

"Wait," Viktoria interrupted. "Are you OK, Teri?"

"Yeah. Why?"

"Well, I've never seen you like this. I can literally see the pulse racing in your neck, you're talking at a million miles per second, and you're sweating as though you sprinted all the way here."

"It's nothing," Teri said, almost jumping while waving both hands like it was no big deal. "I just needed a little pick-me-up today, and Chris had some stuff in his room that did it for me."

"What stuff?" Viktoria demanded. "Seriously, Teri, what are you—"

The distinct, loud squeak of the master bedroom's bathroom door opening signaled that Olivia was out of the shower. Stepping out of the house, Viktoria shut the door behind her.

"Teri, are you high?"

"As a kite," Teri said, giggling.

"What the hell? You know my mom can't see you like this."

"Easy, Nancy Reagan. It's nothing, I promise — I do it all the time." Teri grinned with sarcasm before continuing to rattle off her plans with unbelievable rapidity. "So, we'll go to the party, see the band play, and then come back here. No! We'll stop by 7-Eleven for some good eats first. We'll watch a late-night movie. I'll just spend the night here. Then—"

Viktoria cut her off with a forceful whisper. "Teri, my mom is inside the house."

"So?" Teri asked with an agitated sneer.

Following a deep sigh, Viktoria looked into her dilated pupils. "What's going on with you?"

"What do you mean what's going on with me?"

"I'm just worried," Viktoria said with deep concern. "Over the last few months, you've gone from sneaking an occasional cigarette from your mom's purse or Chris to incessant smoking. There are times I know you've been drinking. You're hiding things from me like going to see Mr. Tailor, and now this."

With a silver flash in her eyes and her lips pressed together, Teri took a step back. "You're not alone when it comes to having problems, Viktoria. I know Dylan was your brother, but it doesn't mean I'm not hurting too. There are a lot of things I'm going through that I would never want you to know."

Viktoria placed her hands on Teri's shoulders. "I'm sorry. I'm just worried about you. All I want for you is—"

A massive, dusty, black pickup truck she didn't recognize was pulling up in front of her house. As soon as it stopped, the passenger door swung open and Chris almost fell out.

"Hey, there's my little sister," Chris slurred as he stumbled onto Viktoria's front yard. "I knew you'd be here. I know what you took from my stash. You can't be out and about with that stuff in you. You need to come home."

The door on the driver's side swung open and Matt ran out, catching Chris before he fell over. "OK, Chris, we found her. Let's get you back in the truck where you belong."

"You need to be home safe with that stuff in you," Chris slurred at Teri again as Matt got him into the truck and shut the door.

"Oops, I guess I screwed up. I better go," Teri said with another giggle before cupping Viktoria's jawline with both hands, pulling her in for a forceful kiss on her forehead. "You have nothing to worry about, I promise. Give your mom a wonderful evening. She deserves it."

With a patient smile, Matt approached Teri. "Well, Chris is hounding me to get you in the truck and back home. Would you like some help?"

Matt held out his hand, inviting Teri to take it. Instead, she stepped around him on her way to the truck.

"Don't touch me," Teri snarled at Matt before turning to Viktoria. "Meet me at my house tomorrow morning so we can walk to school together. And don't forget, tomorrow night's the party, and it's just the two of us."

Teri got in Matt's truck and slammed the door shut as an exasperated Viktoria rested her forehead on her hand. "Oh my gosh! What's going on with her?"

"Now, those two are roostered," Matt said.

"Roostered?" Viktoria asked, looking up with a confused smile.

"On the ranch, that means they're loaded," Matt said with a grin. "Honestly, that's why I never drink, smoke, or anything. I know cowboys are expected to do that, but I don't."

Viktoria smiled back. "Yeah? Well, I'm sure everybody assumes I do too with the way I look, but I don't — my dreams are too big for that."

Matt leaned in with a comforting, soft drawl. "Mine too. You know what? You and I are a couple of misfits — we are definitely not what people think we are. I'm glad I'm not alone."

Viktoria glowed, touching her grandmother's cross. "That makes two of us."

Unbelievable, Dylan. That's exactly what I said when I first met him.

"Well, I better get those two home before a riot breaks out in my truck," Matt said with a smile and a nod. "I'm sorry you had to see all that craziness. I'm also sorry I'm so muddied up. I went straight from trade school this morning to work and then to a very interesting band rehearsal at Chris's, as you now know."

Viktoria blushed. "Hey, look at me — my makeup's smeared from sweat trying to keep up with my mom outdoors all day."

Before turning around to make his way back to his truck, Matt gave Viktoria a heart-melting cowboy wink and grin. "All the smeared makeup in the world can't hide natural beauty."

Before getting in his truck, he gave Viktoria one last wave. "I can't wait to see you at the party tomorrow night."

Viktoria returned with a wave, biting her lower lip.

Just the two of us.

Closing and locking the front door, Viktoria turned around as Olivia entered the living room from the hallway, drying her hair. Looking at Viktoria, she let out a giggle. "Why did Teri leave before I could see her?"

"How did you know it was Teri?"

Olivia giggled again. "There's purple lipstick where she kissed you on the forehead."

Viktoria wiped her forehead, embarrassed that Matt had seen her like that. "She was just stopping by to remind me of the party. Think of a good movie you want to watch. I'm going to take a shower and think of something really delicious to whip up for you."

"I like that plan," Olivia said. "Are you sure Teri didn't want to stay?"

"Nah, she wanted to head home," Viktoria said, playing it off. "She thinks it's cool that we have our mother-daughter days together, so she never wants to get in the way of that."

"Well, that's very thoughtful of her," Olivia said, turning on the TV. "I'm glad she stopped by. I'm sure it was nice for you to see Teri today."

Did I? Was that really Teri? She told me she's fine and not to worry. Still, the chain smoking, drinking, hiding her visits to Mr. Tailor from me, and now drugs? It's getting to be too much — *something's very wrong.*

Chapter 34

Stepping off the sidewalk to cut through Teri's front yard, the cigarette smoke in the air brought Viktoria much needed relief, though her frustration remained. Sitting on the edge of the front porch with her arms around her legs, Teri took another drag as she looked toward the sky as though she had no care in the world.

The gravel underneath Viktoria's marching feet provided more than enough noise to announce her presence, yet Teri remained in her own world, her eyes closed to a warm breeze. Her unresponsiveness only resulted in irking Viktoria even more.

"What the hell, Teri?"

"Hey, there you are," Teri said, impervious to Viktoria's frustration.

"Yes," Viktoria responded, "here I am. Where were you all day?"

Teri shrugged. "Home."

"Are you sure?" Viktoria asked, making sure she got her frustration across. "I rang your doorbell and knocked on your door until my knuckles were about to bleed, and nobody answered. Where were your mom and dad? Where was Chris? I was worried sick all day."

"Take it easy, Viktoria," Teri said with her brow slightly furrowed. "My parents are in Vegas for some stupid work convention, and I don't know where the hell Chris went last night. Look, nobody else was home, and I slept in — that's it, OK? Why were you so worried?"

In complete bewilderment, Viktoria raised her hands to her sides. "Are you serious? Where do I start? You showed up at my house last night, high as a kite for one thing. I don't know what you took, but I thought you were going to have a heart attack. I pounded on your front door as hard as possible this morning while ringing the doorbell to no end, and there was no answer. I was terrified that—"

"What?" Teri asked, cutting her off. "That I OD'd or something and my family had to race me to the hospital?"

Viktoria closed her eyes to dam any oncoming emotions.

Did she really have to go there? After what Viktoria had gone through with Dylan and her dad after the car accident? After losing her grandma just before losing Dylan? Why would Teri make her even entertain the thought of losing her as well?

Opening her eyes to quiet laughter, Teri had stood up, taking a few steps into her front yard to flick her cigarette butt just over the sidewalk.

"You're so dramatic, Viktoria. You need to stop watching so much *Hill Street Blues* and *St. Elsewhere.*"

Viktoria, burning from Teri's thoughtlessness concerning her fears and emotions, made it a point to not smile or respond.

Teri's smile faded. "Viktoria, you know I would never do something stupid like that. Sure, I found some stuff that Chris had, probably for the gig tonight, and I decided to have a little fun and take some."

After a few seconds of uneasy silence, Teri sighed and rolled her eyes. "It was speed, all right? I've tried it before, and I liked it. I guess this stuff was stronger than usual, so I was all over the place last night and didn't crash until early this morning. Apparently, I was so exhausted that I slept through all your knocking and doorbell ringing. So, there you have it — I missed school because I was on drugs. I'm sorry, OK? Are you happy?"

Teri's dismissiveness only served to make Viktoria burn even more inside. Still, she set it aside so she could help Teri truly understand why she was so alarmed.

"Look, you can come to me with anything — *anything*. Please, just don't do what you did last night ever again; no more drugs. I know you think I'm overreacting, but I was just really scared, OK?"

"Of what?" Teri asked, her voice soft and caring again, just as her usual self.

It was impossible for Viktoria to hold back the emotion in her voice as she said, "You know I've already lost Dylan and my grandmother this year. I don't know what I'd do if . . ." It was too much for Viktoria to finish her thought.

With her serene, understanding smile, Teri embraced her like a warm, comforting blanket. "I'm so sorry, Viktoria. I didn't mean to scare you or make you feel that way. I didn't even think . . ." She grabbed Viktoria's hands, and her smile and eyes made the rest of her face glow. "I won't mess around with Chris's stuff anymore, OK? I promise."

"Why did you do it in the first place?" Viktoria asked. "You said last night that you are hurting too. That there are things you are going through that you wouldn't tell me, but you know you can. What are they?"

"Honestly? I don't even remember what I said last night," Teri answered with sincerity. "I'm sure what I meant was all the things you already know, like my parents resenting us and not giving a crap. I'm practically raising Chris, my *older* brother, and you know he's not always a saint. And, you know, I also miss your grandma, dad, and Dylan being around. Your family is my family too."

"Are you sure there's nothing else? Seriously, Teri, please tell me if there is."

With wide eyes and an excited smile, Teri took a firm grip of Viktoria's face, moving it side to side. "No! There's nothing else. So, let's forget all that. It's Friday afternoon. The party starts in just a few hours. Your mom's at work, and our weekend is just getting started."

A smile crossed Viktoria's face as she pushed Teri away. "OK, fine, just don't kiss me on the forehead like you did last night. I'm not going to the party tonight with a purple lipstick kiss mark on my face."

"Oh, I did that?" Teri asked, laughing.

Viktoria also laughed. "Yes! It was embarrassing. My mom wouldn't let it go last night. Let's go back to my house. I have some leftover Norwegian crepes in the fridge."

"Oh yeah," Teri said with a sly grin. "The perfect Friday after-school snack. By the way, how was school? Like I care, but, just in case, did I miss anything?"

"No," Viktoria said with a shrug before another smile crossed her face along with a snicker. "Well, you didn't miss anything in third period, but I wish you'd been there for one thing that was out of the ordinary."

"Oh, yeah? What was that?"

"Jeff. For once, you wouldn't have heard his booming voice or boisterous, meathead laughter cutting into your brain around campus all day. I imagine it was the gauze in his mouth that kept it shut. His eyes were so black he looked like a raccoon with a bandage across his nose."

Not sharing in the humor, Teri's face kept a serious expression. "Yeah? Well, he had it coming. I kept telling him to back off, but he didn't."

"Still," an astonished Viktoria continued, "you're so small. How could you physically, and so fearlessly, land two such devastating punches on him? He's huge! It was like Rocky defeating Thunderlips in *Rocky III*."

After a quick, almost bashful smile, Teri looked at Viktoria with even more sincerity. "I've had their numbers for a long time now. Like I've said before, they're cowards. All you have to do is stand up to them, and they'll leave you alone. You saw it Wednesday with Jeff — he's used to throwing his weight around and walking all over everybody. You saw the shock on his face when he tried it with me, and I literally fought back. In fact, all four of them were so shocked that they didn't do anything about it. They didn't know how to react except to back off. They couldn't handle such a paradigm shift because it had never happened to them before."

Viktoria couldn't hold back her smile. Teri's words, and what she did Wednesday after school to back them up, filled the emptiness in her heart with a comforting thrill of what could have been.

"If only Dylan knew who they really were. You don't know what I would give to be at that junior high dance and see him do what you did on Wednesday. I mean, what would you give to be at the junior high campus that next Monday morning, watching Dylan strut onto campus like a boss while Jeff's little brother, with *his* nose broken, and those other little pricks backed off?"

Instead of an instant, equally zealous response, Teri pulled out and lit another cigarette. Taking a slow drag, her eyes returned to Viktoria with a sincere pain. "Anything — I would do anything."

Like a comforting big sister, Viktoria put her arm around Teri's shoulder. "Hey, like you said, it's just you and me this weekend, and it's just getting started. Dylan wouldn't want us to spend it crying over him. He would want us to have fun and live it up. Let's head over to my house, have some crepes, and find something fun on the tube. I'll look in the *TV Guide* to see if *The Outsiders*, *Rumble Fish*, or some other hot Matt Dillon flick is on, OK?"

Teri's nod and laugh were quick and broken, but they were enough to encourage Viktoria to build on her comfort-by-humor strategy. With exaggerated excitement in her eyes and grin, she grasped Teri's face with both hands.

"I got it! Forget Matt Dillon, we're going to see the band's gig tonight. We need to watch something that'll get us warmed up for their killer set. I bet that if we channel surf all the networks with cartoons on right now, we can find and watch . . . drumroll . . . *Jem and the Holograms!*"

"Oh, barf!" Teri protested with comical disgust. Her good mood was back, and she finished her cigarette with a carefree smile and genuine laughter. Taking it a step further, Viktoria started to sing the theme song to the cartoon, *"Jem is my name, no one else is the same. Jem is my name. But we're the Misfits—"*

"Shut up," Teri said, laughing and pushing Viktoria away. She then took a few steps into the front yard gravel to flick her cigarette past the sidewalk. "Let's get going."

* * * *

Before pulling the crepes out, Viktoria sighed, rolling her eyes at the note Olivia had taped to the refrigerator door.

Looking forward to hearing about the party after work. PLEASE BE SAFE and NEVER LEAVE TERI'S SIDE! I love you — Mom.

With a second, even deeper sigh, Viktoria held her grandmother's cross.

I can read between the lines, Dylan. Yeah, I get it — no boys out of high school. That means no Matt. He's out of high school, but come on. We're only two years apart. Why can't she just let me live my life?

With a plate of crepes in each hand, Viktoria paused on her way from the kitchen into the living room. Sunk into the cushions of the couch, Teri was changing the channels with the remote control, looking for something to watch. It was an almost everyday sight, but it was different that day.

Viktoria couldn't put her finger on it — it was obscure, yet clear. Teri appeared as serene, relaxed, and blissfully unplugged from the world as always. Somehow, though, a certain pain visibly weighed on her — a loneliness, a deep sorrow. Some kind of crisis or disturbance loomed like an enemy surrounding her from all corners.

It was invisible and barely detectible, but it was there: powerful, strong, and closing in. The sweet, nurturing smile plastered on her face, the lively personalities and jingles bringing life to the TV, and the mechanical normalcy of changing the channels were, all in one, Teri's shield, barely keeping the impending darkness at bay.

Last weekend, it was her mom. This weekend, it was Teri. Viktoria would have to wait for another chance with Matt after all.

Ugh, but I don't want to wait.

Chapter 35

The band's equipment and instruments were positioned on the makeshift stage in the backyard just as they were in Teri's garage. Mike's drum set was slightly stage left. To its left rested Grant's bass on its stand. Slightly right, center stage was Chris's mic stand with his guitar just behind it on its stand. And of course, on its stand, stage right, rested the instrument that made Viktoria's heart melt at the mere sight of it: Matt's dark red and black Kay SG electric guitar, the guitar he could play with unbelievable speed and accuracy and look *so* good while doing so.

The band had a large, white banner with plain red block letters above the drum set advertising their name: The Forgotten Ones. Viktoria could only smile and shrug.

A band needs to advertise. It's bland, but it's a start.

With a startled jump, Viktoria pressed her hands over her pounding heart when two arms wrapped around Teri, who was standing right next to her, and lifted her off her feet.

"Here she is! See? I told you my little sister would show up!"

As Chris held a laughing Teri tight while spinning her in circles, Viktoria's feet remained frozen to the ground after turning in their direction and finding herself facing Matt. Her lips managed to quiver a slight smile, and her shallow breaths couldn't keep up with her racing heart. She slowly moved her lips with the hope that the right words, whatever they were, would magically come out, but there was only a beautiful silence. Looking in his eyes, she could only hope he felt the same.

Through his rugged, handsome smile, his Texas drawl emerged, relieving Viktoria by initiating their conversation. "Seriously, now, am I a ghost, or did I actually make it here alive?"

"Wait, what?" Viktoria asked, shaking her head.

"I had to grip the front seat with both hands as Chris drove that van of his through all those neighborhood streets at a million miles per hour — even with all our gear in it. I swear, I was actually praying for a cop to pull us over. The man is out of control."

They both turned in the direction of Chris, who still had Teri lifted in his arms.

"All right, all right! Put me down, you idiot!" Teri yelled, laughing as Chris finally did so.

"The gig is on! Number two! Woo!" Chris shouted as he aggressively high-fived Grant and Mike, causing them both to shake the pain off their hands.

"You see what I mean?" Matt asked.

Viktoria's nose wrinkled in laughter. She hoped Matt found it cute.

The thought then raced through her mind of the amphetamines that, as she learned from Teri, Chris had stashed in his bedroom. She hoped he wasn't on them and was just over-excited for the gig.

"Oh, I love your shirt."

Matt's voice brought Viktoria back into the moment, just where she wanted to be. She couldn't help her shy smile as he continued to look at her shirt.

"Tex & the Horseheads. That's a cool shot of the band. You know I love them."

"When we started talking about all the bands we both liked, they were one of the ones you mentioned," Viktoria said in a quiet voice, still smiling.

Raising his eyebrows to show he was playfully joking, he flashed a flirtatious smile. "Let me guess — you wore that shirt for me."

"I did," Viktoria said, surprised by her own boldness.

Perhaps Matt didn't hear Viktoria after all as he shrugged off his own words. "You know I'm just kidding."

"I'm not. Seriously, I wore this for you." Still shocked by her own boldness, Viktoria forced a brave smile. Matt, unaware of it, had just initiated a challenge in the war, one Viktoria was determined for both of them to win.

Just like Kerry Von Erich on the TV screen, Matt's chiseled face, with a warm breeze blowing in his long, wavy dirty-blond hair, was breathtaking. Still, Viktoria kept her eyes locked on his.

It wasn't more than a few seconds before Matt's glowing grin slowly turned into a soft, kind smile. His voice was sincere and shy. "You know what? I'm very happy that you came tonight, Viktoria."

It was happening. The shared attraction between them was undeniable. With her heart swelling and a captivating excitement rushing through her, Viktoria couldn't stop her words, "I was going to be here no matter what. I was excited to see the band finally play outside the garage. More than that, though, I was looking forward to seeing you. I mean, we've gotten to know each other a little, but not nearly enough. I'm hoping you and I could find a way to spend more time together tonight."

Viktoria forced her mouth shut with a hopeful smile.

I hope I'm not being too forward or revealing too much. Is that going to turn him off? Please say something, Matt — anything.

The burning desire in Viktoria's heart only intensified as Matt responded by being just as bold, "I've been looking forward to this gig, but what I wanted more than anything was for you to be here tonight."

Looking into each other's eyes, no other words came. All they could do was smile. The setting sun combined with the chemistry igniting between them created a beautiful shade of red behind Matt that Viktoria had never seen before.

The spellbinding moment was shattered as Teri came up from behind Viktoria, putting her arms around her. In her hand was a clear plastic cup half-filled with beer.

"Hey, sorry I disappeared. Chris bought a couple of packs of cigarettes for me today and he had them in the van. He also showed me where the keg was, as you can see."

With her chin resting on Viktoria's shoulder, the smell of beer on Teri's breath was strong.

"Thanks for coming, Teri," Matt said, as though he were trying to offer Teri an olive branch. Viktoria's smile faded over the next few seconds of ice-cold silence before the strong smell of beer returned.

"Is he still bothering you, Viktoria? Is he annoying the hell out of you like he did in the kitchen on Sunday?"

Viktoria's heart dropped to the pit of her stomach. Mortified, she pulled herself away from Teri's embrace, turning around to face her.

"What the hell, Teri? Seriously?"

"What?" Teri asked with acidity. "It's true, isn't it? It's like he's trying to attach himself to your hip, trying to impress you with his musical knowledge and Texas charm or whatever. It's just a bunch of boring crap. You know it — I can see it on your face. I'm just doing what a best friend does and trying to spare you from any more of that."

Lifting her hand up to silence Teri, Viktoria, in a panic, turned to Matt.

"No, Matt. That is so not true, not at all. You know that, right?"

No longer a stranger to Teri's verbal jabs at him, Matt, like a gentleman taking the higher road, smiled with an accepting nod.

Turning around again, Viktoria made sure her glare at Teri burned. Teri responded with a bratty shrug.

Chris, standing on the stage with the rest of the band, spoke into the mic, "Matt, it's time to do this. We're just waiting for you."

With a blushing grin to the laughter throughout the backyard, Matt started to make his way toward the stage.

"Wait!" Viktoria called out just loud enough for him to stop. Rushing up to him, she gripped his forearms, looking into his understanding, clear blue eyes. "Hey, I am really sorry about that. I have no idea what's gotten into her lately. Forget everything she said. *None* of that was true — nothing at all. *Believe me*, OK?"

It hurt Viktoria to have to say that about Teri, but it was true. Something was wrong with her, and Viktoria could not let whatever it was invade and disrupt her own life.

A captivating, playful grin formed on Matt's lips. "You've got nothing to worry about. Believe that, sweetheart."

Viktoria's heart, again, melted.

Sweetheart! With that Texas drawl, I can't resist it — not anymore.

"I'll be standing *right here* after the gig. My feet are not budging."

Facing Viktoria as he walked backward before turning around and racing to the stage, Matt's smile broadened as he gave her his Texas-charm wink. "Now I know where to look while I'm playing. Regardless, wherever you'll be after the gig, that's where I'm going to be as well."

An excited rush of blood ignited and over-sensitized every inch of her body. Though Viktoria had been excited for the gig all week, she wished it were already over before it even began.

As Matt jumped onto the stage, the smell of a familiar cigarette brand, mixed with a strong stench of alcohol, filled Viktoria's nose as Teri's arms wrapped around her from behind again.

"Ugh, that hick cowboy is finally out of our hair. *Our* weekend finally starts tonight."

As her smile faded, Viktoria shut her eyes tight as her stomach twisted. What she dreaded and hoped to somehow avoid was now inevitable and on the horizon.

No, Teri — not tonight.

Chapter 36

The warm breeze brought a rock-god liveliness to his dirty-blond wavy locks as Matt turned to face the audience. With his dark red and black Kay SG electric guitar plugged in, he plucked a couple of strings to check his volume. Looking directly at Viktoria, his charismatic smile warmed every part of her body.

"Good evening! We are The Forgotten Ones! Let's see if you can remember any of these songs you rarely or never hear on the radio anymore. We're especially going to stump the girls in the crowd with our first song from the band Rush!" As Chris introduced the band, Viktoria, still trapped in Teri's embrace from behind, cringed, irritated by the screaming in her ear. Wiggling herself free, Viktoria's beaming smile and excitement instantly returned as Matt's powerful fingers ripped into the first song. From the first note, his playing was flashy, fast, and precise.

The guilt of her frustration as she broke herself away from Teri's arms caused Viktoria to turn around to smile and give her attention. Instead of standing right behind her, Teri was on the patio, pouring herself another cup of beer from the keg. Several seconds later, she was back at Viktoria's side with a freshly lit cigarette, taking one swig after another of her beer.

Entranced and fixated on Matt and his guitar playing, Viktoria could only stand, smile, and gaze at him. As the band played on, Teri continued to disappear periodically. Viktoria kept turning around to find her back on the patio, pouring herself another cup of beer.

Staggering back to Viktoria's side each time, Teri would lean on her more and more, putting her arm around her to keep her balance. Every time Matt looked at Viktoria and they both smiled, Teri squeezed her closer.

As Chris announced the final song for the evening, Teri turned to Viktoria with half-opened, glassy eyes, slurring out her words, "Hey, just one more beer and that's it for me. We'll leave after that."

As she tripped on her feet, almost falling over, Viktoria grabbed Teri's upper arms.

"No, Teri, you need to stop drinking, OK? You can barely stand."

As her slow, trembling hands pulled out and lit a cigarette, Teri pointed at Viktoria, still slurring, "No, Viktoria, *you* need to stop. Stop looking at Matt."

"What?" Viktoria asked with a quizzical look, though she knew she was playing innocent in vain. She had to, though; she was walking a razor's edge.

"You heard me," an inebriated yet discerning Teri said, trying not to trip over her own words. "Hey. You. Viktoria. If he's there, what've I got? Nothing. It'd all be for nothing."

"What the hell are you talking about?" Viktoria was confused and frustrated with Teri's sloppy drunkenness.

Placing her hands on Viktoria's shoulders, either to help keep her balance or get her point across or both, Teri's glassy eyes locked with Viktoria's. "Look. Matt needs to go. Besides, you're too young. Too innocent. I'm looking out for you."

Teri then placed her sticky hands, still damp from spilled beer, on Viktoria's cheeks, barely pushing out her words around the cigarette between her lips, "That's what sisters do."

"Ugh, gross," Viktoria said with a grimace as she grabbed Teri's wrists, pulling her hands away from her face. "Stop being so wrapped around the axle about Matt, OK? Stop being so nasty toward him. And *stop drinking*! You're falling all over yourself. Look, they're playing their last song for the night. We've been looking forward to this all week. Let's just forget about everything and enjoy what's left of the show."

Though Teri had been testing her patience beyond measure, Viktoria still stood directly behind her, propping her up with a caring embrace around her upper chest. From over Teri's shoulder, she remained laser focused on Matt as the band ended their set with a blistering performance of a song she hadn't heard on the radio in years. She couldn't recall its name or the band who played it, but it was an epic end to the show.

"Thank you so much! We're The Forgotten Ones! Hope to see you again!" Chris shouted into the mic as if he were in Madison Square Garden. Everyone in the backyard cheered.

Squirming out of Viktoria's arms, Teri staggered up to the stage, giving Chris a loving sister's proud hug and a kiss on the cheek. With a wistful smile, Viktoria took hold of her grandmother's cross as a comforting warmth of longing and hope filled her chest.

I wish that were us, Dylan. Someday, right? We'll be together again, and the war will be won.

Glancing stage right, a giggle escaped her as her smile broadened to the excitement of the here and now. Matt was stuffing his guitar into its case as fast as possible as his eyes remained locked on her. Whenever possible, he held his index finger in the air, mouthing the words, *give me just one minute.*

Rushing to the stage as Matt stood up with his guitar case, Viktoria smiled at him. "Hey, do you need any help?"

"Not at all," he said with his alluring smile. "Don't you worry about a thing — I got this."

As Matt hustled to the van with his guitar and some other small equipment, Viktoria kept an eye on the other side of the stage where Teri was smoking another cigarette, rambling about something to a visibly confused and uninterested Grant.

Rushing back from the van with Mike, Matt hopped onto the stage before looking down at Viktoria. "Mike's going to help me get my amplifier in the van and then I'm all yours."

And then I'm all yours? Forget the amp, I want you now!

As Matt and Mike hobbled the amplifier to the van, Teri's one-sided conversation with Grant was evidently coming to an end as her eyes began to shift between him and Viktoria. Being her best friend, it was impossible for Viktoria to shake the guilt of any possible disloyalty weighing on her. Still, she couldn't help her thoughts.

Please, Matt, get to me before Teri does.

A sigh of relief along with excited anticipation eclipsed Viktoria's dilemma as Matt passed by Teri, who was cut off by Chris, on his direct path to her.

"Not so bad for an obscure garage band, right?" Matt said, beaming.

Viktoria's lips quivered. "You were amazing."

"Well, definitely a huge improvement from last week's gig," Matt continued. "It got a little rough in a couple of spots, but we're polishing it up."

"I'm sure the band did great, but I was only watching and hearing you."

Being so forward worked before the gig, Viktoria. Keep going. Be bold. Fight for what you want!

The kind, soft smile from before the gig appeared on Matt's lips. Again, his voice was shy and sincere. "Well, the rest of the band said the audience loved us. I'll have to take their word for it. I only saw one person out there tonight."

"Was it worth all those hours of practice in the garage to play for that one person?" Viktoria asked.

His eyes gleamed as his smile grew. "Absolutely, without a doubt."

No words came to Viktoria, and she didn't care, because what was building between them said everything.

With a tight-lipped, rugged grin, Matt looked up at the clear, autumn sky. An alluring magic flashed in his eyes as he turned again to Viktoria. "What a beautiful night. The temperature is perfect. How about you and I disappear from this crowd and enjoy it together?" Matt then leaned forward with a chivalrous cowboy nod. "I would love to walk you home."

With her heart dancing, an exhilarating chill overwhelmed her. With the possibilities the dark quiet sidewalks had to offer running through her imagination, her stomach tied up in knots as every part of her body tingled with anticipation.

Teri was stumbling her way toward them, holding another cup of beer. Viktoria's eyes then turned to Chris, who was back to his normal, relaxed self. If he was on anything when he first got there, it had worn off for sure. Teri would be safe with him in the van. Viktoria's decision was hard but painfully clear.

Was Teri so smashed that she wouldn't even remember this night? She was probably better off having Chris drive her home and sleeping it off.

At the same time there was Matt — Matt! — and he wanted to disappear with Viktoria into the night, alone! *Don't blow this chance. Take it! This is the adventurous life you not only promised Dylan but yourself too.* Besides, Teri can no longer even see straight.

Teri was still about twenty feet from them. Chris was only about four feet away packing up his equipment.

Viktoria, trying to sound nonchalant, turned to Chris with a nod and smile. "Chris, your little sister's hammered. There's no way I can take her to my house like that with my mom there; she'd go ballistic. Would you mind driving her home tonight?"

Viktoria knew Chris saw right through her as his eyes shifted between her and Matt, followed by wiggling eyebrows and a mischievous grin. "Don't worry, I'll get her home safe. Make sure you do the same for Viktoria, Matt."

Kind of embarrassed, but not really, Viktoria's eyes returned to Matt as she bit down on her lower lip.

Game on.

Teri had staggered her way toward them. But just a few feet away, she tripped over her feet. Swaying up to the stage, she propped herself up right next to Chris. He was going to take care of her.

Matt extended his hand, ready to take Viktoria's. It was the perfect time, and she had to take it.

Pulling her pressed lips inward to moisten them, Viktoria smiled as she took Matt's hand. Trying to make her hastiness to somehow escape from Teri unnoticed appear playful and alluring, she pulled him in the direction of the fence that wrapped around the yard.

"Come on," she said with a flirtatious grin. "Let's get out of here."

"Hey."

Teri's voice was just quiet enough for Viktoria to pretend she didn't hear it as she and Matt started to make their way to the backyard gate.

"Hey."

Teri's voice grew louder, but Viktoria and Matt were a few steps farther away — enough for Viktoria to attempt to play it off.

Please, Matt, don't turn around. Just keep walking.

"Hey!"

The rage in Teri's shout filled the backyard, stinging Viktoria's heart. No one could have pretended to not hear it.

Frozen and cringing, she gripped Matt's hand even tighter.

Chapter 37

Closing her eyes, the air flowing in and out of Viktoria's lungs felt like a balm before a terrible wound rather than after. Before letting go of Matt's hand to turn and face the unavoidable, she squeezed it to send the message that she wasn't going anywhere — not without him.

With the backyard deathly quiet except for a few inquiring voices, the weight of every stare mortified Viktoria. Hoping against all hope to quickly extinguish the made-for-TV teen drama she was just forced into, she approached Teri with caution and a quiet voice. "Teri, Chris is going to take you home, OK? We'll meet up at the park at our usual time tomorrow and spend the rest of the weekend together like we planned, I promise."

"The hell I'm going home with Chris!" Teri screamed. "We came together. We're leaving together."

Placing her hands on Teri's shoulders, hoping her personal touch would have some sort of tranquil effect, Viktoria looked into her glassy eyes with all the care and love she could convey. "You need to go home with Chris so you can get a good night's sleep in your own bed. You've had too much to drink. I can't take you to my house; you know we can't let my mom see you like this."

"What do you mean I've had too much to drink?" Teri slurred. "I'm not even close to having too much to drink."

Pulling away from Viktoria's hands, Teri clenched her teeth and threw her cup of beer against the stage. The beer exploded in every direction. With dizzy anger, her eyes returned to Viktoria's.

"You see? I didn't even drink *that* one." She then pointed an accusing finger at Viktoria, and a disgusted scowl formed across her face. "And how could you? How could you put this on your mom? None of this crap is about her. It's about *him*," Teri said with a snarl as her finger shifted in Matt's direction. "That bastard."

"You need to stop, Teri." The sudden sharpness in Viktoria's voice reflected the burning in her chest. The embarrassing position Teri put them in was frustrating enough, but throwing Matt into it, especially in such a callous way, was crossing the line.

She also knew Teri was right, though. It was about Matt and not really her mom. Having it pointed out in front of everyone, especially him, and the humiliation of appearing deceitful and juvenile made it even more maddening.

Above all, though, the unfounded hostility and spitefulness Teri constantly hurled at Matt had reached its breaking point. The fact that she was drunk no longer mattered to Viktoria; all she wanted was the truth.

"Seriously, what's wrong with you? Matt has been nothing but good to you. I have never heard him snap back, much less even look at you cross-eyed every time you've put him down or criticized him. Why do you hate him so much?"

Taking Viktoria by the arms and pulling her closer, Teri let out an exasperated, drunken sigh.

"He's in the way."

"In the way?" Viktoria's question was more of an expression of her frustration than an inquiry.

Breaking through her drunken stupor with a momentary sharp, cold stare, Teri's hands gripped Viktoria's shirt. "It's always been just the two of us. For as long as we can remember, through it all, we've only had each other. Nobody gets between us."

"Between us?"

"Nobody. Not again. Never."

"Again?" Viktoria asked, perplexed. "What do you mean 'again'?"

"Not again," Teri repeated.

It was all the beer. It had to be. This was not Teri — not at all. Besides, what was she even talking about? Nobody had ever come between them. Nobody.

A thought popped into Viktoria's head, and it was nearly impossible not to crack a smile, but the last thing she wanted to do was appear to be taking Teri's drunken, though well-meaning, deep concern lightheartedly. "Are you talking about that creepy Brett Eckert who kept following me all around campus last year wanting to go out with me?"

Shaking her head, Teri's pained eyes looked to the ground before Viktoria gently lifted her face to keep her attention. "I know you couldn't stand that guy. Well, guess what? I couldn't stand him either."

"It's not him." Teri's voice trembled as a tear fell down her cheek.

"I know," Viktoria answered with a caring whisper, wiping the tear away. "It's Matt. Well, guess what? Matt's not some weird creep, he's a great guy, and you know that. He wouldn't do anything to get in between us. You really do know that, right?"

Loosening her grip on Viktoria's shirt, Teri lowered her head again. Grabbing Teri's arms to hold her up as she started to cry, Viktoria turned to Chris. "Is the front door to your van unlocked?"

After Chris nodded, Viktoria looked at Matt, quickly holding up her index finger, gesturing to give her a minute. Assisting a stammering, weeping Teri to the van, Viktoria helped her get in the front seat before putting her seat belt on for her.

Taking hold of Viktoria's sleeve, Teri pulled her closer. "I can't do this anymore. We need to get out of here."

"You're almost out of here," Viktoria said, holding Teri's gripping hand. "Don't worry, Chris is about to drive you home. You need some sleep in your own bed, all right?"

"You don't understand, Viktoria, I can't do this anymore."

"OK," an exasperated Viktoria said, pulling Teri's hand from her sleeve. "I got it — no more beer for you, ever."

Grabbing Viktoria's sleeve again, Teri glared into her eyes, speaking through her clenched teeth, "Nobody gets between us."

Viktoria gently took Teri's face in both hands. "Stop saying that, Teri. The more you do, the worse I feel. Just like you tell me all the time, don't worry about it."

Getting Teri to rest her head back, Viktoria wiped her tears away before giving her a kiss on the cheek. "Look at all we've been through. Believe me, nobody will ever get between us. Let it go, all right?"

Chris got in the driver's seat of the van as Grant and Mike climbed into the back.

Looking at Chris, Teri then turned again to Viktoria. "I need Matt d . . . I need Matt d . . ."

Don't say it, Teri. I know you're drunk out of your mind, and you wouldn't really mean it, but please don't go that far. That would be too much.

Before her head fell back and she passed out, Teri turned again to Chris. "I need Matt Dillon."

The heaviness and tension in the air disappeared as Viktoria and Chris looked at each other, bursting out in laughter.

Teri, you're right, I am too dramatic, but still, don't ever scare me like that again!

After turning on the van, Chris looked at Viktoria. "Don't worry about Teri. She's been like this quite a few times at the house. She says the weirdest things when she's drunk. Tomorrow morning, I'll get her some coffee, throw *The Outsiders* in the Betamax so she can get her Matt Dillon, and she'll be back to what *she* considers normal. In the meantime, *your* Matt is still waiting for you in the backyard, *anxiously*."

Viktoria blushed. "Shut up."

"Ha!" Chris shot back. "I'll see you tomorrow."

As the van made its way out the back gate, Viktoria looked up at the clear starry sky. She then took hold of her grandmother's cross. Moistening her lips, she smiled.

Guess what, Viktoria? Matt's waiting. Remember June 1? This is just the beginning. This weekend can only get better.

Chapter 38

The strength of Matt's hand alone blanketed Viktoria with the warmth of complete, undoubted security. The bright silver moonlight accentuated the muscles on his arms.

A familiar, powerful roar of an engine approached from behind. Racing past them was the same extremely large pickup truck from the Sunday before. The dent and chipped paint were undeniable — it was Cody Rutherford's truck. This time, though, no beer bottle was thrown, the truck didn't stop, and there was no altercation. With Matt by her side, the enemy held its fire.

Whether it was Matt's tall body, rugged and strong from his outdoorsy, cowboy lifestyle or, perhaps, appearing as an adult couple to be respected that made Cody ignore them, Viktoria didn't know. She didn't care either. The truck just kept driving, leaving them alone, and that was enough. Viktoria couldn't help but squeeze Matt's hand a little tighter, causing the two of them to look at each other with reserved, wanting smiles.

"I love clear warm nights like these," Matt said, gazing up to the heavens.

"Does it remind you of home where the stars at night are big and bright?" Viktoria snapped and pointed the index finger of her free hand at Matt and flashed a silly grin. She hoped falling back on her goofy humor, her best defense in a nervous situation, didn't jeopardize the romantic tension between them.

"Yep, deep in the heart of Texas," Matt responded with an exaggerated drawl and wink as well as a flirtatious smile that assured Viktoria the playfulness undoubtedly went hand in hand with the building heat between them. "Nights like this remind me of those summer nights on my grandfather's ranch outside of Paris."

"Paris?" Viktoria echoed with humorous confusion.

Matt smiled with another wink. "Paris, Texas."

Laughing with slight embarrassment, Viktoria used it as an opportunity to push up against Matt.

Matt snickered, playing innocent. "What?"

"Next time be more specific," Viktoria playfully demanded as she pushed up against Matt again, but this time, she kept her body closer to his.

"Well, OK, then," Matt said with an old-fashioned, western cowboy nod. "If you want, I can share with you a little secret about that ranch that nobody knows."

"Really? All right," Viktoria said, keeping the side of her body up against his as they walked.

Clearing his throat as though he was going to disclose some earth-shattering information, Matt flashed Viktoria a mischievous grin. "At my *paternal* grandfather's ranch, located approximately 33.6 miles southwest of Paris, *Texas—*"

Viktoria laughed, nudging Matt's arm. "Shut up. Don't be such a brat."

Matt's enchanting smile shined in the moonlight, and the butterflies went berserk in Viktoria's stomach as he continued, "Fair enough. With my dad being a high school teacher, he would spend summers working on my grandfather's ranch. As soon as we were old enough, he would bring me and my two brothers with him while my mom and my sister held down the fort at home. We spent countless nights sleeping under the stars. Around a fire, before retiring for the night, my dad and my older brother, Steve, taught me how to play countless amazing country-western riffs and scales on an old acoustic guitar. They were so hard to learn, especially on that old beast of a guitar. Once I got them down, though, a whole new world opened up to me.

"Those old guitars make your fingers mighty strong and calloused, but I couldn't stop playing. For hours on end, I would work on those scales and riffs, getting them wired to the point where I could even build around them and come up with some crazy stuff — I soaked it all in. Well, when I got back to Dallas after each summer, I would plug in my electric guitar, amplify and distort all the chops I learned, and blow away all the kids in the neighborhood along with all the local bands my friends and I formed in our garages."

Passing under a streetlamp, Matt looked into Viktoria's eyes with another mischievous grin. "What everyone thinks I play is not speed metal or groundbreaking rock 'n roll fury and genius. It's just good old country-western licks, enhanced and brought to life by electricity, electric guitar pedals and effects, and a stack of Marshall amps. Nobody else knows my secret. Nobody in Texas or Arizona — not even The Forgotten Ones — only you."

Viktoria smiled, keeping her eyes on his. "I'm honored."

She really was honored; it was special for him to share something so private with her. She also liked the feeling that she and Matt had a secret between them.

Taking it a step further, Viktoria reached over, placing her free hand on his arm. "Your secret to guitar playing is similar to the tricks I use that makes everyone think I'm a genius in the kitchen."

"Oh, yeah? What's that?"

"It's a trick I learned from my grandma that she taught herself when it was just her and my dad alone during World War II in occupied Norway — how to make something filling and delicious out of almost nothing. When it came to ingenuity in the kitchen, she was unmatched. As soon as I was old enough, she would take me to her house and the diner at my dad's truck stop as often as possible. She saw how much I loved working in the kitchen and she was determined to teach me all of her tricks. I soaked it all in. Anyway, adding all I had learned from my grandma to all the ingredients and products in my kitchen at home and the diner at the truck stop, I can really blow people away with cakes, stews, casseroles — you name it."

Matt smiled. "Well, I'm honored to know that secret."

"I don't think it's a secret. It's just a trick."

"Really? Well, what is something about you that you would consider a secret?"

Looking down at her feet, an embarrassed laugh escaped Viktoria.

"What's so funny?" Matt asked with his amazing smile.

She licked her lips as her stomach tightened. Her hands gripped his hand and arm even tighter as she leaned over, trying not to laugh.

Matt broke into laughter himself. "Is your secret really that hilarious?"

Viktoria braced herself. "OK, I'm going to tell you something that *nobody* knows about me, not even my mom. But you have to promise not to laugh or abandon me on the walk home. You also have to swear you'll *never* tell a soul — not Chris, nobody."

"I promise," Matt said with a warm smile. "You have my absolute word."

Shocked that she was revealing it to him, Viktoria took a deep breath before looking into Matt's eyes. "I absolutely love professional wrestling."

Matt stopped, turning Viktoria to face him with the biggest eyes and smile. "No way! Are you serious?"

Viktoria cringed, nodding with nervous excitement. "Yes."

Matt clapped his hands as he turned in a complete circle. "Whew! Finally! I'm not alone!"

Viktoria almost jumped out of her skin as she grabbed Matt by the shirt. "Wait, are *you* serious?"

"Of course!" The veins in Matt's neck bulged with elation. "World Class Championship Wrestling? Every week, my parents thought I was playing some gig downtown. Heck no, I was at the Sportatorium! And you won't believe this, but people used to always ask for my autograph because they thought I was Kerry Von Erich."

Viktoria, overwhelmed with excitement, pushed him off the sidewalk. "That's because you look just like him, you hotter than hot cowboy!"

The next several blocks were spent talking about current and past favorite feuds, storylines, and matches. The two of them couldn't stop talking about the Von Erichs, the Four Horsemen, the Koloffs, all of them. They especially discussed the tag team they both loved the most: The Road Warriors.

On North 53rd Avenue, the lights of the park appeared in the distance on the left. Reality pierced through Viktoria's romantic haze.

"The park's coming up," she bemoaned. "Ugh, I don't want this to end!"

"No kidding," Matt said with an equal amount of disappointment in his voice. "I know from yesterday your house is right up the street."

Viktoria sighed. "It's about three blocks to the right."

"That's too close," Matt said, letting go of Viktoria's hand to put his arm around her, pulling her in tight.

My house is too close, but not you — not by a long shot.

Viktoria knew Olivia was home and waiting for her. The urgency within her mounted and multiplied with each step, causing frustration to bleed in.

Passing the park, the wood fence separating the backyards from the sidewalk was passing by too fast. Crossing another street, Viktoria's backyard was now on the other side.

We can't go beyond the fence. What if my mom has the curtains open?

"Which house is yours again?" Matt asked.

"My front yard begins at the end of this fence," Viktoria answered gracefully, surprised she could hide her urgency and frustration so well.

Their night together would have to end there, no matter what.

It's now or never, Matt.

Chapter 39

They were about twenty feet from the end of the fence. At that point, the front yard began, along with a heartbreaking and frustrating remainder of the weekend if nothing happened. Hoping beyond hope, Viktoria slowed and shortened her steps.

With only five feet of opportunity remaining, Matt stopped, turning Viktoria by her shoulders to face him. His hands moved down to her upper arms, gently squeezing them.

Oh yes.

The tip of her tongue moistening her lips as her eyes locked on his, Viktoria's heart raced as her body tensed with an exhilarating itch in her stomach. She knew it was coming.

Without saying another word, Matt's hands lifted her face and pressed his lips against hers. He looked at her again. "I would never forgive myself if I didn't do that before the night was over."

Viktoria could only let her eyes and smile gleam in the moonlight, inviting and enticing Matt to do it again.

Matt took Viktoria by her shoulders, pulling her even closer. Pressing his lips against hers again, every muscle on Viktoria's back constricted as his hand warmed the back of her neck. She didn't want it to stop.

I can't believe this is happening.

Her head resting on his chest, held by the firm softness of his hand and fingers running through her hair, the slight smell of his cologne was teasing and rugged. While its scent added to the powerful blanket of security she was basking in, it also made her want to challenge it.

Gripping his shirt with both hands, Viktoria breathed Matt's cologne in deeply through her nose, rising to her challenge. Lifting her head, she bit her lower lip, locking eyes with Matt. With a kittenish smile, she backed him up against the fence, pressing her body to his.

Her hands taking his face, she pulled it toward hers, locking their lips together again. Moving her hands down to his chest, she kept him pushed up against the fence, pinning him between it and her.

Her lips and hands moved in the directions of her imagination and past fantasies of that moment. With no other experience to go by, she was surprised and encouraged by Matt's mirrored responses and the undeniable chemistry they shared. She met the challenge head on; her greatest battle to date won.

Returning to the security of his embrace, Viktoria again rested her head against his chest. With his heart beating against her ear, she closed her eyes, pretending they were lying down, sleeping in that position all night. She then looked up at the bright moon and stars.

Now I know what they mean by — I can't believe I'm actually thinking this — magic. That word has always made me want to gag, but this is undeniable. I wish time would stop right now.

Time!

Her eyes opening wide, Viktoria let out a quick gasp as she looked at her watch. It was 11:52. It was a great relief, but also an embarrassing, infuriating one.

Crap! I only have eight minutes. I hate, hate, hate curfew! This sucks!

Placing her hands on Matt's chest, she pushed her body slightly from his, looking up at him with a well-masked smile. Matt held her face in both hands again.

"Is it getting late?"

Viktoria hoped Matt was merely curious and not picking up on her sudden sense of urgency. The last thing she wanted was for the word *curfew* to even enter his mind. She wanted him to see her as an equal, a woman, and such a juvenile word being associated with their relationship would have been mortifying.

"It's almost midnight," Viktoria said with a casual shrug.

Matt sighed. "Ugh, you are going to hate me, but I need to go. I promised my uncle I would help him replace the brakes on his truck. He wants to meet at his garage at eight o'clock."

Whew!

"I understand," Viktoria said as nonchalantly as possible. "Besides, my mom has an early workday tomorrow. I promised I'd be home by midnight to tell her how it went tonight."

"Oh yeah?" Matt returned with a nervous, mischievous grin. "What are you going to tell her?"

"Only what she needs to know," Viktoria said with another kittenish grin.

Gently holding her face again, Matt rested his forehead on hers. "I'll walk you to your doorstep."

With quick thinking, Viktoria smiled and shook her head. "Nah, if the curtains are open, my mom could easily see us and would want to come out and meet you. This is our night

— let's just keep it between us. Besides, if my mom could see us, we couldn't end our night like this."

Grabbing his shirt again, Viktoria pulled Matt into her for the most passionate kiss she could give.

Looking into Matt's eyes again, she lightly licked her lips.

"I'm sure you'll be at Teri's house tomorrow to practice with the band like every other Saturday afternoon."

Matt smiled. "Like clockwork."

Viktoria flashed a sly grin. "You know I'll be there. We're going to have to find another way to be alone again."

She pulled him in for a strong yet playful kiss before pushing him away gently. "Get yourself home and get some rest. This continues tomorrow night."

With his charming nod and wink, Matt turned around and made his way down the street, looking back to smile at her again under a streetlamp. As he disappeared into the dark, Viktoria looked at her watch — she had a few minutes to spare.

Pressing her arms against her chest as though she were still holding him, she gazed up at the clear night sky. The bright moon and stars were shining down on her. They were the only other ones who knew the secrets and beautiful moment the two of them shared. Not too far away, they were shining down on Matt, guiding him home.

Lifting the neckline of her shirt to her face, she could smell his cologne. Closing her eyes, she only allowed Matt to appear in front of her.

Viktoria looked up at the moon and stars again, gleaming in return with gratitude for such a perfect night — a night created just for her and Matt.

Chapter 40

The girl looking back at Viktoria in the mirror couldn't help but give her a warm, triumphant smile. Dylan's bright vision of the future, symbolized by her glowing face from her foundation and light powder, had truly been glimpsed.

With her black eye shadow, eyeliner, and mascara, it was as though Dylan was looking back at her. Her bright, blue eyes — the eyes they shared — glistened with pride.

Her black lipstick in the mirror's reflection was the most pleasing sight of all. Not only did her lips say what was necessary to achieve what she desired the night before, they also *did* what she wanted more than anything with Matt.

The May 1986 issue of *Pro Wrestling Illustrated* rested on the edge of the bathroom counter. With her makeup applied for the day, she picked up the magazine, gazing at the two monsters, Animal and Hawk, on the cover.

Looking back at the girl in the mirror, her eyes were beginning to form the same attributes as the fearless, focused, determined ones of the two monsters. Just like them, her eyes pierced through her makeup — *her* war paint. She was becoming one of them: a Road Warrior.

Olivia was at work, her chores were done, and she was ready for the day. Viktoria checked her watch — she had ten minutes. Giving herself one last look over in the mirror, she placed her hand over her grandmother's cross.

It's Saturday afternoon and you know what's next, Dylan. This is our time.

With a sandwich and a glass of chocolate milk prepared, she had a few extra minutes to call Teri. She tried two other times that morning but there was no answer.

Though their Saturday afternoon meetups at the park were a given, Viktoria couldn't help but call and confirm it that day. Despite Teri's incessant smoking over the past four months and dabbling in alcohol and, as it was revealed Thursday evening, Chris's substances, Viktoria had never seen her actually drunk, much less plastered.

She had seen Chris hungover thousands of times after a night of heavy drinking or indulging in narcotics, at least the ones he admitted to. It was always an awful sight. If Teri felt nearly as bad as he always looked, she would definitely not make it to the park.

Dialing her number again, Viktoria waited a good minute before hanging up. Still no answer, not even Chris.

What's going on? Are they still sleeping? Are they both really that hungover? Chris must've taken more speed than I thought.

Taking Teri's advice from the day before to not be so dramatic, Viktoria turned her thoughts to other more positive scenarios.

Perhaps they'd been in the garage all morning reassembling the band's gear so they could get right into practicing once the other guys got there later. Teri was really good at helping Chris with that.

Maybe they slept in a little, and then they went out for lunch or to the record store. Viktoria decided she'd go to the park after watching wrestling. If Teri wasn't there, she'd just go to their house.

246 • *The Cross I Bear*

Convinced and even a little proud of her second, more rational conclusion, Viktoria made her way into the living room with excitement and her lunch. It was the time of the week she lived for, with just herself and Dylan. Still, with a smile, she wondered if Matt was also watching. She was going to have to quiz him later.

Instead of an electric sold-out crowd at the Sportatorium in Dallas, Texas, the matches took place that week in front of a sparse crowd at the city's Cotton Bowl Stadium. It didn't matter to Viktoria — she was still on the edge of her seat, ready to keep Dylan updated with all the story lines, feuds, and, of course, the play-by-play action of each wrestling match.

Kerry Von Erich was still out of action that week, but it didn't sting Viktoria as much because she now had Matt. She also knew other wrestlers were on the card Dylan would be excited to see. Dingo Warrior and Steve Simpson, two other mesmerizing wrestlers he idolized, were on the program as a tag team.

Though the two riveting wrestlers lost by disqualification, the show went on to redeem itself, especially with the three final matches. Viktoria could not contain her excitement as she, like a color commentator herself, called the matches. Move after move, slam after slam, she knew she kept Dylan on the edge of *his* seat.

As the show ended, Viktoria's head rested against the inviting back cushion of the couch with thrilled exhaustion. She placed her hand on her grandmother's cross.

I'm also bummed that Dingo Warrior and Steve Simpson lost, but what about those three last matches? Those were awesome, Dylan. Ricky Steamboat beating Mighty Zulu. Kevin Von Erich winning over Black Bart. That main event topped it all off. Bruiser Brody defeating Abdullah the Butcher. In a steel cage with Fritz Von Erich as the guest referee? That was insane!

Viktoria smiled as she looked at the spot on the floor where Dylan used to sit to watch wrestling. Just above where Dylan's head used to be, something looked different. It was as though the air shifted or changed form. It was invisible, yet clear — Dylan's big, excited smile, the one he always turned to Viktoria with whenever an amazing performance took place in the ring or one of his heroes won.

With a wistful, comforting burning in her heart, Viktoria got off the couch and sat on the floor right next to where Dylan used to sit. He was there. Resting her hand on the floor right where he sat, she closed her eyes, gripped her grandmother's cross tight, and tried with all her might to touch him, to feel him just one more time.

Sniffling, she let go of the cross to wipe the tears falling from her eyes. She knew Dylan could no longer touch her physically — only spiritually.

Though the physical and spiritual worlds were right next to each other, as Mr. Tailor said, they too often felt a million miles apart. At that moment, though, in an all too rare moment, the two worlds were not only connecting, but also somehow overlapping. Keeping her hand where Dylan used to sit, Viktoria held on to that brief intersection of both worlds where the two of them could comfort each other in an embrace that was imperceptible, but nonetheless too real.

Though Viktoria knew she was going to be late to the park, she could not let that moment pass her by. Standing up, she took a deep breath of commitment to go out and face the day.

All right, Dylan, let's do this. I know it's been well over four months since June 1, but we're starting to finally gain momentum — let's keep it going.

Back in front of the bathroom mirror, Viktoria touched up her makeup. Dressed in black and studded silver, like Animal and Hawk, she was ready for battle.

The world awaits us, Dylan.

The girl in the mirror smiled back at her.

And Matt awaits me.

As she turned off the bathroom light, a relentless, loud knocking on the front door started and only increased in intensity, just as it had on Thursday evening.

What the hell? It was obviously Teri. Was she high again?

"OK, OK! I'm coming, Teri! Relax!"

Swinging the front door open, the words she had to express her annoyance were gone as her heart sank to the pit of her stomach. The disheveled individual standing in front of her was not high, but visibly distressed. It wasn't Teri; it was Chris.

Chapter 41

At first, no words were said. Reeking of cigarettes, Chris's T-shirt was wrinkled, along with his Levi's. He had most likely pulled them out of a pile of dirty laundry and thrown them on. His long chestnut-brown hair looked the same — unkempt, like he had just rolled out of bed. But most disturbing of all were his weary gray eyes. Their exhaustion was more emotional than physical. Despite her earlier effort to heed Teri's advice and not jump to dramatic, tragic conclusions, Viktoria couldn't deny her instincts: Something was wrong.

"Chris? Are you all right?"

Viktoria truly was concerned for him. He never just showed up at her doorstep alone. She also hoped, though, that his answer would include a relieving, usual update on Teri as well. The unease in his voice proved to be as disturbing as his troubled eyes.

"Hey, Viktoria, is Teri here?"

"No." Viktoria's response stirred relief, concern, and curiosity within her.

Chris pulled out a cigarette, his hands shaking as he lit it. "I didn't just want to show up at your house, but I tried calling a few times, and I kept getting some guy who said I had the wrong number."

"Our phone number was changed a couple of months ago; Teri must've never written it down."

"Oh," Chris said before his voice began to strain with emotion. "Look, do you know where Teri could be right now?"

Her stomach tight and burning with alarm, Viktoria grabbed Chris's arm, getting him to look directly at her. "Chris, you're scaring me. What's wrong?"

Nervously rolling his cigarette between his fingers, he took a deep swallow as he turned to look into the distance. Viktoria shook his arm to get him to look at her again.

"Is it Teri? Is it your parents? Please say something."

Still, there was no answer. He kept his blank, pained stare on her face, but not on her eyes. With frustrated concern, Viktoria locked the front door and proceeded to pull Chris toward his van.

"She's got to be at the park. Let's go."

In the less than two minutes it took to drive to the park, there was only the hum of the van's engine, nothing else.

Viktoria jumped out of the van when they got to the parking lot, not waiting for Chris. Her chest was tight with an awful, sick worry as she rushed from the parking lot to the tree where she and Teri always met.

Please, please, Teri. Please be there.

Turning the corner at the outdoor racquetball courts, she looked through the chain-link fence toward the tree. Her heart wrenched even tighter — Teri wasn't there.

Not knowing what to do or where else to go, Viktoria slowed her pace, eventually resting against the rock under the tree where Teri usually sat waiting for her. Chris caught up with her several seconds later.

"I don't know, Chris," an exasperated Viktoria said, breaking the tense silence. "She could be anywhere. Do you have any ideas?"

She folded her arms as though they could provide a shield from the dreaded unknown. Turning to Chris, his silence was unbearable.

"Chris," Viktoria almost shouted to get him to see the frustration and fear on her face. "Any ideas?"

He shook his head and shrugged, lighting another cigarette. That was enough; Viktoria couldn't take his silence anymore.

"Hey!" Viktoria marched up to within inches of Chris's face. "In case you haven't noticed, I am freaking out right now. I can't tell you how scared I am, and you know something you're not telling me. It's pissing me off! So, put out that freaking cigarette, man up, and tell me what the hell is going on!"

Chris exhaled his smoke reluctantly, and his voice remained flat as his upper lip stiffened. "I don't know where Teri is."

"OK," Viktoria responded with raised eyebrows to let him know that answer wasn't enough. Chris then glanced toward the sky, as though he were trying to think of the right words to say. "I need more than that, Chris. Whatever it is, just say it."

Taking another drag, he finally looked Viktoria in the eye. "You saw it last night, how Teri says the craziest things when she's drunk."

Viktoria refused to smile or even nod in agreement. She kept her eyes and serious expression on Chris, showing her need for him to get right to the point.

"On our way home last night, Teri was so blitzed her head kept swaying back and forth. She kept turning to me, saying, 'I can't do this anymore.'"

"She said that to me before you got in the van," Viktoria said. "Do what?"

Again, Chris hesitated, causing Viktoria to ask with more urgency, "What?"

"That's what I asked," Chris said, shaking his head as though he were lost. "She said she couldn't live with hiding it anymore. She said it was killing her, and she deserved it."

"What? What's the 'it' that she's been hiding?"

Taking another drag, Chris shook his head with his eyes shut tight as though he were trying to dismiss a thought as a mere irrational misunderstanding. "Look, Viktoria, sometimes, when people are as drunk as Teri was last night, it really messes their heads up. They're not even themselves, and whatever pain or grief or demons they're dealing with get really twisted within them. They will then say or express anything it takes to purge them out, like some sort of perverse exorcism, and—"

"What are you saying, Chris?" Viktoria's question took on an even sharper demanding tone.

Chris capitulated with a deep breath. "When we got home last night, Teri, being so out of it, said something so twisted I took it as drunken stupor nonsense. It was so ridiculous I even laughed. When we finally woke up this morning, I laughed again and teased her about what she had said. Being the stupid idiot that I am with my dark humor, I said jokingly that the truth was finally out, and she better let you know before I do. She didn't smile, respond, or anything. I then went out to the garage to reassemble all our equipment from last night. Teri never came out to help me. When I went back in to check on her, she was gone. I searched throughout the house — she was nowhere. When I checked the bathroom, her toothbrush, makeup, shampoo, everything was gone."

"Stop trying to avoid it and tell me, Chris," Viktoria demanded, not able to bear it any longer. "What did Teri say? What did she do?!"

He closed his eyes while taking a long, shaky breath, and then opened them. "I don't think Dylan committed suicide."

Chapter 42

A reeling dizziness overtook Viktoria, leaving her head spinning. Her stomach felt weighed down with what she could only imagine was a combination of vomit and warm thick blood as she kept her empty stare on Chris, waiting for him to finally admit it was all a sick joke. He gazed at her with sad confusion in his eyes, but his lips didn't move — there was no admission or punch line.

"There's no way. She could never do something like that. Please tell me I'm right, Chris."

Except for Chris's trembling chin, there was no other response.

"Chris?"

Again, no response.

"But *why?*" Placing her hands on Chris's shoulders, her voice held no strength. "This is all just a big misunderstanding; she wouldn't do that."

With tears welling in his eyes, Chris couldn't move his tight, quivering lips. As a tear finally broke loose, falling down his cheek, he turned around, facing away from Viktoria. Covering his face with his hands, he wept uncontrollably. He forced his words out between sobs with terrible pain, "I screwed up so bad. All I cared about was my music, the next party, the next time I could get drunk, high, or stoned again. I'm the big brother. I should've stepped up and cared for her when nobody else would, not even our parents. All Teri did was try to take care of me. What did I ever do for her? Nothing. Look at the path I chose. The world I opened her up to. She never had a chance. Now look at what's happened."

Viktoria went to place her hand on Chris's back. The way he stood as his back convulsed was just like Teri. She had also never seen him cry, as it was with Teri before Dylan's death.

Before Dylan's death.

With a sickening chill shuddering her whole frame, Viktoria pulled her hand away, stepping back as she reeled with dizziness and nausea. The horrifying pieces thrust together — all of Teri's weeping since May, and only when Dylan came up; going from sneaking an occasional cigarette from Chris or her mom's purse to incessant chain smoking, heavy drinking, and drugs over the last four months; usually laughing Sherry off until she said the previous Saturday that Dylan was better off dead. That was when Teri fiercely lost it.

The final piece that completed the horrifying image was the increasing bond Viktoria and Dylan shared after losing their grandmother, combined with the words a drunken Teri uttered through determined, gritting teeth just the night before. The words now pierced Viktoria's heart like a knife: *Nobody gets between us.*

Crossing her arms against her chest for any form of comfort whatsoever, she stepped farther away from Chris, whose presence lost all significance. All around her, everything appeared darker, even the Arizona sun.

"I need my mom."

Chris removed his hands from his face, turning to Viktoria with eyes of sorrow, shame, and understanding.

Again, Viktoria said the only words she could, "I need my mom."

Chris nodded as he pulled out another cigarette for his own solace. Viktoria's voice shook with horror as she turned to leave the park, "I need to go. I need my mom."

Though it was a bright early afternoon, everything around her only seemed to get darker as Viktoria kept her head down and her arms folded. A panicked sob escaped her as she longed for her mom's comfort, and her tears blurred the cracks in the sidewalk as she quickened her pace toward the Safeway supermarket.

With each step making it seem even farther away, Viktoria's trembling hand took hold of her grandmother's cross.

I need Mom, Dylan — so much. Please tell me it didn't happen. Please tell me this is all a bad dream. Please make this all go away.

Wiping her eyes as she crossed the parking lot, she looked straight at Olivia's usual cash register as soon as she walked in the store, but she wasn't there.

Gabrielle, a girl who had graduated the year before, and who, seeing right through the wealthy, beautiful enemies' facade, had buddied up with Olivia at work, was on the next register over. Unsuccessfully trying to conceal her panic, Viktoria walked up to her.

"Gabrielle?"

The taller, lean girl looked at her with instant concern. "Viktoria? Are you OK?"

"Is my mom in the breakroom?"

"No," Gabrielle answered with extreme worry in her voice. "She worked the early shift today — she already left."

Turning her head to the side, Viktoria shut her eyes tight. Added to her horrific grief was the sudden self-anger burning in her stomach.

Mom told me last night she was working the earlier shift. How did I forget that? Now I have to walk all the way home, but I need her now.

Gabrielle's hand on her upper arm caused Viktoria to turn.

"Something's wrong, Viktoria, I can see it. Is there anything I can do? I can call your house and see if your mom is there."

A gruff voice growled from Gabrielle's register. "Young lady, aren't you open? Your light's on but you are apparently not in the game."

Viktoria turned toward the voice. Mr. Thompson, Olivia's perpetual complaining customer, now stood at Gabrielle's register, ready to give *her* hell. His presence only added to Viktoria's panicking — enough to send her over the edge.

I need to get out of here. I have to get home. Please be home, Mom.

"I'm on my way, Mr. Thompson," Gabrielle reassured him before turning again to Viktoria and speaking under her breath, "I can't stand him."

Plastering a weak, half-smile under her tear-filled eyes and sniffling nose, Viktoria could barely speak, "I need to go."

Gabrielle gently nodded, giving Viktoria's upper arm a comforting rub and quick squeeze. "OK, I'm here if you need me."

Viktoria kept her head down and her arms folded as she walked. Her heart felt increasingly tight and broken. Cars and trucks roaring by, people's voices, honking horns, and all other sounds only served to aggravate her grief. With each step closer, the farther away she felt. Grabbing her grandmother's cross, her chest tightened and convulsed.

Please, Dylan, tell me it didn't happen.

Crossing the intersection of North 53rd Avenue and West Poinsettia Drive, her front yard appeared in the distance. Her panic and pace increased as her bedroom window grew closer and closer.

Please be home, Mom. Please be home.

As her house came into full view at the corner, the relief of the garage door open with Olivia's car parked inside made Viktoria cry even harder. She sobbed as she ran to the front door, and her hand shook while forcing her keys into the deadbolt and the doorknob.

Shutting the door behind her, Viktoria leaned her exhausted body against it. "Mom!" With no response, she cried even louder, "Please, Mom, where are you?"

Again, there was no answer. She started to walk toward the kitchen, but halfway through the living room, in anguish and frustration, she cried out again, "Mom, please!"

On the couch rested a half full white bag she recognized from when Teri would bring her belongings to spend the night. Before Viktoria could make anything of it, the stench of a familiar cigarette brand drifted through the air.

The living room spun as curiosity overshadowed heartache and shock. Her nightmarish emotional whirlwind was stilled by her gasp. Stiffened and paralyzed by the innate desire for survival, Viktoria could not breathe as the cold sharp blade of a knife pressed against her throat.

With a hand gently pulling her hair downward, Teri's shaking voice whispered in Viktoria's ear, "Get on your knees."

Chapter 43

Viktoria slowly dropped to her knees.

"Teri," her voice shook. "Teri, please don't."

From the end of the hallway, Olivia's voice called out weakly, "Viktoria!"

"Mom!" Viktoria cried.

Gently pulling Viktoria to her feet by her hair, Teri's voice was still quiet, but more determined. "Get up. Get up. Get up."

Again, Olivia's weak voice came from the hallway. "Viktoria!"

"Mom!" Viktoria shouted again before an aggressive tug on her hair forced her head back. Within an inch of her right ear, Teri's quiet voice grew forceful. "Not another word. You got that? Now move."

With the blade still tight against her throat and her hair gripped in Teri's fist, Viktoria gasped for air as she was pushed from behind into the kitchen, then to the sliding glass door leading into the backyard.

"Unlatch and open the door," Teri demanded.

Viktoria's fingers nervously fumbled with the door's latch before she could finally get it to open. Forced outside, farther away and cut off from her mom, Viktoria could no longer suppress her fear.

"Please, Teri," she pleaded through her clenched teeth and building sobs. "I'm begging you, please don't do this."

Her hair yanked again from behind, and with each quiet, angry demand, Viktoria could feel Teri's lips move on her right ear. "Shut up! You hear me? I said shut up! Now, *slowly,* and *quietly,* turn around, facing me, and put your back against the wall."

With her pulse pounding and her eyes shut with dreaded anticipation, the knife's sharp blade remained pressed against her throat as she turned. Teri's small, strong hand gripped Viktoria's shirt, pressing her up to the wall.

"Sit down."

The knife followed her down, forcing Viktoria to still her sobs for fear of any sudden movement forcing the blade to cut her neck.

"Look at me," Teri's quiet, strained voice demanded.

Opening her eyes, Viktoria saw the kind and nurturing look in Teri's eyes was gone, replaced by a stone-cold maniacal glare. It was Teri, but it wasn't.

"We're leaving, Viktoria."

Teri's words were clear, but Viktoria could not comprehend them. In confusion at first, and then with a sickening concern for Olivia, she could only slowly shake her head.

"Viktoria," Teri said in a strangely comforting, normal tone that also insisted she got her point across, "I have to leave and I'm taking you with me."

Viktoria's unbearable concern for Olivia inside the house, alone and hurt, eclipsed the fear of the sharp blade against her throat. No longer able to hold in her sobs, she could only let her tears fall as she shook her head again.

The pressure of the blade was suddenly reduced to a light touch. The chilling glare in Teri's eyes faded just as fast, replaced with a caring, concerned expression.

"Viktoria, can you hear me?" Teri asked with a warm, soft voice. "Please say something."

It was Teri. Though the girl in front of Viktoria was still holding a knife to her neck, the caring, nurturing best friend she always knew was breaking through. She could only hope enough of Teri was there. Through her sobs, Viktoria could barely get her words out, "Teri, I need my mom."

The warm concern in Teri's eyes yielded to alarm and panic as well as her voice. "No, no you don't. You don't need your mom anymore. Look, we have to leave. From now on, we only need each other."

"Please, Teri. Please don't do this. This isn't you."

Shaking Viktoria's shirt as though she didn't already have her undivided attention, Teri's face came within inches of hers.

"Please understand me, Viktoria. *I need you!*"

Teri's panicked plea, divulging her codependency so willingly, cautiously emboldened Viktoria with a sense of leverage — she needed it for Olivia; she needed it for the truth. Her shaking voice was soft and calm, hoping it would have the same effect on the girl holding the knife to her neck.

"Whatever your reasons are for doing this, it's not worth it. Please, just talk to me, Teri. Tell me what's wrong."

Her breath was shaking, along with her hand holding the knife. A tear escaped Teri's eye. "I can't."

"Why?" Viktoria asked with as much concern as she could express. "Why can't you tell me?"

Teri then wiped another tear from her cheek with her shoulder. "It would hurt too much."

"Chris was here earlier today," Viktoria said, though she cried as she spoke, already knowing the answer deep inside. "He told me what you said last night. Is it true?"

Shutting her eyes tight, Teri broke down weeping. She rested the knife on Viktoria's lower neck.

"Why did you do it?" Viktoria could barely ask through her tears. "Why did you take my brother away from me?"

"It was an accident," Teri forced out through her sobs.

Viktoria could not breathe as her body locked in agonizing grief. With the first gasp of air her body finally allowed, she found her jaw in Teri's grip. Forcing Viktoria to look at her, the alarm and panic within Teri returned.

"Viktoria, I swear, you need to believe me! I didn't mean to do it. I thought you and your parents would be home by the time I got there that night, but you weren't. When I got to the front door, I heard Dylan in the living room, crying. He wouldn't answer the door, so I used my key to get in."

Teri wiped another tear with her shoulder as her chest convulsed. Her face frozen with pain, she could only choke on her sobs before she continued, "It was so terrible. He had no shirt on, and his body was so bruised and beaten. He just stood in the middle of the living room, holding your dad's gun, crying uncontrollably. He looked so frightened when he saw me. He screamed at me to go away. He kept crying 'I want to die! Just let me die!' I begged him to give me the gun, but Dylan just shouted no and ran out the door. I chased after him, but I couldn't catch up until I finally cornered him at the canal."

Chewing on her lower lip as her face trembled, Teri gripped Viktoria's jaw even tighter.

"Please, Viktoria, please, please, please believe me. When I had Dylan cornered, I begged again for him to give me the gun. He didn't say anything, he just sniffled. When I slowly reached my hand out, he shook his head, putting the gun up against it. I couldn't let him do it. I grabbed for the gun and tried to take it away from him, but he refused to let go."

Teri shook her head with a hopeless, helpless shrug. "I did all I could to get it away from him, but the gun went off."

With her mind twisted and torn between what Teri had just told her and the horrifying pieces that all came together earlier at the park, no words would come to Viktoria. Her silence only brought more distress to Teri's face and voice.

"You *do* believe me, don't you? Please say something, Viktoria!"

The words were finally forming, but with the hand gripping her shirt still holding the knife close to her neck, Viktoria's lips remained quivering and shut. Pulling Viktoria's jaw and shirt forward, Teri then thrust her back against the wall.

"Viktoria! Please say something! Please!"

The words she desired to say grew too strong, forcing her lips into motion. Viktoria *needed* to know the truth, no matter what. As the words boldly came out with her shaking voice, whether voluntarily or involuntarily, she could only hope Teri's need for her continuing presence and support, the leverage, was as genuine and vital as she expressed. "If it was an accident, then why did you hide it? Why did you let us believe my brother killed himself? Think of everything that happened, Teri — the court case, all that my family went through. Tell me why."

The agonizing pain Teri expressed disappeared with an instant fit of anger as she tightened her grip on Viktoria's jaw. "Stop, Viktoria, just stop! It was an accident. That's all you need to know."

Viktoria jerked her head side to side, loosening Teri's grip on her jaw. "It was an accident? That's all I need to know?"

Grabbing Viktoria's hair, Teri pressed the back of her head against the wall, repositioning the knife closer to her throat. "That's right, Viktoria. That's all you need to know."

Her stomach twisting and burning, Viktoria couldn't stop her lips from moving. She didn't want them to stop. "When I helped you into the van last night, you were angry about me leaving with Matt. You grabbed me and said, 'nobody gets between us.' Was that about how close Dylan and I got between my grandma's death and his? Were you thinking that then?"

Teri's face lost all emotion.

"Tell me what you were thinking," Viktoria demanded through clenched teeth.

The silence that fell over Teri grew thicker and darker before a silver streak reignited life to her eyes with a chilling flair. Within her serene smile and voice was a sickening acid. "Leave it alone, Viktoria. It's what Dylan wanted: to not be here anymore. Even after I got the gun away from him, I know that's all he wanted. He didn't have to say anything. I could see it on his face. After all he'd been through? What else could I do for him? Trust me, it was for the best."

Viktoria reached up, gripping Teri's shirt. "Teri! I know what you did! How could you—"

"Viktoria!" Olivia cried out in pain from inside the house.

Viktoria gasped. "Mom!"

She tried to break away from Teri's grasp, only to be thrust back down and against the wall. The force and pain reminded her of the freakish strength of Teri's small body.

"No, no, no," Teri commanded in a rapid panic. "We're leaving. Now!"

Viktoria struggled to resist. "No!"

"Hey!" Teri growled through clenched teeth. "Don't fight me!"

Viktoria's head was pinned against the wall, and the blade pushed tightly against her neck. With even a single ounce of increased pressure, it would cut through her skin. Gasping for air as fear crushed her body, she gripped her grandmother's cross.

I need you, Dylan. Please, please help me.

"Stop doing that!" Teri shouted as she reached around Viktoria's neck, yanked off her dog collar, and held it to her face. "You see this? You have this because of me. I'm the one who got it back from Sherry. I see you always sharing some deep thought or secret with this, an inanimate object. Why not me? You don't need this or anybody else. You have me!"

Teri threw the dog collar to the ground and grabbed Viktoria's shirt while keeping the knife close to her neck with her other hand. "Let's go!"

As she was pulled to her feet, Viktoria tried with all she had, but she couldn't reach her dog collar.

Please, Dylan, don't let her take you away from me again.

Chapter 44

She desperately reached for her dog collar again, but the upward pull on Viktoria's shirt forced her face within an inch of Teri's.

"Didn't you hear me?" Teri scolded through her teeth. "Let's go."

"Viktoria!" Olivia cried out again. Viktoria knew she was close, most likely in the kitchen.

"Mom!" she shouted as she tried to pull herself from Teri's grasp.

Turning to run into the kitchen, Viktoria was stopped by Teri's strong grip on her hair from behind. Yanked back and down with powerful aggression, Viktoria fell to the ground. Again, her back was pinned to the wall with the knife's blade pressed against her throat.

"Why are you doing this to me?" Viktoria cried. "Just disappear and leave us alone! Why can't you just do that without me?"

Taking hold of Viktoria's jaw again to force eye contact, Teri's face strained with heartbreaking sorrow before she could answer in a quiet, strained voice, "Because you are all I've got. My parents? They would love to see me finally disappear. I don't have Chris. *I* take care of *him*. I can't rely on him. Hell, look at me — look at the wreck that I am. I can't even rely on myself. *You*, Viktoria. You are the only stability in my life. I can't lose you to someone else. Without you, I'll die. I won't let anybody do that to me."

Her face twisting in angry determination, Teri leaned in even closer. "Do you understand what I'm saying? Nobody gets between us — not your parents, not Matt. *Nobody!* Not even Dylan. It was sheer survival, Viktoria. It was my life or his! He had to go."

"Teri!" Viktoria shouted. "I swear I'm going to—"

On the other side of the sliding glass door, a kitchen chair fell to the floor, along with a body. Viktoria heard Olivia groan painfully. She grabbed Teri's wrist, trying to break the tight grip on her jaw.

"Mom!" Viktoria tried to yell through her tightly shut teeth as she grabbed Teri's shirt, attempting to wrestle out from under her. "Let me go!"

Viktoria's frame shuddered and stiffened in excruciation as she was slammed against the wall twice before being thrust down again. Whether it was Teri's fist or the knife's handle, the hit to the side of her head that followed left her reeling with a sharp nauseating pain.

Her head was forced upward against the wall by Teri's grip on her chin, and the blade trembled as it pressed against Viktoria's throat with such force, the sting of skin about to break eclipsed the pain shooting through the rest of her body. As Teri's face approached Viktoria's right ear, the knife's blade followed with increased pressure. The warm trickle of blood beginning to run down the side of her neck was enough for Viktoria to gasp with panic.

The sharpness in Teri's growl revealed zero concern. "What did I say? Don't fight me. Look at what you're making me do! Without you, I have nobody. Nobody! I'm as good as dead. What makes you think you deserve to keep on living if I can't? This is it, Viktoria. Right now! It's your choice: Either we live, or we both die."

From the corner of her eye, Viktoria could see the dog collar. She tried desperately to reach it, but it was too far away. The nausea was building. The backyard was beginning to spin.

Please, oh please, Dylan, I can't reach you. I need you. Mom needs you. Please, please help me.

"What's your choice!" Teri screamed as she pushed Viktoria's head harder against the wall.

The blade pushed deeper into Viktoria's neck.

No, Dylan, please don't let this happen.

The trickle of blood gained a flowing momentum.

Dylan! Dylan!

Her eyes opening wide, the nausea and spinning vanished as an extraordinary, burning surge shot down Viktoria's spine. As it rapidly expanded, the stunning, powerful warmth electrified the muscles in her back. Spreading across her shoulders and down her arms, the indescribable force shot down her core and into her legs. In her heart, it only magnified.

Her grandmother's cross. Her war paint. The challenging stare of The Road Warriors on the magazine cover. June 1. The girl staring back at her in the bathroom mirror that morning was ready for war, and, at that moment, more than ever, she could taste victory.

Her greatest enemy never lurked in the school halls and subdivisions, dressed in cheerleading uniforms, letterman jackets, and all the other latest styles. Since war was declared on June 1, her greatest enemy had been right beside and in front of her, disguised as her best friend and greatest ally. Viktoria had no other choice, not only for herself, but also for Olivia. This battle was, by far, the most crucial in the war and she had to win, no matter what.

Gritting her teeth, Viktoria grabbed Teri's wrist, pulling the blade downward from her neck. With a grunting shout for strength, her hand gripped Teri's neck, pushing her away.

Struggling with Teri as she rose to her feet, Viktoria forced a second grunt as she clenched her teeth to resist the shock of the blade piercing her upper hip. Teri refused to lose her grip on the knife as Viktoria pushed her. A shout of sharp pain escaped her as the blade was yanked out of her hip. Choosing to ignore the pain, Viktoria knew she had to keep fighting.

Grabbing Teri with both hands, Viktoria swung her around, slamming her against the wall, pinning her knife-wielding hand tight against it.

"Viktoria!"

Fighting to keep Teri pinned against the wall, Viktoria turned in the direction of the voice. Just outside the sliding glass door, on her knees with blood soaking the bottom half of her shirt, Olivia lifted her shotgun to take aim.

"Mom, no!" Viktoria shouted.

"Viktoria, please!" Olivia begged. "I don't know if the police will get here on time."

"Mom, don't do it!" Viktoria shouted back.

With the distant sound of sirens and Viktoria's distraction, Teri fought loose, pushing herself away from the wall. Taking two punches to the face, Viktoria still refused to let go of the hand holding the knife.

Taking a third punch to the face, Viktoria gritted her teeth. Grabbing Teri's shirt, she pulled their bodies together. Reaching behind, she grabbed and yanked Teri's hair, forcing her to the ground and on her back.

Staying on top of her and holding the knife-wielding hand down with her left hand, Viktoria lifted her right hand and punched Teri as hard as she could.

"Hey!" Teri screamed as blood rushed from her nose.

Struggling to hold her down, Viktoria responded with two more punches to Teri's face.

"I'm going to kill you, I swear!" Teri shouted as blood leaked from the corner of her mouth.

"The hell you are!"

The sirens pierced Viktoria's ears. Still, she refused to lose focus on the fight.

Slamming Teri's knife-wielding hand against the ground over and over, she still wouldn't let go. Gripping Teri's neck with her right hand and squeezing with all her strength, Viktoria raised her torso and repeatedly rammed her knee into Teri's ribs as hard as possible until her coughing and loss of breath forced her to lose her grip on the knife.

With a hell-bent grunt, Teri reached up and grabbed Viktoria's neck. Pushing her arm away, Viktoria lifted Teri's head by her hair before thrusting it against the ground with such force she lost her position on her knees.

Just as her torso fell against Teri's, Viktoria was pulled to her feet by two strong hands. A police officer kicked the knife farther away from Teri before he turned her over and hand-cuffed her.

The two strong hands were gentle as they steadied Viktoria. She turned to see kind eyes and heard a comforting voice that she had never before associated with Officer Blanchard. "Viktoria, are you OK?"

With heartbreaking concern, she could only say two words, "My mom."

With a slight smile, Officer Blanchard nodded.

"Please don't worry," Olivia whispered as Viktoria broke down in her embrace after rushing to her. "We're going to be fine."

Her mom's blood-soaked shirt peeled from Viktoria's skin as a paramedic lifted her carefully. Lying on the gurney, Olivia's eyes beamed as she held Viktoria's arm.

After the paramedic cleaned and bandaged the stab wound on Viktoria's upper hip, she limped back to Olivia, taking her by the hand. Olivia then turned to her with a weak voice, slight shrug, and a longing, helpless smile.

"I guess it won't be dinner from Angelo's and a movie tonight. How about a Saturday night at the hospital? Amazing cuisine with reruns of *Laverne and Shirley* on a small fuzzy TV screen."

Her thoughtful, slight smile toward Olivia faded as two officers led a handcuffed Teri from the backyard. Still, Viktoria's desire was the same as always — the same as Dylan's — to be strong for her mom. Her smile returned as she squeezed Olivia's arm.

"The ambulance is out front," the paramedic intervened.

"We need to get you to the hospital."

"Wait," Viktoria said. "There's something I need."

Limping over to where Teri had thrown it to the ground, Viktoria winced as she bent over and picked up her dog collar. Dusting it off and holding it in her hand, she focused on her grandmother's cross.

Thank you, Dylan. I needed you and you were there. Look at the hell we went through today. It was our greatest battle and we won. We did it together. There's no stopping us now.

This war is ours to win — together.

Chapter 45

Closing her eyes with a peaceful smile as the breeze blew through her hair, Viktoria loved the perfect temperature Phoenix offered in mid-December. The early sun welcomed another promising Saturday morning.

Sitting on the front porch, just having waved as Olivia drove off to work, Viktoria held her dog collar in her hands. Gazing at her grandmother's cross, it was a quiet moment to reflect on all the changes, both exciting and sad.

The hole in Viktoria's heart over the last two months left by Teri's absence proved to be too similar to the one left by Dylan. She was her best and only friend since kindergarten, but all the time, passions, and love they shared with each other had vanished. Viktoria still shuddered to think of how quickly their inseparable, beautiful relationship had crumbled into irreparable pieces.

At the same time, she couldn't help but wonder when she truly said goodbye to the Teri she knew. It had been much longer than she had ever realized, she just didn't know exactly when.

It was more of the little things Viktoria longed for. The way Teri — the one she knew — sat on the rock as she waited for Viktoria at the park. The little faces they made at each other in class. The way Teri's eyes lit up when anyone mentioned Matt Dillon or one of his movies. The distant sound of the band practicing in the garage as Viktoria entered their neighborhood.

The band — oh, how I miss the band.

The Forgotten Ones were no more. Though it was Chris's brainchild and everything he had been betting his future on, he was the one who dissolved the band. What happened with Teri hit him hard. Realizing his excessive codependency on her and drugs, he knew he needed to change.

A loving, hopeful smile formed on Viktoria's face with the thought of Chris. Knowing that he, like Teri, was also sick, he took it upon himself to get his life together. Seeing him cleaned up, sharing an apartment with Grant Coleman and working at the gas station while studying for his real estate license completely blew Viktoria's mind. He even quit smoking, which was a miracle in the Allardyce family.

Teri's trial was set to begin in January. It wasn't how Viktoria wanted to start off 1987. After what happened with Dylan and everything that followed, the last place she ever wanted to visit again was the courthouse.

What weighed on her even more was having to testify at Teri's trial. She was dreading having to go into the courtroom and see her. Teri was not only a total stranger now, but also a monster — one Viktoria despised. It saddened her to question whether or not she wanted to see Teri, the one who was her best and only friend, ever again. The pain was too deep to think about all she had lost for too long.

The one thing that comforted Viktoria concerning the trial was the fact that both Olivia *and* Henrik were going to be there. Having her dad home with her and Olivia every night after work again meant the world to her.

Before Olivia was even released from the hospital, Henrik had already trucked in from the East Coast and stormed into his boss's office, demanding that he be switched from interstate back to local trucking. After his passionate *my mom and I, a small boy, were left to survive alone in occupied Norway during World War II, and I, as a man, will protect my family and never abandon them* lecture, his wide-eyed, overwhelmed boss was more than willing to switch Henrik right on the spot.

Since then, the smile on his face had been priceless at the dinner table every night as Viktoria set a plate of nostalgic Norwegian dishes from her grandmother's recipe book in front of him. It was also priceless to see Olivia so rested, healthy, and happy since Henrik had been home. Even the house had regained the light, love, and solace it had provided them when Dylan was there.

The scar on Viktoria's upper hip, like the one on Olivia's stomach, was there to stay. The mere thought of it, though, brought her the same rush of confidence and anticipation that strengthened her each time she saw it on the girl in the bathroom mirror.

Her moment of reflection magnified as she looked down at her grandmother's cross.

It definitely was the new beginning that day I had to fight Teri, Dylan. There was so much I learned, not only about myself, but also about us.

You were right there with me. You were always there. But we were closer than ever on that day when I needed and cried for your strength. That was when I learned my most powerful lesson, the one that changed everything. Do you know what that is?

Your arms are always reached out to me, but it's up to me to reach for you. The deeper I dig inside of me to reach higher and higher, the more I feel you. Who knows? Maybe someday I'll be able to reach high enough for a full embrace.

Do you know what's so amazing? Now that I'm reaching higher and higher every day, everything is better — school, home, everything — and it's because I'm closer to you.

A childlike grin formed across Viktoria's face.

I can't stop looking at that picture of Animal and Hawk on the cover of Pro Wrestling Illustrated. *Their eyes still challenge me to go out and keep fighting, but they now look different. In their eyes is also a look of pride and unity with me — with us, actually. I know why, Dylan. It's because, just like the two of them, we fought through hell and won! Together!*

Sure, I have a scar, but Animal and Hawk have their share too, right? Now we're like them.

People see it without even realizing it. Everything changed at school, in these subdivisions, and even for Mom at work after the fight with Teri. The enemy is no longer lurking; they are retreating.

Sherry Davis and her group? They leave me alone. I even get smiles and respectful nods in the hallway from Jeff, Vince, and all those guys. Can you believe it?

Keeping her eyes on her grandmother's cross, a short, excited laugh escaped Viktoria.

You and I know why, though. Right, Dylan? They don't even know it, but the enemy sees us as one of them — The Road Warriors — just like you always wanted. Your dream has come true.

We've been unleashed, and we're just getting started. There's no stopping us. Just like carrying Grandma's cross above my heart, I always carry you in my heart, and I know you'll always be there by my side to carry me. That is how we are going to win this war, Dylan.

Viktoria looked up as a large black, dusty pickup truck turned the corner, stopping in front of her house. Viktoria peered into the cab as she stood, biting her lower lip with a playful grin.

The tall, rugged driver jumped out, racing around the front. Opening the passenger door with his strong hand like a gentleman, he turned his eyes toward the house, laser-focused on Viktoria. His dirty-blond wavy locks blew in the breeze as his bright, charismatic smile melted Viktoria's heart.

Believe it or not, Dylan, Mom and Dad are actually seeing me not as a girl anymore, but as a young woman. Viewing me in that light, they finally concluded that dating a guy who's only been out of high school for one year isn't such a scandal after all.

Latching her dog collar around her neck, Viktoria's mind went to the girl looking back at her in the bathroom mirror just a half hour before. Her makeup — her war paint — with all that it stood for, was perfect. Stepping off the porch, she paused, gazing at him with a smitten smile.

"Did you bring your mom's recipe for her slow-cooker cheesy potatoes and smoked sausage?"

Matt reached in his back pocket, pulling out and unfolding a piece of paper. "Absolutely — called her last night."

"Did you stop by the store to pick up the ingredients?" Viktoria asked as she met Matt at the truck with a tight embrace.

"I sure did," said Matt. "Well, I couldn't find a couple of things."

"Oh, yeah? What was it you couldn't find?"

Matt shook his head with a shrug. "Onion and garlic powder. I hunted high and low all over the produce department, but they were nowhere."

With a quick nod, Viktoria raised her eyebrows. "Huh. Did you look in the aisle with the seasonings?"

Matt's face turned red with an embarrassed grin. "Uh . . . nope."

With an understanding smile, Viktoria gave her eyebrows a quick raise again. Taking his unbuttoned flannel shirt with both hands, she pulled him in for a kiss.

"All right, cowboy, let's make a quick stop at the store. The gang at the truck stop has been looking forward to trying your mom's dish all week. 'The Master Chef' can't disappoint."

Matt took a deep breath. "Saturday's the busiest day of the week — hope I can keep up."

"You will," said Viktoria with a reassuring smile. "You're getting better every week. Don't worry, we'll be out of there before noon as always."

"Oh, no worries about that with this big, faithful machine. We'll be back here well before one," Matt said, placing his hand on the hood of his truck before turning again to Viktoria with a warm smile and a wink. "We'll be in that living room right inside there tuning in to the Sportatorium and World Class Championship Wrestling. I'll be spurred, whipped, and branded before I let Dylan down."

The comfort of Matt's drawl, smile, and words brought a soft, emotional laugh to Viktoria. She couldn't help pulling him in for another kiss.

"I know you. I know your heart. You and Dylan are too similar — you won't let him down, and neither will I. In one way or another, the war continues, and the three of us are in it together. We have to win."

Made in the USA
Columbia, SC
20 May 2022

60694864R00157